THUMBPRINT IN THE DOME

Brian Bennett

CONTENTS

CHAPTER 1

John Stratton, aged thirty-four, stretches his finely tuned muscular body as he wakes from a good night's sleep. It is a warm summer Monday morning in late June, and he lays there listening to the dawn chorus as the birds call for their mates. With the sun streaming through the newly fitted skylight, the rays warm his tanned body. He watches his beautiful new wife, as she slowly surfaces from a deep, satisfying sleep. He gently taps the side of her leg with his foot in a bid to rouse her.

Without opening her eyes, she smiles broadly to herself in a knowing sort of way and whispers in a low raspy voice, 'Good morning husband.' She turns her head and flicks a strand of her long blond hair out of her sparkling green, passion filled, eyes and, looks deeply into his eyes. She opens her mouth to speak, and he sees the gold stud in her tongue. This reminds him of the untold pleasure that she gave him only a few hours ago. Soon they are lost as they begin to make love the way only newlyweds can, both of them full to the brim with passion and lust. When they are totally spent, they lie together, their bodies fully entwined, damp with sweat, and if possible even more deeply in love than they had been before their marriage only a few weeks ago. Little did they both know, that sadly, this would be the last time they would make love for a very long time.

Sarah at five feet six, is athletically slim with long blond hair. She has large sparkling green eyes, and is so stunningly beautiful that she could grace the cover of any top fashion magazine. Sarah is the most perfect spouse, a woman that any man would be proud to have as a wife and lover. They have talked about having children and if it happens, he knows that she will be the perfect mother.

Having had her shower, Sarah walks down the stairs, her hair wrapped in a white fluffy towel, giving off the scent of freshly squeezed lemons. Smiling to herself as she glides into the kitchen and sidles up to John. Reaching up she links her fingers behind his neck and pushes her tingling body into his. She feels very proud as she looks into the blue eyes of her handsome husband. John breathes in his wife lemony scent He has a full head of short black hair, and bright blue eyes that have sparkled from the first time that they met all that time ago at her workplace. And from that wonderful day to this, she always smiles to herself as, whenever she looks into his eyes, they always seem to be undressing her. 'Will you wake me up like that every morning for the rest of our lives, my darling, even when we are old and grey?' she asks hopefully.

He smiles down at her and whispers seductively, 'Especially then, but it may take a little longer,' came the honest reply. Pulling her to him he kisses her passionately.

As they leave for work, John winks and smiles lovingly at his wife as he folds himself into his shiny black BMW, Sarah climbs into her Golf GTI. She follows him through the streets of Oxford to the junction with the M40. Waving to each other, Sarah heads north towards Banbury and John turns down the slipway to begin his hour long journey towards London. He smiles to himself as he watches her red car in the rear view mirror, as it quickly fades into the distance. Almost as soon as he drives onto the motorway, he groans out loud as he sees a flashing yellow road sign, telling him that the road ahead is closed, due to a serious accident. He slaps the steering wheel in frustration, knowing that the next exit is a long way down and he could be stuck there for hours. Traffic is very light at this time of the morning, but give it another hour and he would be into the daily grind of rush hour traffic and hours of stop-start travel. He takes his foot off the accelerator and moves to the inside lane to contemplate his options. He decides to phone the office and tell his boss that he is going to be late, but he smiles to himself as coming up on his left-hand side he spots a 'police only' exit sign. Thinking to himself that he hadn't noticed this particular exit before, he shrugs his shoulders, checks that there are no marked police cars in sight, slows down and takes the exit - after all he works in the Fraud Squad.

He drives up the long, winding slip road until he reaches a T junction that joins a main A road. Not being sure where he is, he sets the cars sat-nav for Baker Street, London.

He smiles to himself because he has chosen his favourite, deep voiced Irish woman to relay his route to him, he likes her because she definitely has some devilment about her. She instructs him to turn right, without even thinking about it he turns the steering wheel and does exactly as she instructs. He smiles as almost immediately he is informed by a road sign, that London is forty-eight miles ahead. He cruises along the A road at the correct speed limit and selecting a Don Williams track begins singing along to 'You're My Best Friend', John begins to think about Sarah and just how lucky he is to have found the perfect woman. Deep in thought, he is informed by his invisible Irish guide of a left turn just 200 yards ahead which he needs to take. He slows down and takes the left turn as instructed and immediately finds himself on a single-track concrete road. He follows the deserted road for few minutes until he comes to a large white sign to the side of the road, which in large black letters, tells him that he is on a strictly private road and to go no further.

He looks forward into the distance, then into the rear-view mirror, thinking, this surely can't be right. As there is nowhere that he can turn around, with no thought of reversing all the way back to the main road, he has no other option but to carry on driving straight ahead. The narrow single track road seems to be heading nowhere but must lead somewhere, because every 400 yards or so it has speed humps built into it. He stops again and looks ahead, but something tells him to continue forward. About a mile further down the narrow track, he slows down to, gently ease over a rather high speed hump, and comes to a sudden, juddering stop.

'What the bloody hell?' he asks out loud thinking that he must be stuck on the speed-hump. With the car still in gear, he revs the powerful engine to no avail. He puts the car into reverse and tries again, nothing. He puts the automatic into park and climbs out, looking all around in every direction. He sees that he is totally isolated, alone amongst many acres of cornfields and high hedgerows. Taking out his mobile phone he tries to contact his office but finds he has no signal. He places his hands on his hips and swears out loud in frustration. He then gets down on all fours and looks underneath the car. Strange, he thinks to himself because he doesn't appear to be caught up on anything, so why won't the bloody car move? He takes a quick look all around the car, and finding it clear, he decides that it must be mechanical. With no phone and no car, he is lost in the middle of nowhere and can't believe that this is happening to him and curses his Irish guide.

He looks back to where he has come from and can see nothing, no farm house, no main road, just the straight concrete road surrounded by dark green corn fields. He turns around and looks in the direction that the car is facing and sees more of the same. The Irish woman has sent him in this direction for some unknown reason, so placing his trust in her, he begins to walk along the private concrete road, to where he doesn't know. After only a few paces, he bumps into what appears to be an invisible wall of some kind. He places his hands on the clear bumpy material of whatever the obstacle is. It feels like silk, but the surface is completely covered in tiny raised bumps. He is further confused because although can clearly see through the invisible wall to the tree covered hills in the distance, if he places his face against the unseen obstacle, he can see nothing at all. Suddenly there is a loud click and the rushing sound of escaping air. Just to his right, as if by magic, a previously unseen doorway appears. He moves tentatively towards the opening and is instantly terrified when he is suddenly sucked forward, into an unknown world.

He falls forward onto his hands and knees, turns his head and looks back, momentarily stunned, he stands up. He can see no car, no road, nothing. Looking down, he sees that somehow his clothing has changed and he is now dressed in a dark blue smock over blue trousers, and has white flip flops on his feet.

'What the bloody hell is going on here?' he asks himself, as he turns back to find the opening again, but there is nothing there. He reaches into his pocket for his phone only to find that he no longer has any of his personal possessions.

'I must be bloody dreaming,' he says, now very confused.

CHAPTER 2

John looks around at his new surroundings, at what can only be described as a modern looking small purpose built town, full of square, sterile looking, white two storey buildings. All of which are surrounded by well kept, lush green grass, in which are planted a spattering of well nourished, fully leaved, trees. People, dressed in exactly the same clothes as he, are walking amongst the buildings. Each seemingly going about their daily business as if in some sort of trance. In the distance he can see two couples dressed in white playing tennis, whilst a group of joggers disappear out of view behind a white buildings. Looking to his left he sees a stranger approaching. The man is smiling broadly. He is dressed in the same dark blue clothing as himself. He's of short stocky build and aged somewhere around forty. His thin grey hair is combed over a shiny bald pate. He wears small, round, gold rimmed glasses that are somehow perched on the end of a pitted, deep purple, bulbous nose A nose that is the centre piece of a pale, sunken cheeked narrow face, his grey eyes look as if they have been pushed deep into his fat face. 'Has to be a drinker,' thinks John to himself.

'John,' the man waves his left hand as he calls out his name.

'How the bloody hell do you know my name?' he asks the man who is now holding his outstretched right hand towards him, in welcome.

'Welcome to the Dome. My name is Joe.' As he reaches out and takes hold of John's right hand with his own sweaty limp hand, the man begins to shake John's hand vigorously.

John asks angrily, 'What the bloody hell is going on here?' Whilst for some unknown reason, continuing to shake the man's hand.

'Ah, yes, please walk with me and I will try and explain what is happening to you,' offers Joe.

As the two men begin to walk towards the group of square white buildings, Joe begins trying to explain what is happening to John. 'Well, the best way to begin is to say that for you to be here at all, must mean that you have been selected as you have a certain skill that is required by the controllers of the Dome.'

'But, I don't want to be here in this bloody Dome. I was perfectly happy with my life, thank you. I have only been married a month for God's sake,' snaps a very unhappy John.

'I'm afraid that there is nothing that you or I can do about it now because there is no possible escape from this place. Many have tried, all to no avail. If you are lucky, you will only be with us for two years, and by us, I mean the five hundred fellow inmates, all chosen for our own individual skills. From what I have been told, you are a serving metropolitan policeman, currently stationed with the fraud squad, correct?' In a state of shock, all that John can do is stand open mouthed and nod his head whilst wondering how this complete stranger, can know so much about him.

'I have also been told there is, amongst our small community, a certain criminal element, committing a very serious crime and your expertise is needed to investigate it, and you are to bring those responsible to justice.'

'But I don't want to be here, I want to speak to the person in charge. Now,' demands John.

'That I am afraid is one thing I cannot help you with, simply because there is no one person in charge,' answers Joe.

'But, there must be someone in charge, for you to know that I was here, who I am and what I do for a living,' John replies

Joe takes John gentle by the arm and says reassuringly, 'Let's sit down at a bench and I will do my best to explain what I can. You see what will happen is that when you have settled in and are ready to begin your investigation, you will receive your instructions, as if by some sort of invisible telepathic voice. A thought will come into your head and that thought is what you will act upon. Take this suspected crime that I mentioned earlier, all will be explained to you, and only you by some silent voice. Now let me take you to your new apartment, and I will explain the rules of the Dome as best I can.'

For some unknown reason all the argument seems to leave John as he simply turns and follows this strange little man. He can't for the life of him figure out what the bloody hell is going on, it is as if he is somehow doing everything on auto pilot and he hates the thought of not being in control

They enter a three story apartment block that is marked on the outside with a large black letter A, and walk along a whitewashed corridor with brown wooden doors on either side at regular intervals. They stop outside room number three. Joe opens the door and lets John enter the simple rooms, He gives John a short but informative tour of the rooms, which contains a fully functional, white tiled bathroom, a simply furnished one person bedroom and a comfortable sitting room with a large flat screened TV although there is no kitchen, John asks why, Joe smiles and explains that there is no need for a kitchen, as he can eat out anytime at no cost, 'In essence, you can eat whatever and whenever you want. Although there are coffee and tea making facilities in the main living room, exactly as if you were in a three-star hotel.'

John looks at Joe and pleads with him, 'Can I please contact my wife now, she will be very worried about me?'

Joe shrugs his shoulders. 'I'm sorry, John, but there is no way to contact the outside world, there are no phones, no computers, no post and no daily news papers. Now please sit down and I'll explain the rules of the Dome. Firstly, let me tell you about the currency here in the Dome, you have a daily allowance of 250

Dome points. We have all the normal shops here, which means that you can purchase almost anything you like, to pay for your chosen items you simply scan your right thumbprint on the scanner provided. There is a scanner placed in each shop and at the end of each day, any points that you have not used will go into your final account. Your target in this account will be 10,000 points, if you should reach the target by the end of your two year stay with us, you will be released. Now, if for whatever reason you don't reach the target, you will remain here until you do eventually reach it. In the main square you will find normal clothes shops, you are more than welcome to buy these clothes but you are only allowed the wear them in the evenings after six, or if you are going to, lets say, have a meal with a friend or go to the cinema.

Other than that you must remain dressed as we are now, is that understood? Hopefully this next item will not apply to you, but I have to inform you of it anyway. If you are in any way involved in any crime, no matter the severity, for a total of three times, you will be forced to face punishment in the tube, and I can assure you that you don't want to do that, for reasons that will become abundantly clear in time. The only thing that I can tell you about the tube, is that no-one has ever come back from the experience and having witnessed the deadly event myself, I wouldn't recommend it under any circumstances.

Now should you be fortunate enough to have enough points when you do come to the end of your two year stay, on your release you will go through a scanner, after which you will remember nothing of your time here at the Dome, or of the Dome facility itself. The final thing that you need to know is this; you are more than welcome to have a sexual relationship here at the Dome, but if it is just sex that you require, we have certain young ladies that will provide that particular service, you can find these ladies in the pubs and don't worry, you can't miss them.

This service is again to be paid for with your thumbprint, so basically you can get anything you desire, whenever you desire it. Taking everything into consideration it is a perfect life here at the Dome.'

CHAPTER 3

Sarah sits quietly at her desk trying to concentrate, but she is beginning to seriously worry about John, he always contacts her at least once a day, but today she has heard nothing at all from him and his phone has been switched of all day, which isn't like him at all. She has called his office repeatedly, only to be told by his work colleagues that they have heard nothing at all from him all day, they have tried but cannot contact him by phone or their police radios. They are trying to locate his vehicle by using the tracker device, that he has fitted to his car.

Sarah returns home and begins to prepare spaghetti Bolognese for their supper, she stops what she is doing to call John's best friend Jimmy. It turns out that Jimmy is also very worried about John, as they were supposed to meet for lunch that very day, but John never turned up. Jimmy tells Sarah that if he does hear anything, day or night, he will call her immediately. Sarah continues to prepare their meal even though she is worried to death about her absent husband. She sits on the settee chewing her nails with the cold untouched meal on her lap, it is then that she breaks down and begins to cry uncontrollably.

After she clears up the remnants of her untouched meal, she begins to get a really bad feeling about John, so she decides to contact the local police and report him missing. She speaks to the desk sergeant, who tells her that he isn't supposed to act on a call about a missing person for the first twenty-four hours, but as John is a serving police officer, he will make an exception to the rule and check all the local hospitals. He also tells her that if she has not heard from John by the same time the following evening, she is to call back, they will then take things to the next level and contact CID.

She tries John's dead phone one last time before she climbs into a cold lonely bed and cries herself to sleep.

Joe takes John on a tour of the Dome facility. The first building that they enter is the bank, where John is asked to register his thumbprint, which when done will enable him to make purchases. He is then introduced to the bank manager, Mr Andrews. Andrews is in his early sixties and has a large pot belly that stretches his black waistcoat to it's limit, each of the small black buttons are straining so much that it looks as if the whole lot could explode at any time. The fat man has piggy little eyes sunken into his fat face. His bright red cheeks and the sweat beads that line his forehead suggest that he has very high blood pressure. He is sitting behind a large oak desk, on which stands hardly anything that you would associate with running a bank.

There is a large writing pad covered in blue shaped doodles, by its side is a blue pen. There are three plain white pots, one contains pencils, one contains different coloured pens and the other is full to the brim with paper clips, most of which seem to have been joined together. A plain white coffee mug, a black remote and that is everything. There are no filing cabinets, papers, computers, just a few boring landscapes on the wall. The fat man stands to greet them and John gets his first look at the man's short bowed legs, after shaking hands Andrews makes his office chair creak under the strain as he flops his huge bulk back down. Once he is comfortable he informs John that they will be working closely together in solving a very serious crime, a crime for which he has been specifically chosen. John is suddenly fascinated by the fat man's thick lensed glasses, they magnify his grey eyes and remind him of Brains from the children's TV show Thunderbirds.

After their meeting with the bank manager, John and Joe continue their tour of the facility, on the way they pause at a large ornate pond filled with exotic looking Koi carp of many different colours and sizes. They stop and watch as inmates male and female sit around on the small wall and feed the fish by hand, the thick fish lips making a slurping sound as the suck the white pellets deep into their mouths. They continue their tour and Joe shows him all the shops plus the three Dome pubs, The Bell, The Swan and the Dome Central, John stops walking and turns to Joe and asks, 'How can all this be happening Joe, there must be someone in ultimate charge, I just don't understand what I am doing here? I just want to go home to Sarah, back to my normal life.'

Joe shakes his head, 'As silly as this may sound, John, you will eventually get used to life here and I know that two years sounds like a very long time, but I promise you that the time will soon pass, just try and accept that there is nothing that you can do about the situation, so think positively. Life here really is the perfect life if you give it a chance, the grass somehow gets watered at night, the sun shines all day, every day, even though you know it isn't real, the sky is always blue and the clouds change shape constantly, just like a normal sky.'

Joe admits that he only has a few months left at the Dome as he has almost reached his points target, but if he is totally honest, his life is so good here that if he had a choice, he would stay for ever, and live out the rest of his days here.

The two men part company and John decides to wander around on his own. Feeling very isolated, lonely and somewhat depressed he walks to the nearest pub which just happens to be the Swan. The building, just like all the others is white and square, although the inside looks just like any normal bar, it even smells the same as any normal high street pub. He orders a pint of lager and a rare steak, when the smiling blond waitress delivers his drink to his table she brings with her a silver scanner. She holds the scanner out to John and he places his right thumb onto the black screen, there is a high pitched beeping sound and he has paid for his meal. He thanks the waitress and takes a sip of the cold lager as his mind automatically turns to the last time that Sarah and he sat in a pub just like this one and enjoyed a meal together. He just knows that she will be out of her mind with worry, and wishes there was some way of contacting her.

He returns to his sparse lonely room and sits in front of the television. He scrolls through the index and finds that not only are there the normal TV channels, except the news and weather, but also a futuristic music centre with a list of thousands of CDs listed by categories and built into the system. He also finds that he can select any book that he fancies reading, and discovers that by simply pressing a button, the pages of the virtual book will turn automatically. He wishes that he could have this system at home. He chooses to watch an old Kojak movie. He sits through the whole film but if someone were to ask him what the film had been about, he wouldn't be able to tell them. When the film ends he flicks through other stations and notices that there are no adverts whatsoever, just perfect.

He climbs into a cold single bed and thinks of his darling Sarah. He can't think of another woman, real or fictional, that he would rather spend the rest of his life with. How he would love to have her warm, willing body in his arms now. He suddenly feels very sorry for her because she must be going out of her mind with worry. He switches the light off and lies in the darkness, thinking of her, as a single tear makes its lonely journey down his cheek.

CHAPTER 4

Sarah wakes early the next morning. The first thing she does is climb out of bed and look out of the bedroom window to see if John's black car is there. In her heart, she knows it won't be, there is only an empty space where his car should have been. She takes a shower and dresses ready for work, deciding to go to work because, if she remains at home she will only worry herself to death. Before she leaves, she writes a note for John, telling him to ring her should he come home before she returns. Deep down, she knows that the note is written in the desperate hope the he does eventually come home. But, she knows in her heart of hearts that he will never read her note. She then rings his office yet again, to find out if they have heard anything. On being told they have heard nothing, she again leaves her mobile phone number, just in the hope that John does eventually turn up at his office.

She leaves yet another message on his phone, and looking around her perfect new home; she suddenly bursts into tears and drops to her knees and sobs her heart out. When she leaves for work she follows their normal route until she reaches the M40, as if by habit, she looks in the rear view mirror to where John's car would normally be, there is just a big empty space. Sarah cries uncontrollably, and through the tears, she asks for the hundredth time.

'Where are you, my darling John? Please come home to me.'

John wakes up in the strange bed and automatically turns to find his wife. Realising she's not there, everything about his strange situation suddenly comes flooding back to him. Drying himself in the bathroom after his shower, it is as if someone is suggesting that he goes to see Andrews at the bank. Dressed and ready for another day in this strange place, he makes himself a cup of tea, and out of habit switches the TV on. On the screen, there is a message telling him that he had spent 75 points the previous day and that 175 points will be carried forward to his final account. He flicks through the channels and thinks how strange it is not to be able to watch the news. How will he ever know what is going on in the outside world? But trapped in his new world, does it really matter? Ignorance is bliss, according to the old saying.

Feeling bored, John looks in a few of the apartment's many closets and finds a small pile of blue underwear and on a higher shelf a brand new pair of the latest Nike trainers in his size. On a lower shelf, he sees a brand-new pair of black slip on shoes, again in his size. On hangers in another nearby closet are hanging three spare pairs of blue trousers, and by their side hang three spare blue smocks, all neatly pressed.

'Not much choice here for a good night out then,' he thinks to himself. As he leaves the apartment, he suddenly realises that there are no locks on any of the doors. Very strange, he thinks to himself, as he makes his way to the bank, trying to sort things out in his mind as he ambles along. He thinks through everything that has happened to him so far. As he looks around at the other inmates, he realises that all the women are wearing black smocks and trousers. The men are all dressed the same as he is. He thinks back to the dirty cup and the clothes that he had left strewn on the floor of his apartment.

'Sod it,' he thinks, as he makes his way to the bank. Everyone who passes him nods and smiles a welcome, which is definitely one thing that would never happen on the streets of the real world.

He stops at a plain-looking building which turned out to be a bakery. The sweet sugary smell of fresh baking makes him feel suddenly hungry, so he enters the well lit shop. There doesn't seem to be anyone serving but he can hear someone working in the rear. Laid out in front of him are rows of freshly baked cakes and buns, all displayed so as to tempt the inmates. In a warming oven are freshly made hot bacon rolls, sausage rolls, pies and pastries. Not sure what to do, a pretty young girl walks into the shop. She smiles a welcome and helps herself. He watches her out of the corner of his eye. She is maybe in her late twenties, with shoulder length brown hair, with blonde streaks near the bottom edge, her wide smile and bright white teeth making her look beautiful. Having made her selection of two bacon rolls, she then places her thumb onto a silver scanner standing at the end of the counter. There is a ping as the scanner does its thing.

'It's a very hard choice, isn't it?' she says, smiling in a friendly way, as she takes her rolls, turns and leaves the shop.

John finally chooses a Chelsea bun and places the warm cake into a white paper bag before placing his thumb onto the scanner when again there is a ping. John enjoys his Chelsea as he makes his way slowly along the rubbish free street, on his way to the bank. The policeman in him takes in everything, appraising each person as they come into his eye-line, As he walks along, taking in his new surroundings, he notices for the first time that there are no cameras watching his every move, unlike in the real world where there are cameras on every street corner. The footpaths in the Dome are very clean and chewing gum free and, more surprisingly, there isn't a single piece of graffiti anywhere. As he takes a stroll across the lush grass, he marvels at how well kept the grass appears, not a brown patch to be seen anywhere. On top of that, black litter bins are located on every corner and by the side of every picnic bench. The whole place looks exactly what it is, and that is totally artificial, almost sterile. When he looks around at the other inmates, there doesn't seem to be any urgency in their demeanour unlike in the real world. Everyone seems to be very friendly. Groups of people are sitting around chatting and enjoying each other's company. It is as if they have resigned themselves to the inevitability of their situation. John slowly turns around on the spot and takes in everything that he can see. He smiles to himself as he thinks. 'If only life on the outside, could really be like this.'

He walks unhurriedly into the bank, and with a great deal of effort Mr Andrews lifts his great bulk from his creaking chair in a bid to greet him. They shake hands, and Andrews asks him to come through to his private office. John follows the fat man as he waddles along in front of him to enter the inner sanctum. John glances around at the modern looking décor of the small but well-furnished office. When he is sitting down, the bank manager asks him if he would like a drink of any sort.

'No thanks, I have just had one,' answers John with a sarcastic smile, as he studies the fat mans small mouth for the first time. The man's mouth is more a slit than a normal mouth and when he talks, John can just about see small, bad teeth.

'Where are all your staff?' asks John.

Andrews looks at him and smiles. 'Why would I need staff, John? Let me show you this.' He picks up his small black remote and aims it at the huge wall mounted screen, which must be at least six feet by four almost filling one wall of the small office. A list of forenames both male and female appear on the screen in alphabetical order. Each name has a number by its side.

'This is a list of residents of the Dome, all five hundred or so of us. You'll notice, there are only their first names shown, and these forenames are all separated by apartment blocks and room numbers. Let me demonstrate.'

'Let's look at your account shall we, John?' The bank manager scrolls down the long list of names until John and the symbol A-33 appears on the large screen, on the bottom right hand corner of the screen, shown in green is what must be an image of John's finger print. On the top left hand side of the screen the word account is written in capital letters. Below it, outgoings – 75 points – then, taken forward to 175 points, then, total credit: 175 points.

'Everything is done automatically; don't ask me how, because I honestly don't know.'

'What if I were to accidentally forget to scan my thumb?' asks John.

'Well, you might get away with it on one occasion, but then you will get a televised warning, don't ever forget, John, crime, no matter how small, counts as one of your three strikes. So ask yourself this, would it really be worth trying to cheat the system, when everything is already free of charge in the first place? Now, John, the main reason that you're here is known only to Joe, myself and the powers that be, let's call them the management. Firstly, let me give you a warning, they, may or may not test each of us as to our honesty, during our stay here, the only problem is that none of us knows when we are being tested. Now, you have been brought here because you have specialist skills as a fraud squad officer, and because of these skills, it will be down to you investigate a problem that has come to the attention of the management.

I have been told that a certain group of men that were brought into the Dome as a sort of trust-greed experiment, but the experiment seems to have gone seriously wrong because it looks like these men, there are three of them, have found a way to infiltrate the Dome's banking system and are somehow using other peoples' thumbprints for their own benefit. I don't understand how they are doing it, but they don't use any of their own points, therefore their points are amassing at an alarmingly fast rate. Your job is to find out why and how they are doing this. Now to come to the reason why you were chosen to carry out this investigation, it is simply because the management have discovered that you have first-hand knowledge of these men, and you were very close to apprehending them three years ago in south London. I believe that you named them the Honda gang, because they always used large Honda motor cycles, to make their escape after robbing jewellery shops in and around London.

This group of jewel thieves were brought into the Dome, firstly to see if they would carry on stealing expensive jewellery, even if they can obtain these same items for nothing and secondly, and more importantly, if they were to steal these precious stones, and we know that they are, how would they do it, and how would they expect to get the stones out of the Dome from which there is no escape?'

So the question I have is this, do we allow them to keep stealing these items or do we stop them now, with very little evidence, and make them face the tube? If we allow them to carry on and they do manage to get the diamonds out of here, it means that they have discovered a weakness in the our security, and we can't have that, can we John? Also, we would like you to test the Dome's security systems yourself and see if you can find any form of weakness, if you do discover that there is a way of escaping from this place, I don't for one minute expect you not to take the opportunity to leave us. But, should you decide to leave us unannounced, I would appreciate it very much if you would leave me a note detailing how you managed to escape and then the necessary action can then be taken, to rectify the problem.'

'Now, as you will discover in the near future, there are a series of hidden doors in the Dome, but don't get too excited, none of these lead to the outside world. Your thumbprint will open these doors because you are beyond reproach by reputation. We have to stop them John, the future of the Dome and its security may depend on it.'

'Yes, I understand what you want from me, all that is quite clear, but how will I find these hidden doors? How do I open them? And do you know how the 'Honda gang' are collecting these diamonds?' John asks.

Andrews smiles broadly. 'You and only you will be privy to this information and you will be informed in due course, meanwhile, I suggest that you take a few days, and get to know the layout of the Dome, and its hidden secrets. When you have done this, we will meet again. At such time, if needed, I will give you a pointer as to where you can start your investigation. Now do you have any other questions?'

Without hesitation John says, 'Yes, I have two questions. Firstly tell me who is in charge and how do we receive our instructions? Secondly, have there ever been any successful attempts at escape?

Andrews looks at John, smiles weakly, and spreads his pudgy hands wide in defeat and saying, 'No-one here knows the answer to the first of those questions, John and don't think that I haven't contemplated this myself over the time that I have been here. The best solution that I can come up with is that in all honesty, I think it best if we don't know who controls the Dome. Ask yourself this, John, is it one of the superpowers or perhaps an even greater power? If it is a superpower, are they searching for a new way to control the human race? If it is an alien power, are they trying to take control of us by studying and controlling our thoughts, that is one thing that they can do for certain. If that isn't the case, then how do we know what action to take next? Here is another thought, how are the facilities supplies brought in without us knowing? How is the grass watered? The rubbish bins emptied, repairs done, shops restocked? In all the time that I have been here, I have never seen it rain, so how do they keep the grass so green and lush? The sun shines every day, all day. Life here is to perfect, which begs the question, will we all die en-masse one day, are we all being cultivated for food or will we all be zapped some day, so that we no longer remember any of this experience and then dumped in some unknown place to fend for ourselves?

These are all questions that need answers, John, but how do we find the answers, when there is no-one to ask? As for the second question, well, when we first arrived here there was a maintenance man here, his name was Gary Seadonly, he was obsessed with the thought of escaping, he tried cutting, burning and drilling the outer shell of the Dome, all to no affect. He spent hour after hour every day rubbing his hands over the outer wall of the Dome's shell trying to find the hidden doorway, but as far as we know he never did locate it, in the end it drove him mad and one day he simply disappeared and was never seen again. We don't know if he was removed by the management or whether he did eventually manage to escape.'

CHAPTER 5

John takes a seat at a bench, in the park area. The bench is situated under a fully leaved tree, somewhere in it's many branches he can hear small birds chattering away to each-other. He chose this particular wooden bench so that he can, not only watch the young men passing the time playing Frisbee, but also to eavesdrop on a group of suspicious looking men holding a secretive conversation at a nearby table. He seems to recognise the men from security footage that he'd seen some time ago back in London, and that footage had been taken from a high end jeweller's shop in Kensington High Street, that had just been robbed.

They sit with heads close together as they whisper to each other, whilst at the same time cautiously looking around, to make sure that they cannot be overheard. His police training and experience, tells him that the trio are up to no good. He is listening so intently to the men, that he doesn't notice a young woman who is standing by his bench, he looks up to see that she is holding a small cardboard tray, which holds two large coffee containers.

'Can I join you?' she asks him nervously. He points to the seat opposite him and says, 'Please, be my guest.'

The young woman nervously takes a seat opposite him and places a coffee in front of him. She then holds her hand out. 'My name is Elsa.'

He takes hold of her hand and squeezes it rather than shakes it. 'John, very pleased to meet you.'

'Are you new?' she asks.

'I arrived only yesterday. What about you?' he asks, and can't help himself as he looks deep into her large chocolate brown eyes.

'Two weeks ago. Is this place weird or what,' she asks with a seductively broad smile. He nods his reply, then adds, 'I don't think weird exactly covers it.' John tries not to look too obvious, but does take the opportunity to study her fine Spanish looking features, while she is looking down at the table as she sips her coffee. She is fairly tall, with tanned olive skin, long straight black hair, which is held back with a bone slide, in the form of a red butterfly. Her large doe-like eyes are dark chocolate brown and are the most beautiful eyes that he has ever seen. He knows without looking that her legs will be long, slim and just about perfect. His thoughts are maybe wrong because of Sarah, but she is definitely a very beautiful woman. He feels guilty as his eyes drop to her ample breasts as they rise and fall, under her black smock. John, on one hand wants her to go away so that he can carry on listening to the three men, but on the other hand, she is a stunningly beautiful woman and he definitely wants to get to know her better.

They drink their coffees and chat nervously about the Dome. The three suspicious men stand up, shake hands and leave in different directions. A disappointed John watches the men as they walk away, he would dearly love to know what they are up to. He and Elsa arrange to meet at the Dome Pub at seven for supper. They part company, and John takes a casual look around his surroundings and decides that, seeing that he is trapped here, he needs to find out what and where the boundaries are. He walks in a straight line from the park, away from the buildings, after maybe two hundred yards, he comes to a well used running track. He looks in both directions and can see, in the distance that the track curves inwards giving the impression that they are imprisoned in a large circular construction. He chooses to turn to the left, for no other reason than he is left handed. He places his right hand against the seemingly transparent outside wall and feels its strange, silky texture which is covered in tiny hard pimples.

He begins to walk along the track that veers slightly to the left. He manages to keep in contact with the silky skin of the outside wall at all times. Keeping his hand on the wall, it takes him the best part of an hour to complete a full circuit. Then he is back in the park area where he began his journey. He stands still and uses his imagination to visualise the full shape of the Dome. He is a bit bewildered that he hasn't felt a door or any sort of recess in the outer wall, but he will continue searching. There just has to be a way out of this infernal place and he is determine to find it.

Detective Constable Molly Wright has been dispatched to John's home to investigate his disappearance. Sitting with Sarah in the kitchen, drinking coffee, she is a typical, confident female police officer, about five foot eight, slim with short chestnut brown hair, she is wearing a smart two piece black suit. The image that she portrays is one of efficiency, intelligence and total control. The first question that she asks Sarah is, 'Can you tell me please, was John happy when he left for work the day that he went missing?'

'Yes, he was very happy. You do know that we have only been married a month?' Sarah answers.

She nods her understanding. 'I'm sorry, but we have to ask these questions, and please call me Molly. Had John any plans to travel abroad, or any problems at work, any financial worries?'

Sarah shakes her head, and when Molly asks about their marriage, a slightly embarrassed Sarah tells her that they had made love that very morning, before they both left for work. Sarah asks Molly about John's car and is told that the police are still looking for it. They have made active the tracker system, but it doesn't seem to be working.

'So what happens now?' asks Sarah.

'Well, obviously, we will keep looking and hope that John turns up sooner rather than later.' The policewoman studies her notes and says, 'that's all I need for the moment. Is there anything that I can do for you before I go?' Sarah shakes her head.

'I must be going then, but I will keep in touch.'

With that, she places her business card on the kitchen table before standing to leave. Sarah opens the door for her and watches her walk back to her car. She takes a quick look at the nearby houses to see that her neighbours are watching from behind twitching curtains, but not one of them has offered her any kind of support. She blames herself for that, as she hasn't made any effort to get to know them as yet, simply because she has been so wrapped up in her own tiny, precious world. Sarah walks back into her quiet, lonely home, closing the door on the outside world. She then sits on the settee and sobs her heart out.

'Oh, John, where are you?' she asks herself for the hundredth time. She rings John's mother to tell her what is happening, John's mother, Joan, is a widow, and kindly offers to come to stay with Sarah until John turns up. Sarah put's her mother-in-law off by saying that she will keep her informed and will ring her immediately if there is any news. Sarah wishes that she could do something, anything, but she knows that all she can do is hope and pray that John will eventually turn up. She picks up her mobile phone and rings the number that she has been ringing all day, and still there is no news.

She has a shower and crawls into her cold bed saying a silent prayer and holding the phone against her chest in the faint hope that someone will ring with good news. Once again she cries herself to sleep.

CHAPTER 6

John sits in the Dome pub, patiently waiting for Elsa, he glances at some of the other customers and realises that they are dressed in normal casual clothes, he thinks back to what Joe had told him about this and resolves to go clothes shopping in the morning. He looks out of the window trying to figure out that, if the hidden doors aren't in the outside walls that he has already examined, then where are they?

In the inside walls, maybe, there could even be one in this very pub? Without actually knowing what he is looking for, how will he ever find them? It is then that he spots the three men from the park standing closely together at the bar, whispering again. Each of them constantly looking around, making sure that they aren't being over heard. His mind travels back to the case file back in his office, and the CCTV photos of the three. They've changed their appearance slightly, but he's pretty certain that it is the same three. This is where he will begin his investigation, starting first thing in the morning.

That will give him the whole night to come up with some sort of plan. Just then, he notices Elsa smiling down at him as she stands by his table, she looks absolutely stunning, wearing a bright yellow dress that seems to illuminate her olive her skin in some way, with matching yellow shoes. She is obviously bra-less by the way that her ample breasts are being displayed. He stands up smiling as he looks her up and down, she has gone to a lot of trouble to make herself look good and he feels suddenly very under-dressed and waves her to the seat opposite him and stuttering, 'Sorry, I was miles away, would you like a drink?' He knows that he has been caught out looking at her breasts again and his lower body has reacted accordingly. He is embarrassed as he tries his best to cover himself, because he knows that she had seen his reaction and having done so, had quickly lifted her eyes back to his but he could see her cheeks turning pink as she began to blush.

'Do you think they do a merlot?' she asks with a slightly nervous stutter, she smiles to herself, because she knows that her efforts to make herself look good have been worthwhile by the way that he looked at her and the sparkle in his eyes as he had looked at her upper body. She wants him sexually, knows that she is very desirable and from the reaction that she had seen in him, he feels the same way and she can't wait to get back to the apartment.

John calls the waiter over and orders a bottle of merlot.

They eat a very good meal of rare steak, fries with all the trimmings and after a short break, enjoy a fresh fruit crumble and custard, the whole meal is just perfect and made better still by the sexual tension so obvious between them. As they sit chatting after the meal, she asks him what he did for a living before being brought into this place as from what she has been told, everyone in the Dome has some sort of unique skill.

Not wanting to give too much away, he says, 'you go first.'

Elsa glances about the room to make sure that no-one is within earshot, she leans over the table and whispers, 'I am a sergeant in the Metropolitan police.'

She looks at him nervously; picks up her glass and takes a large swallow waiting for some sort of response, when he says nothing, she continues, 'I don't know if this makes sense, but I somehow just knew that I had to come and talk to you in the park earlier.'

John sits, looking at her, she is looking down nervously and swirling the dregs of her drink around in the bottom of her glass. He then makes his mind up and says quietly, 'I think that we are supposed to meet. You see, I'm in the Fraud Squad, and believe that we have been brought here to solve a major crime and at the same time, check out the Dome's security. But what I can't figure out is this, if someone can create all this, bring us together, then why can't they solve the crime themselves?'

Changing the subject to their personal lives, John tells her that he has only been married a month. She reaches across the table and grips his hand tightly, and says, 'You poor thing.' As she continues to hold his hand. John returns the gentle grip unable to help himself as he rubs the back of her olive skinned hand with his thumb.

The smiling waiter comes over at that moment, with the scanner and breaks the spell, John release his grip and is suddenly very embarrassed. He places his thumb onto the screen. There is a ping. Realising that they are the last people in the bar, he stands and asks, 'Shall we go?'

They leave the pub and head back, reaching the apartment door they stand looking nervously at one another, 'Please, come in, John. I need to talk to you.'

She leaves the door open for him to follow, he nervously walks into the room trembling because he isn't stupid and knows what she wants from him, and whilst he wants the same thing knows he must stay loyal to Sarah.

'Coffee or wine?' she asks him.

'Coffee, please,' he answers. While she makes the coffee, he looks around her apartment, it is exactly the same as his own.

Elsa places the drinks on the glass-topped coffee table and nervously sits down. 'Please sit down, John. I have something to ask you.'

Nervously, as he joins her on the black leather settee, making sure that they aren't touching. As they silently sip their drinks, she turns to him and asks with a slight tremor in her voice. 'John, will you stay with me tonight, please?'

He gives her a worried look as the last thing he wants is to upset her in any way, but loyalty to Sarah is at the forefront of his mind. 'I'm a very recently married man, Elsa, you know that. It just wouldn't be right,' he answers.

'We don't have to do anything, John, but if you did want to, then we can. It's just that I am so bloody lonely. You're the only person that I have had a conversation with since I have been in this awful place. Please, don't go. Stay with me, John. If only for one night, I will never ask you again,' she pleads.

'Okay, I will stay, but nothing will happen between us, is that clear?'

She nods in agreement, and says thank you. She is disappointed but she will respect his decision. Looking away from him, she stands and heads for the bathroom. Saying quietly, 'Just give me a few minutes, and then you can come through.' He sits on the settee wringing his hands together and thinking to himself, I shouldn't be doing this. I really ought to go. Then the bedroom door opens ever so slightly. He sees the overhead light go out. He stands nervously and thinks, last chance. He turns his head and looks at the apartment door. He shrugs his broad shoulders, turns back and heads for the bathroom. When he has finished there, he walks slowly into the large bedroom. He can see Elsa lying on the far side of the bed, facing away from him.

He undresses down to his boxer shorts and slides into the warm bed. When he is settled, Elsa turns to him and lifts his arm and places it behind her head, resting her head on his hairy chest. She whispers, 'Good night, John.'

'Good night,' he whispers. He lies awake, he can feel her warm body pressing against him, her firm breasts against his naked torso. Her nipples feel rock hard through the thin material of her nightdress. He tries his hardest to ignore all these things, but is finding it very difficult as he breaths in her scent, his body begins to respond and he isn't so sure that he can resist her. He is relieved when Elsa begins to breathe soundly. He feels her stir as she drapes her arm across his waist. He begins to have thoughts that he knows he shouldn't be having.

With his lower body responding the way that it has, he knows that with the slightest of touches in the wrong place she would give herself to him willingly. So he tries his best to lie still and change his thought process and think about his present situation and the future, anything to take his mind off the lovely Elsa.

CHAPTER 7

DC Molly Wright rings Sarah first thing the following morning to tell her that although there is no further news, she will need see her again to ask her some more questions. She arranges to be at Sarah's house at seven that evening, When she arrives Sarah opens the door with a glass of red wine in her hand. 'Any news?' she asks hopefully.

'I'm afraid not, but as I said, I do have a few more questions, if you don't mind?' asks Molly.

Sarah lift her glass towards Molly and asks, 'Want one?'

'Why not,' she replies.

When they are sitting side by side on the settee, Molly says, 'There is something I have to tell you Sarah, but as it is not common knowledge, I must ask you to keep it to yourself. Will you promise to do that?'

Sarah agrees and Molly continues 'What has happened to John isn't an isolated case.'

Sarah's mouth drops open, 'What do you mean not an isolated case? You mean the same thing has happened to someone else?'

Molly holds her hands up to calm the other woman and continues, 'Well, to be perfectly honest with you, it has happened quite a few times recently, and it has nearly always been in the same area. However, there is some good news. Some of the people who have gone missing have eventually turned up again, but not one of them can remember where they have been or what has happened to them.'

Sarah looked aghast and asks, 'How long were these people missing for? Was it days, weeks or months. Just how long are we talking about here?'

'Well, from what we know so far, it ranges from a few months up to two years, but I have to warn you that some of the missing people have not turned up at all,' answers Molly.

'So, what do we do now?' asks Sarah, who is beginning to get slightly irritated.

'Well, there is nothing that we can do, other than wait and hope that John turns up safe and sound.'

Sarah stands up and looking down at the policewoman. In desperation, she says,

'But you must question these people again. Surely one of them knows something. Can't you use some sort of hypnotism, truth drug, anything… you must be able to try something.'

Molly shakes her head and answers, 'We have tried everything that we can think of to get more information from them, and we are doing all that we can. Unless his car or John himself turns up, Sarah, we will just have to wait and hope for the best.'

Molly leaves Sarah curled up on the settee. Sarah has turned her back to the other woman and ignored her completely, after her unintentionally flippant answer. The police officer feels desperately sorry for the depressingly sad woman, but she can do nothing more for her until her husband turns up, either dead or alive!

When Elsa wakes the following morning, she is very disappointed to find she is alone, but she sees a handwritten note on her pillow, which reads:

See you at our usual bench.

I will have breakfast ready and waiting for you.

John

Having showered and dressed, she leaves the apartment and walks across the lush grass, her wet hair flattened against her head and hanging limply. John looks her up and down as he watches her walk towards him in her drab black clothing. He knows that if he were to close his eyes the vision of her standing before of him the evening before would be there, his eyes linger on her bouncing breasts with their erect nipples, he turns his head away because he has been caught out looking at her for just a fraction to long. When he lifts his eyes up to her face, he can see that she is blushing bright scarlet, but at the same time she is smiling coyly because she has achieved what she set out to do, and that was to get John to notice her and her ample attributes.

'Hi,' he says, feeling slightly uncomfortable at being caught ogling her.

'Hi, yourself,' she replies, looking deep into his sparkling blue eyes as she lowers herself onto the park bench directly opposite him.

'Have you by any chance noticed that there are no children in this place?' he asks her. She tears her eyes away from his and looks around at the other residents and shakes her head.

'No, I hadn't noticed, but now that you mention it…'

John says, 'Take a look around and tell me what you see.'

Elsa looks around and says, 'I must admit, it does look rather busy today compared to other days. Maybe I just hadn't noticed before.' As they sit together, they look around. Every person, man or woman, that they can see, seems to be very busy. The shop windows are being cleaned, the grass is being mowed, people are engaged in a variety of mundane, every day useful things.

Elsa asks, 'Have you seen the whole complex? Have you been into the main square yet?'

'No, I've only really walked around the track that runs around the perimeter wall, to the pub, this bench and back' he answers her.

Standing up, she smiles down at him and holds her hand out to him, saying, 'Come on then let's go and explore.' Standing, he automatically take her outstretched hand as they turn and head for the heart of the complex.

After only a few paces, Elsa releases his hand and casually links her arm through his, and looking down at the ground as they strolls along, asks, 'John, may I ask you something?' He glances at her and gives a single nod.

She speaks without looking at him. 'Is it true, as has been suggested to me, that when we do eventually leave this place, we won't remember a single thing about our time here?' Without waiting for a reply, she carries on, 'Just say for arguments sake that we did take our relationship just a little bit further, well, we wouldn't remember it anyway, would we? So, looking at it like that, means that there wouldn't be any harm done to anyone, would there?' She stops him and looks deep into his eyes, with a lopsided grin on her face, showing her true intentions. She wants him badly and fully intends to get him.

'Well, don't you agree?' she asks in a husky voice.

'I hadn't looked at it like that, but I have still been married for only a month, don't forget that either!'

They enter the main street, where she tells him that the street they are now on will eventually lead them to the main square. As they stroll along, they see a group of other inmates sitting on some stone steps, and they all seem to be painting. John glances to where the artists are looking and says sarcastically, 'Once you have painted one white square building, surely you have painted them all.'

Elsa smiles, 'Look at it from their point of view, what else is there to paint, a building or a few trees. Another thought for you, what do they do for fun? I mean how many inmates have you seen actually laughing or having a good time? Not one have I seen, not since have I've been here anyway.'

They look around the small spotlessly clean street. It looks like any other normal boring street, in any other boring town, shops, cafes, pubs and a few people carrying shopping bags. One of the big differences, is that there are never any delivery vans, cars or lorries. People are busy working in a few of the shops, restocking shelves or sweeping floors but in most of the shops, although you can hear people working somewhere at the rear there is no need for anyone to serve as you just walk in and simply help yourself.

When they reach the square, he tells her to find a seat whilst he fetches coffee. She sits and watches two elderly gentlemen playing chess with large wooden pieces which take all their strength to move from square to square. Sitting on nearby steps are other elderly men discussing each and every move made, as they wait for their turn to play. Two men and two women walk past dressed for tennis, which surprises Elsa as she hasn't seen a tennis court, although, obviously, there must be one somewhere. John heads for the Dome Cafe. On his way there, he spots one of his three suspects pushing a square cart with maintenance worker stamped on it's side. That's definitely worth knowing, he thinks.

He returns to the square. Elsa has chosen the end wooden bench on which stands a normal sized chess board with all the pieces in position, as if waiting for a game to begin. He knows why she has chosen this particular bench, so that she can observe the whole square and see what is going on in all areas, who is doing what, and notice if anyone looks at all suspicious.

Clever girl, he thinks as he walks around the chess players, towards her. Her eyes never leave his every step of the way, and now it's her turn to study him as he walks towards her, and his turn to blush as her eyes linger on him. He can feel himself turning bright red as he sits down beside her.

'Bacon sandwich?' He offers her one.

'Just what the doctor ordered, thank you.' She says, taking a huge bite seemingly unembarrassed at being caught out ogling him. Within seconds of her taking a bite of her sandwich a pair of robins appear by her side and the brighter coloured male begins to sing whilst looking at her, as if singing for his supper. Elsa smiles down at the birds and breaks small pieces from her sandwich and tosses them to the birds, which they snatch up and fly into a nearby tree. She watches one it holds the bread under its claw and breaks small pieces off with its beak and eats them. Elsa looks at John and says, 'When you just sit and look around this place, it has everything you could possibly need to make life here comfortable.

I went into the chemist yesterday, and they have everything, all the top brands of make-up, hair products, body lotion, perfume, anything a woman can want. You have to admit that whoever created the place, has gone to a lot of trouble to make sure that everyone's incarceration is as comfortable as can be possible. They even have a nurse, Ellen, working in a small pharmacy. Her main job is to sort out minor ailments. Anything more serious and it has to go through the bank manager, and he sorts the problem out. Apparently he can contact the appropriate person, and a doctor is brought in from the outside, who then treats the patient in a room behind the pharmacy. If it is anything serious, apparently the patient is taken out at night.'

He looks all around him, opens his arms wide and asks, 'But why? What is this place in aid of, there must be a reason for it's existence?'

Elsa shrugs and says, 'I have no idea, John, but we have no choice but to stay here. We will just have to make the best of it, won't we?'

They sit close together, unintentionally touching, the sexual tension between them is more than obvious. John tries his best to ignore the sensation but the heat emanating from her body is driving him mad with desire, as they sit quietly eating their breakfast, each distracted by their own thoughts. They watch other inmates wandering by all seemingly resigned to their fate.

Without looking at him, Elsa asks, 'Where does all the stock for the shops come from? Who orders it all and who pays for everything?'

It's his turn to shrug his shoulders as he ponders the question, and says, 'I don't think we will ever know the answer to that question, do you? I don't think that this is anything to do with the government. This place is way beyond them.' They sit and ponder the problem as they watch the inmates busying themselves, as they go about their daily routine. A pretty young woman walks past and passes Elsa a flyer telling them that the latest James Bond, Goldfinger, is being shown at the Odeon cinema that evening.

'Do you fancy it?' Elsa asks him.

'Why not?' He smiles.

They stroll around the whole complex arm in arm, sometimes hand in hand, like two lost souls in an unfamiliar land. Every now and then, he will stop and look at a few things in the shop windows, but the only thing that interests him at the moment is an unmarked stone building he can see in the distance. A concrete structure that stands completely on its own, he can see no windows or door, this fact alone makes the building stand out suspiciously from the rest of the complex. He gently eases her towards the building, guiding her towards a stone path that leads directly to what looks like a large square block of painted concrete. Once they arrive at the strange building, they walk around the small square construction using the concrete path built around its base.

He quietly asks her as she stands out of view from watching eyes, 'Have you by any chance spotted the hidden cameras yet? I have seen three so far.'

She shakes her head and waits for him to continue talking but his attention has been drawn to something else. A constant humming sound is coming from the concrete building. Also, he can feel a slight vibration when he touches the white walls. On one side of the building, he finds a thumb pad. Looking around to see they are not being observed, he places his thumb on the pad. There is an instant click and a hidden door opens just a fraction. He pulls the door opens just a tiny bit more but can see nothing because of the darkness within.

He turns to Elsa and says, 'When it is a bit quieter, we'll take a look in there.' They walk back to the square, buying two torches just in case it is completely dark in the strange building, a large drawing pad, and a pack of different coloured felt tipped pens. When they arrive back in the park area, they see John's three suspects sitting at a bench, again in deep and urgent conversation. Their eyes are constantly scanning in all directions, making sure that they aren't overheard, making it rather to obvious to everyone around them, that they are up to no good.

John leans close to Elsa, takes a deep breath of her body scent and says, 'See those three over there?' He uses his eyes to indicate the direction in which to look.

She has had a quick glance, he carries on. 'They have been acting very furtively ever since I have been here. I think that we ought to find out a bit more about them, I know what the one with the ginger hair does, but as for the other two, I haven't a clue about them, as yet.'

'I can help you there. The one with the pony-tail works in the flower gardens. I spotted him there earlier, planting some large red flowers.'

Keeping his previous knowledge of the three to himself, he thinks back to what his boss told him on his first day in the fraud squad, 'Trust no-one, not even your best friend, because everyone has a breaking point when being tortured.'

John says, 'That just leaves Baldy, let's watch and see where he goes?' While they wait for the bald-headed man to leave the other two and walk away, John draws a quick map of the Dome's buildings and where he has seen the three hidden cameras.

They turn to each other at the same time, each with their mouths wide open. 'Have you just received an invitation?' he asks in amazement.

She smiles broadly as she nods her head excitedly. 'Please, John, let me tell you, we have just been offered the chance to move in together, apartment 74, Block D.' Elsa looks at him as he sits there with his mouth wide open and his eyes are suddenly wide with excitement.

'That's amazing, how do they do that?' he asks, she grabs his hand excitedly and says earnestly, 'Who cares, lets go and find it.' With that, she pulls him up, and they quickly head for Block D.

They find room 74, their new apartment easily, simply because it is the first door that they come to as they enter the block. They walk into the apartment and are immediately struck by the sheer size of the rooms, this apartment has everything that they will possibly need. A fully equipped kitchen, and the lounge has a white leather three piece suite and a giant flat screen TV mounted on the wall. Against another wall stands a fully stocked bar. On the coffee table in the middle of the room is an envelope marked for John's attention. The word private stamped on it's front.

He is just about to pick the envelope up and open it when an excited Elsa calls out. 'Wow, come and have a look at this, John.'

He walks into the bedroom, and she is standing with her hands on her hips, looking around the impressive-looking room. He feels his eyes grow wide because standing in the centre of the room is the biggest bed that he has ever seen, it has a royal blue silk spread that has a gold crown emblazoned in its centre.

He walks slowly around the bedroom looking in drawers and opening cupboards. At the bottom end of the bed another huge flat screen TV is fixed high up on the wall. Below the TV, on a shelf, stands a state of the art music centre, with rows of CDs, which cover all tastes of music. Row after row of books completely fill another wall, and every other available space has been taken up with mirrors.

He walks into the en-suite which has everything that you could ever want in a bathroom, a giant heart-shaped bath and jacuzzi, which is in its centre, his and hers wash basins and matching towel rails. As he walks back into the main bedroom, Elsa is giggling playfully. She is lying down on the giant bed, pressing buttons on a control pad. 'Come and lie down and try this out?' She shouts excitedly. He walks over and jumps onto the bed and lays down by her side. She presses a button, and a ripple moves slowly up the bed. She presses another button and the bed begins to vibrate, which makes her giggle even louder.

'Hours and hours of fun,' she shouts playfully. They play with the buttons for a while until John climbs of the bed and walks into the lounge. After a couple of minutes, he calls Elsa, 'Come and have a look at this.' When she walks into the main living room, she slips her arm through his as he stands looking down at pictures and a printout of his three suspects that he had spread out on the coffee table.

The ginger haired man's name is Ted. He stands at six feet tall. He is very thin with weasel-like feature, he lives in apartment 3, Block B. Baldy's name is Eric. He has big wide shoulders and a narrow waist, and long shoulder-length hair with startling blue eyes. He is a good-looking guy, and looking at his smirk on his face, he knows it. His apartment number is 2, Block B. Tom is a strange-looking chap with brown hair, which is pulled back and caught up in a long ponytail. He has dwarf-like features, beady eyes, and bowed legs. Tom hasn't a lot going for him in the looks department. He has grey sunken features, stubby nose and bright, rosy red cheeks.

'Someone is trying to help us, don't you think?' asks John.

CHAPTER 8

Joan Stratton, John's mother is a widow of many years. On hearing of Sarah's plight, she drops everything and invites herself to stay with her daughter-in-law. Just from hearing her voice, Joan can tell that Sarah is in a very bad place and desperately in need of her help. John's mother is a kind, slightly plump woman in her late fifties, who always dresses very well. She has curly grey hair that has just a hint of blue running through it.

Sarah can't sleep no matter what she tries and has also begun missing meals. She has made the decision to stop going to work mainly because she just can't concentrate on anything. She spends her days on the computer, constantly moving from site to site trying to find out all she can about missing persons, past and present. Joan is getting seriously worried about her daughter-in-law. When Molly rings with a no news update, Joan tells Molly her concerns about Sarah. Molly also says that she is worried that Sarah is slipping fast into a state of deep depression and that she will call around later with the family doctor, but she isn't to tell Sarah what she is doing.

John walks to the bank to see Mr Andrews, taking with him the list of his suspect's names. Andrews looks at John as he sits down in front of him. 'I suppose you want to see their spending records, am I correct?'

'Yes. If that is possible. I think it may confirm my suspicions.'

Andrews presses a few buttons on his remote and a list of names and numbers appear on the big screen. It reads:

Ted, Apartment A3, Block B.
Day 426. Points out 24. C-F-226
Day 427. Points out 47. C-F- 203
Day 428. Points out 39. C-F-211
Total points carried forward = 7,019

Eric, Apartment A-21, Block B.
Day 482. Points out 48. C-F-202
Day 483. Points out 44. C-F-206
Day 484. Points out 21. C-F-229
Total points carried forward = 8,071

Tom, Apartment A-16, Block B.
Day 462. Points out 74. C-F-176
Day 463. Points out 60. C-F-190
Day 464. Points out 19. C-F-131
Total points carried forward = 6,119

They both study the numbers on the screen, and Andrews says, 'Impossible, just impossible, you just can't get by using so few points. Looking at the points used, they are living on one tiny meal a day and nothing else, and yet we know that all three of them have bought anything that they have wanted, plus plenty of diamonds, watches, necklaces, so how are they doing it?' He turns his face from the screen and looks at John, saying, 'You must find out what they are up to, John, and quickly.'

John rubs his chin, while he sits looking at the carpet, deep in thought. 'There is another way. What about closing down all the shops that stock expensive jewellery, that way they can't buy any more diamonds,' he suggests.

Andrews replies, 'No, I don't think that will work, John, I think we will need the shops open to be able to catch them doing whatever it is that they are doing.'

As John leaves the bank, he walks straight into Joe, who says, 'Ah, there you are. Can you come with me for a minute, please, there is something that you need to see.' Without waiting for a reply, Joe turns and walks away.

John catches up with the other man as he heads for the inconspicuous stone building, that he had discovered earlier. Joe places his thumb onto the scanner and the door clicks open. They both enter the building, and then make their way through another metal door, which leads them to a round, futuristic looking, lift. Once inside, Joe presses a button and the lift begins its silent descent to a lower floor. The lift stops and the door opens into a large, cool, eerily silent, sparsely furnished room. Situated against the wall to the left are a row of wooden seats. Against the wall to the right is what can only be described as a court room dock. Against another wall, standing on a four inch high silver plinth, is a clear round tube, about four feet in diameter, which reaches from where the glass tube fits snugly in the plinth, all the way up to the ceiling and beyond. The whole room has been fitted out in dark wooden panelling and made to look like a replica court-room.

Joe whispers to John, 'Do you remember me telling you about the tube?' When John nods his head, Joe uses his eyes to direct John's attention towards the tube. John studies the clear tube which looks quite harmless from where he stands.

'Today, we have a candidate for its use, and we want you to witness the severity of the Dome's justice system in action,' says Joe. A few minutes later, a door opens behind the dock and a subdued, tall, gaunt-looking bald man enters the court room and stands solemnly in the dock with his shiny head hanging down as if he is embarrassed. He lifts his head momentarily and glances at the tube, shakes his head from side to side and then looks down again and waits for his fate to be announced. Through the same door that they had entered the courtroom through, Mr Andrews enters wearing a pale white wig and a black flowing legal gown. He walks to the centre of the room and nods at John and Joe and then turns to the man in the dock, he lifts a card and begins to read 'Are you David from Apartment 1, Block C?'

The man in the dock confirms that he is indeed that man, by a single nod of his narrow head. And Andrews continues, 'David of Apartment 1, Block C, by the rules of the Dome you have been charged with three crimes, two of violent conduct and one of violent theft. Can you please confirm that you were given a final warning only seven days ago and when you were given that warning, were you reminded of the consequences of your actions.'

The man in the dock seems to ashamed to even look up, he just nods his head again, as if he is resigned to his fate Andrews then asks.

'David, do you know the true consequences of your actions?' Again David doesn't look up, he simply nods his head for the third time in answer. Mr Andrews then asks. 'Can you tell me why you had to use violence to acquire something that you could have acquired for nothing? It makes no sense to me.' The man in the dock, David, just shrugs his shoulder and gives a slight shake of the head. 'Now let me ask whether you have anything at all to say in your defence?'

David shakes his head in resignation. Andrews walks over to the condemned man, and takes him gently by the arm, he leads him towards the clear tube. A soft windy sound begins overhead, the hissing sound increases and becomes a sucking sound. It is as if a seal has suddenly been broken. The tube slowly rises to a height of around ten feet. The condemned man is placed directly below the tube on the silver platform. He looks up as the tube slowly lowers around him, forming a seal as it sinks into the platform. He looks up as the wind noise slowly increases, growing ever louder until it sounds like a tornado in the room with them. The condemned man rises ever so slowly upwards inside the tube with a silent scream. There is a look of shear panic on his terror-ridden face as he seems to hover ever so slightly before suddenly shooting upwards. To where, no one knows. Just like that, he is gone, it is all over. The sound of the wind slowly lessens as they watch another clear tube lower into position, once a seal has been formed around the base the wind slows and slows, until the room is left deathly silent.

Andrews bows to the tube and leaves the courtroom the same way that he had made his entrance. When John and Joe leave the building, the bank manager is nowhere to be seen. John turns to Joe. 'What just happened in there?' he asks.

Joe says, 'That is the Dome's justice system in action, when David first arrived here he was informed of the rules, just as you and I were and if you break the rules, that is the consequence, the system is strong but fair.'

John has a deep frown etched across his forehead as he tries to take in what he has just seen, 'What do you think has happened to him?' he asks, somewhat concerned.

Joe simply shrugs his shoulders and says nonchalantly, 'I don't know, but it can't be anything good, can it?' As the two men enter the lift, Joe presses the '0' button, John sees a silver flap below the lift button and wonders what is concealed underneath it? I had better have a look at that later, he thinks to himself.

When John locates Elsa again, he takes her hand and asks her to take a walk with him to the jewellers. When they arrive, they find a very tall, handsome elderly man with very long thin fingers and manicured nails, smiling at them. He is standing behind a very large display of fine looking jewellery, clocks, rings; merchandise such as you would find in any upmarket shop. 'Can I help you, sir?' he asks John hopefully.

'Yes please. I would like to see some diamond rings and any loose diamonds that you may have,' They are shown a tray of diamond rings. Elsa begins to try the rings on, moving her hand this way and that, watching the false sunlight reflecting in the bright stone.

'Do you like this one darling?' she asks, as she holds the ring in front of John. John raises his eyebrows and gives her a withering sort of look and then ignores her. It is strange to see every item marked for sale in Dome points, rather than real money.

John asks, 'as the rings are so many points, such as this one at 7065 points, how does anyone ever pay the asking price, on only 250 points a day?'

The man smiles and explains, 'Well it's quite simple really, we can accept your running total as a down payment. It just means that you will have to stay with us a little while longer, until you pay off the balance.'

'And tell me, what about someone trying to steal them?' asks John.

'People have tried, but the powers that be,' he looks skyward, and opens his hands wide. 'Well, the ruling forces will surely know. Anyway, that is why I am here, not only to advise but to stand guard over this magnificent display.'

John then says, 'Thank you. We will think about it.'

They turn and leave the still smiling man as he waits for his next customer. 'That's interesting. I have just seen another hidden camera,' he says, as he glances at her.

He sits her down at a quiet bench and tells her about David and the tube. Even about the seemingly minor charges that the victim had faced.

Elsa says, 'I can't understand how they can know that he or anyone else has done something wrong, in the first place. And if he is that violent, how did they get him into the courtroom. They must have some way of subduing a person. I mean, who reports a crime and who to, let's face it, there are no police around to do that sort of thing. I would love to know how they do it and who is behind it all.'

They are strolling back towards the benches in the park area when a commotion over to one side catches their eye. One of the Frisbee players is lying inert, on his back, on the lush grass. As they move closer to have a look and see if they can help, all the people that have gathered around the unconscious man, as one, slowly begin to move back out of the way. They try to move closer to help the stricken man, when they are advised subconsciously to stay back. Seconds later a white, battery operated, flatbed truck with a single blue flashing light and a warning beeper comes into view driven by nurse Ellen from the pharmacy. Sitting by her side is a squat, oriental-looking man dressed in white. The medics pull to a stop by the side of the prone man, step down from the truck and kneel by the his side of the man. Ellen examines him, first listening to his heart and then taking his blood pressure, and from her black bag, she takes out a transparent plastic mask and places it over the man's face.

Then attaching a small white unmarked metal canister to the bag she and her assistant turns a black handle and the sound of escaping gas can be heard. As everyone stands around looking down at the poor young man, he slowly opens his eyes, blinks a few times before they fully refocus. He stays like this for a few seconds before the nurse removes the mask, he takes a deep breath, then sits up, looking around at everyone as they stare down at him. 'What?' he asks, as he stands up, seemingly having made a full recovery.

People standing around him look at one another mystified. The watching crowd chat amongst themselves for a few minutes. Some look skyward, some just shrug to each other and walk away. Those inmates that remain watch the truck as it drives away, and then return to whatever it was they had been doing before the commotion had begun. The Frisbee players soon take up their positions and go back to playing their throwing game, just as if nothing had happened.

CHAPTER 9

Now back at work, Sarah has made the decision that, since there has been no word from John in the few weeks since his disappearance, there is a very good chance that he will never will turn up at all. Molly seems to have forgotten her all together. On top of everything else that is going on, she thinks that she might be pregnant. She is only four days late, but that is very unlike her. She thinks it would be prudent to do a test. The sound of the phone ringing on her desk makes her jump. She can see from the caller display that it is Molly, so she snatches up the receiver and asks, 'Hi, Molly, any news?'

'Hi Sarah. No, not yet, but I was wondering if you could possibly come down to London sometime soon. There is someone that I would very much like you to meet. There's no hurry, but if you can let me know when you can make it, I will set everything up.'

Sarah suggests that she go down that same day, after leaving work. Molly agrees and gives her the address and post code of the person she wants her to meet and asks, 'Shall we say seven this evening?' They say their goodbyes, and Molly ends the call. Sarah's mind instantly slips into overdrive, trying to imagine what information, if any, she will learn later that day.

Sarah heads down the M40 motorway towards London, which, during rush hour is always very busy. The sat-nav is programmed to the post code that Molly has given her, and going by the displayed destination time, she will just about make it on time. When she arrive at the address in Hendon, Molly is waiting outside the terraced house, but she doesn't seem to be her normal self. Molly asks Sarah to sit her car for a minute, as she would like to have a little chat with her before they go into the house. She begins by saying that the man that they are about to meet is named Andy Norman, and he was missing for fourteen months until one day, he unexpectedly retuned home, he simply walked into the house one day as though he had just been down to the shops.

'I'm not saying that this is the same situation as John is in, but I think that you ought to meet Mr Norman, just in case, okay?'

Sarah agrees and follows Molly as they walk up to the front door of the house, which is opened by a plump, grey-haired, homely little woman with thick legs, beady eyes, and a very long pointed nose, who says, 'Ah, Molly, come in dear, and this must be your friend Sarah?' They shake hands and the lady of the house asks to be called Mary.

'In there, in there,' the little old woman says, as she ushers them into a stiflingly hot living room. Every inch of shelf space has been taken up with tiny ornaments, from brightly coloured birds to small thatched country cottages. There are so many of them, that it must take a month of Sundays to dust them all. Sitting in the corner, by a roaring log fire, is a weather-beaten old man who must be a good seventy years old. Resting on a small table by his side, is a well-used brown pipe, smouldering away in a match filled ashtray. In his hands, he holds a mug, full to the brim with steaming hot, strong, tea and on the side of which are printed the words, Worlds Greatest Gardener.

Mary offers them both a cup of tea, which they gratefully accept, and as she leaves the room to make it, Molly introduces Sarah to Mr Norman. Molly bends over the old man as though he is deaf and senile. As she rests her hand onto his arm, she says.

'Hello again Mr Norman, do you remember that I told you about my friend Sarah and her husband who has gone missing?'

Andy Norman nods and asks to be called Andy. Molly then asks him to tell them again what had happened to him.

'Well, there is not much to tell really. I went down me allotment as usual, and when I came home, the missus said that I had been gone for more than a year. I said don't be daft, woman. She was crying and hugging me. She phoned our Jack, that's our boy, and he said that he was coming right over. Then she phoned you lot and, well, here we all are. I still don't know what happened, and I didn't believe it all. That is until I went down the allotment and saw the state of the land. Well, it looked like it hadn't been worked on for an age. I am very proud of me bit of land, you know.'

When the old man stops talking, they see Mary standing in the doorway with a tea tray in her hands, as if rooted to the spot, just staring at her husband, she seems so relieved that he has returned home. On the tray sits her best china. Molly walks over and takes the tray from Mary and places it on the coffee table. Mary pours the tea and hands them both a cup, and then passes round a plate of rich tea biscuits. 'And you say that you don't remember anything at all?' asks Sarah.

'No, not a darn thing. It was just like I had just come back from the allotment. Fourteen months she said I was gone. I still can't get me head around it all,' replies Andy Norman as he shakes his head in total bewilderment.

Sarah and Molly finish their tea and politely leave. When they are outside, Molly asks Sarah if she is hungry and Sarah suggests an Indian restaurant. Molly smiles and says, 'Come on then, we'll take my car. I know a place not far from here.'

When they are sat down eating, Sarah asks, 'Why did you bring me to see Mr Norman, Molly?'

The police woman thinks for a minute before answering, she then says, 'Well, I guess I just wanted to prepare you in case John should suddenly turn up out of the blue one day.'

Sarah nods her head in understanding. On the journey back up the motorway towards her home, all Sarah can think about is fourteen months. He may not love her after all that time and if she is pregnant, the baby will be five months old when he finally does return home. She received one piece of good news from Molly, and that was that the police are still going to pay John's salary because, as far as they are concerned, he is still on active duty. That means that at least the mortgage will be paid. She drives home on auto pilot, and before she knows it, is sitting on the driveway outside her lonely home, not really knowing how she had made it there.

John and Elsa stroll down to the pub for a meal before going to the Odeon to see the James Bond film. They have both chosen rare steaks, and again, a bottle of merlot. They are enjoying their meal when the three suspects stroll into the pub. They stand at the bar and order three pints. They then each order a meal and sit down at a table in full view of John and Elsa. John doesn't know if he's being paranoid, but he has a feeling that Ted, the ginger-haired one, keeps glancing at him. He decides to ignore him and goes back to enjoying his meal with Elsa. They talk about Bond films, the ones that they had already seen.

They have a very enjoyable meal and leave the pub to walk to the cinema. As they stroll along the street, Elsa takes hold of John's hand as if it is the most natural thing to do. It is at this moment that he realises that he hadn't thought about Sarah for a couple of days. He guiltily let's go of her hand and pretends to look at some books in a shop window. As he is looking in the shop window, he catches a slight furtive movement from behind him, on the other side of the street. He waits and watches the reflection because he knows that whoever it is will show themselves eventually. Sure enough, Ponytail is in a shop doorway watching them. So John takes hold of his date and kisses her deeply, all the time watching Ponytail in the shop windows reflection. Elsa kisses him back hungrily and pushes her willing body against his. After a couple of minutes, ponytail walks back towards the pub. When they end the kiss, she is breathless and asks where that had come from, not that she was complaining. He tells her about Ponytail, and rather than let things spoil their evening, they still go and see the film, surprised to see that the small cinema is almost full.

Having enjoyed the film, they make their way back to the apartment. She has her arm draped through his and he is very conscious of her firm breast rubbing against his arm. She looks at him and says jokingly, 'You can be my James Bond tonight, if you want to,' she giggles.

When they arrive back at the apartment, John goes into the kitchen to make coffee. When he carries the coffee into the living room, she is sitting on the couch in her flimsy royal blue dressing gown, watching a nature programme presented by David Attenborough.

He passes her the hot coffee and sits down by her side. He can't help but notice that every time she lifts her mug to her lips, he can see the whole of her naked left breast. She obviously knows exactly what she is doing because at that point, she just sits there holding her mug to her lips. John takes a big gulp of his coffee and swears at himself for having the thoughts he is having. He is becoming very aroused, and hates himself for it. Elsa leans towards him and kisses him on the cheek. She intentionally does this so that her left breast is fully exposed to him. She smiles a knowing smile and leaving him sitting there goes into the bedroom.

He is forced to sit there on his own for quite a while until he has calmed down, he has to wait until things are back to normal but hates the fact that he is acting like some back alley tomcat.

When he does eventually walk into the bedroom, he nervously takes his clothes off, and without looking at Elsa, he slips into the huge bed. She immediately turns over to lay against him, she lifts her head, which allows him to place his arm behind her head. She then moves closer and rubs her naked body against his, she then bends her leg and places it onto his hardening manhood. With a husky voice says, 'Come on Bond, don't fight it.' With those few simple words, he is lost. The new lovers make urgent passionate love, over an over until they are both totally spent. They finally sleep soundly, lovingly wrapped around each other.

CHAPTER 10

A month and a bit has past since Sarah has seen her husband and she has discovered that she is indeed pregnant. Over lunch, Sarah tells Joan, who is very excited at the prospect of becoming a grandmother. Although, unknown to Sarah, her mother-in-law has already guessed as much. Joan, deep down is very pleased, but also slightly concerned at the good news.

'Now you have something to look forward to, dear,' says the older woman, but when she looks around at Sarah, who is lying down on the settee, with her back to her, silently crying uncontrollable tears which roll down her red cheeks. Joan sits by her daughter-in-law and holds her tight in a bid to comfort her.

'John will be soon be back, dear, you'll see,' says Joan. Sarah looks around at the older woman and whispers.

'It's not that I don't miss him terribly, Joan, it's my mum and dad. They would have been so proud at the news of the baby, had they still been alive.' Joan affectionately rubs Sarah's back and says, 'Yes, dear, they would have been very proud. Very proud indeed.'

They sit quietly holding each other until Joan says, 'we will Just have to make the best of it until he returns home, dear.'

As Sarah looks at the large framed picture of her parents that hangs in pride of place above the fireplace, she knows in her heart that they would be happy for her, and that from up in Heaven, if it is at all possible, they will look out for her and protect her. She then thinks back to when she was only ten years old and her granny, whom at the time she was spending the day with, telling her that her mummy and daddy had gone up to Heaven. She did eventually find out, years later, that a drunk driver had driven head on into their car, killing both of them instantly. Not long after that, she also found out that her other granny had died from a broken heart. Sarah then went to live with her aunty Gwen in South Wales until she was eighteen years old. She then moved to London to stay with her cousin Alison, who worked as a secretary. Alison managed to get Sarah a job in the same car distribution company.

The company had, at the time, a very large fraud problem. That was when Sarah met the tall, dark haired, man named John Stratton. The rest, as they say, is history.

John is making toast when Elsa comes up behind him and slips her arms around his waist, 'I only have one regret about last night, John.'

'What's that?' he asks, smiling. 'I regret that when I do eventually leave here, I won't remember our love making.'

He turns around and looks deep into her eyes. He slips his arms around her waist and asks, 'What if you become pregnant, Elsa?'

She smiles broadly and looks into his sparkling blue eyes, and says, 'I had a subliminal message last night saying that I will not become pregnant, because the powers behind the Dome have taken care of the problem by adding something to the water supply. That's why there are no children in the Dome.' She smiles at him and says, 'So, fire away, James.' So with that, he takes her deep and slowly, right there and then on the kitchen table, all thoughts of Sarah gone for the moment. When they are both completely spent, they leave the kitchen and have a long soak in the giant bath where they begin making love all over again.

Sitting at their usual bench in the park, John looks at his plan of the Dome and tries to work out the possible positioning of any other hidden cameras, as he is convinced that there have to be more of them placed in other strategic positions. But there is the added problem of finding out where the control centre is hidden. He looks up at Elsa as a sudden thought strikes him and asks, 'How do you steal someone's identity in a place like this, when your only identity is your own thumbprint?' He lowers his eyes from hers, and then sits there deep in thought looking at his thumb.

'Let's take a look around the shops,' he suggests. She asks if they are looking for anything specific. He replies that they are looking for some sort of scanner. They do a complete tour of the shops and find nothing, except another hidden camera. But the trip isn't a total waste of time because Elsa takes John clothes shopping, the casual clothes that he buys are for a night out at one of the pubs. Sitting back at the bench, he marks the camera's position on his map of the Dome. After some thought, he says, 'Thinking about it, there can only be two possible explanations. The first is that ginger, the maintenance man, has made a scanner to scan the thumbprints, or the second, well, I don't even want to think about that because is to gruesome to even contemplate.'

Maybe I should go and see Andrews again, he thinks. He suggests to Elsa that she take a walk to the shops and buy the ingredients for their evening meal, which he will cook when he returns to the apartment.

'Are you trying to get rid of me?' she asks with a smile on her face. In response, he smiles back at her and walks away towards the bank. He strolls into the bank where Andrews smiles at him and, without standing up, reaches out and shakes his hand.

'I had a feeling that you were on your way to see me, John. Come, let's go into my private office.' The fat man heaves himself out of his chair and leads the way inside. As John follows close behind he notices a strange musty odour coming from the bank manager and decides that the smell isn't very nice at all. He holds his breath and allows the other man to sit down before he enters the office When they are both seated, Andrews asks John what he can do for him.

'Is there any way that you can tell if someone is almost at their end release date and for no apparent reason at all, has suddenly spent all their points, And can you tell if these people are still physically visible inside the facility?'

Andrews sits with his pudgy hands clasped together on his huge stomach and looks at John, 'There are many questions there, John, and it will take some time to answer them all, although what you are suggesting does sound rather, sinister. Come back tomorrow and I will see what can be done.'

John stays where he is and says, 'I thought you said that there are no cameras in the Dome. But I have located a few hidden ones, and if there are cameras, there has to be a control centre, and it has to be around here somewhere.

The bank manager looks down and smiles. 'You really are very good, aren't you, John? You see, I have looked for cameras myself but have never found any. We had a man named Colin Rothe staying with us a while ago. He was a skilled surveillance officer, and he was on the same mission as you are. He came to me one day and began trying to tell me that all of this is some sort of undercover military operation. Well, to be honest, I didn't believe him. Two days later, he just disappeared. I have asked myself a thousand times; did our Mr Rothe find a way out of the Dome? If he did, then the others who have gone missing must have found a way out also, which means there is definitely a security problem.' John stands and leaves the office and takes some deep breaths of fresh air before he walks straight to the unmarked building. He stands with his back against it, deep in thought. After a very long time, he says to himself, 'I wonder.'

On his return to the apartment, he finds Elsa in the middle of making a Bolognese. When she sees him, she says, 'I have couple of films for later if you fancy it.' But he doesn't hear her. He has a bottle of wine open and is sitting with a full glass held to his lips, untouched, and again he is deep in thought. He is still sitting in the same position when she brings the meal through. She looks down at him. 'Are you okay, John?'

He shakes his head and says, 'Sorry, I was miles away. Oh, that does look good.' He says, taking the meal from her. They sit side by side and eat with their plates on they laps, just like an old married couple. When they finish, he asks her, 'Fancy a spot of detective work later?'

She looks at him with a crooked smile and says, 'I had something else in mind for later, but I suppose it can wait.'

He keeps watch out of the window until all is quiet. He then takes the two small torches that he had bought earlier. He turns to Elsa and asks, 'Are you ready?'

She takes the torch that he offers and flicks it on and off to make sure it is working. She follows him out of the door and make their way to the unmarked building. After a final look round to make sure they aren't being watched, he places his thumb on the pad. There is and instant ding, and the door clicks open. When they are in the lift, he lifts the hidden wall pad and presses the button that he had seen earlier. The lift begins it's silent descent. They pass the courtroom and go deeper into the bowels of the facility. The lift finally stops, and when the doors open, they are looking down a long, shadowy corridor. Only the first light is on, but as they move along the corridor, more of the lights come on. At the end of the corridor stands an uninviting white wooden door. John places his thumb onto the pad, another ping, and the door opens into complete darkness. They switch their torches on, and the first thing that they see is a red car. As they sweep their torches around, more and more cars come into view. John turns and shines his torch onto the wall, looking for a light switch. Finding one he places his thumb on the pad and, with another ping, all the lights come on. They are standing in a huge underground car park and staring at hundreds of cars. They have found the car park containing every inmate's vehicle.

'My God,' exclaims Elsa. John begins to walk quickly between the cars. He tries the door of a couple of and finds them all unlocked and each car has its keys in the ignition. He quickens his pace, his eyes darting this way and that. Eventually, he finds his own car. He opens the door and reaches for his phone.

'Shit,' he exclaims out loud as he finds the phone is dead. He knows that he has no charger in the Dome anyway. He tries to start the car's engine. Nothing.

Elsa leans into the car and says, 'can we go back now, it is bloody freezing down here.'

He hadn't really felt the cold until she mentioned it. He suddenly realised just how cold it is and begins to shiver. He takes her hand and leads the way back to the door. Before they leave they stand and look around the giant car park once more. The car park itself must be as big as a football field and at least forty feet high.

Back inside the apartment, he stands at the window and looks in every direction to make sure that they aren't being observed. Sitting next to Elsa on the leather settee, she turns to him and says that she can't believe what she has just seen.

He looks at her, 'If they can get cars in, then they must be able to get cars out again. Maybe there is a way out of this place. We must go back down there soon and do a proper search.' He grabs her hands in excitement and says, 'but first, we need to buy some warmer clothes.'

CHAPTER 11

Sarah and Joan spend their days either shopping for baby things or decorating the nursery. When Sarah is left in the house on her own, she sits on the floor of the nursery and cries her eyes out. Early one Sunday morning, she feels the baby kick for the first time. She wishes that John were there to share this precious moment with her. She has been given sick leave from work, mainly because she looks so ill. She is painfully thin now, so much so that she looks almost anorexic.

All that she does these days is sit and stare into space as if she has nothing to live for. When Joan tries to bring her out of it, Sarah will just sit and cry because she says that she misses John so much. As the long days pass, she becomes more convinced that her husband has gone forever. At that thought, she begins to sink into a deep state of depression. Joan tries her best to support her, but it is getting increasingly more difficult as the days wear on. Joan has made her mind up that she will have to call Molly again and see if she can help in any way because Sarah can't go on like this. Not only for her sake, but for the baby's, as well.

The older woman also want's to call Sarah's GP because she is worried about the unborn baby's health, with Sarah being so painfully thin she feels she may have to be sectioned, so the doctors can apply to the courts and get permission to force feed her if necessary. Joan realises that she hasn't seen her daughter-in-law eat anything at all in the last few days.

The next day, John and Elsa go shopping for the warmest clothing they can find. They go back to the apartment and stow their newly bought items away. They will leave their investigation until much later that night, when things are a lot quieter.

'What shall we do while we wait for it to get dark, then John?' Elsa asks with a hint of excitement in her voice.

'Lets take some precautions first. Let's hide a few things in certain places. That way we will know if someone has been in here, someone who shouldn't have been.' John suggests, trying his best to change the subject.

After arranging different items in a certain way, he says, 'Let's go and see what our friends are up to today, and I do have to go and see Andrews today, at some point' They make their way hand in hand to the park. John goes to fetch breakfast from the bakery while she sits and watches people going about their daily business, not one of them is smiling, not one of them seems to be very happy. Of their suspects, there is no sign whatsoever, which, is, in itself, very unusual and slightly worrying.

John walks over to the bank to see Andrews. When they are seated in his private office, John tries his best to breath in and out of his mouth because the odour is a lot stronger today, the fat man intertwines his short stubby fingers on his huge belly and says, 'I have some very disturbing news for you, John. You asked me to find out if any of our people have accumulated a lot of points and suddenly, for no apparent reason at all, began to spend their points. Well, I have to tell you that there are eight inmates who have, that we know of so far. And you asked if they are still in the confines of the Dome Well, the truth is, we cannot locate them. I have asked Joe to look into things and to keep me updated. Tell me, what do you think is going on, John?'

John sits still and thinks for a while, and then asks, 'Exactly how many points have gone missing in total?'

'Altogether, there are at least 495,000 points so far, but there could be a lot more, we are still checking, and they have all been used in the same shop, the jewellers shop, and they have all been used to buy diamonds, rings, necklaces, and broaches.'

John sits and thinks over this information and asks, 'Can you tell me where the maintenance man has his office?'

'That's easy. It's at the rear of the Bell.' He smiles.

John asks, 'If I needed to take a look in his workshop, can you find him something to do that will keep him busy for an hour or so?'

'No problem. We know that you have bought some warm clothing. Not many people wear warm clothing in the Dome, and you may wonder why we have such clothing shops in the first place, as the climate is so constant. Well, it's because, at some unspecified date, we will wake up one morning to find that the temperature in the Dome has dropped dramatically, it will be so cold, that mist will come out of your mouth, when you breathe. When we go into the park we'll find that a huge ice rink has been erected and the shop where you acquired your warm clothing today is suddenly stocked with ice skates. Whenever this event happens, it makes me think of Christmas and my family.

I sometimes think that this is some sort of test, a test to judge us by, to see how we would manage in a certain type of catastrophe. But it is quite entertaining to see all the inmates suddenly rush to the shops to buy warm clothing. Part of the test being that, although the clothing has been in clear sight day in and day out for months on end, and the inmates have walked past those shops hundreds of times, not one of them has ever paid them any attention. They then panic as they search the shops for anything warm, when the clothing has, in-fact been on sale all the time that they have been here. That's my theory, anyway.

I also see that you have discovered the underground car-park. That is rather clever of you. You have obviously noticed how cold it is down there. Well, I can tell Ted to do a temperature check because a hot spot is showing on the monitors, shall we say, one o'clock today? Oh, and by the way, you will have to be quick in your investigation of the workshop because there is no security coverage down there, so we won't know when Ted is returning until he reaches the surface again.'

With that, the fat man smiles, as John nods his head in thanks, Andrew's smile widens as he returns the nod. Happy with the way that the investigation is going he says, 'Splendid. I find the whole affair quite exciting. Please, let me know if you find out anything useful.'

John watches the maintenance man push his trolly towards the stone building. With Elsa keeping watch. John makes his way to the man's workshop. He searches every nook and cranny but can't find any sort of scanner. He does however, find a small metal box that has been securely fixed into the base of one of the lower work benches, The steel box has a rather large heavy duty lock on the front.

They are sitting at their usual bench eating an ice cream when they see the ginger-haired man returning from his underground work. John watches him every step of the way and wonders what will happen next.

CHAPTER 12

Molly arrives at Sarah's house and knocks on the door. Sarah opens the door and is surprised to see the policewoman standing there holding a large bag of fish and chips, smelling strongly of heated vinegar.

'Supper?' Asks Molly, smiling broadly. Sarah sniffs the air as she stands to one side and lets her visitor enter. Joan and Molly dish out food onto plates. A knowing look passes between the two, because as Joan had secretly rung Molly earlier in the day to tell her what a sorry state that Sarah is in. When they carry the food into the dining room, Sarah sniffs the air hungrily, showing her first real interest in food for a long time. She falls on the food and devours hers before the two women are even half way through theirs. She even asks her mother-in-law if there is any chocolate ice cream in the freezer.

Molly sits and holds Sarah's hands and tells her that she has to start looking after herself because of the baby, if for no other reason. She goes on to say that if she has to bring her fish and chips every night, then that is what she will do. Sarah nods her head and says, 'I'm so sorry, but my head's been all over the place lately. I miss John so much, you know, and the thought of him being missing for all this time. I don't think that I could stand it if I have to give birth to our baby without him being there. I don't even want to think about going through all that on my own. I just don't think I can' Molly pulls her into her shoulder and whispers into her ear, 'You don't have to go through it all alone. I am here for you, Sarah. I will be by your side every step of the way, that is if you want me to be?'

Sarah pulls away from the police woman and says, 'Oh yes please, Molly. I would love for you to be there, thank you. Oh, thank you.'

And from that moment on, Sarah begins to improve both mentally and physically. She begins eating more regularly and it shows in her demeanour. Molly accompanies her to each of the scans she has to undergo and attends all the prenatal classes. Joan seems to be a bit put out at first, but seeing the effect that Molly is having on Sarah, she bites her tongue and secretly thanks Molly for her help.

John and Elsa wait until all is quiet before pulling on warm clothing and heading for the underground car park. They hold hands as the lift makes its way silently underground, John uses his thumbprint to gain access to the car-park. With the lights turned on, they walk in different directions in their search for a way out of the Dome. They run their fingers along every inch of the strange feeling outside wall. When they meet in the middle, they look disappointedly at each other. John looks around and says, 'There just has to be a way out of here.' In a fit of temper he smashes his fist against the unfeeling outside wall. They walk back towards the door and John spots a green van with the name Colin Rothe on it's side. Underneath the name is written 'Surveillance Officer.' John makes a mental note to come back as soon possible to take a closer look at Colin's van. They make their way back up to ground level. They step out of the door into the daylight to see that they are being watched, yet again.

They make their way back to their apartment and remove their warm clothing, Elsa says, 'Someone has definitely been in here, John, things have been moved.' John looks around and finds that his plan of the inside of the Dome is missing, but, he wonders, will the thief be able to figure out the significance of the crosses, the ones that mark the position of the hidden cameras? As they make their way to the Bell to eat, they are again followed every step of the way by the three criminals. They sit at a table and order a meal and a bottle of red wine. The trio sit at the bar close to them and order three beers. The ginger-haired one then takes John's drawing out of his pocket and spreads it out on the bar. All three bend over the sheet of paper. Quiet conversation passes between them. Ginger keeps glancing at John. Occasionally he will say something, and the trio will all laugh. John and Elsa take their time over the meal. They finish the wine before standing and nodding at the trio as they leave. They make a point of slowly walking around the perimeter wall. They don't need to stop and look back, because they know that every step that they take is being noted by three pairs of inquisitive eyes.

Once back in their room, John places a chair under the door handle to keep out any uninvited guests. They go to bed and make passionate love, soon afterwards Elsa falls asleep, but John lies awake deep in thought. He tries to make up his mind about going back down to the car-park, but can he make it down there without being seen? He knows that he needs to have a look inside Colin's Rothe's van.

The next thing he knows, it is early morning. Having showered and dressed, the pair make their way to the park benches. They no sooner sit down, than the villains turn up and sit down at the next bench. They open the sheet of paper again. All three of them bend over the drawing, looking deeply at the paper, trying desperately to learn it's secrets. John and Elsa spend the day walking around the main square, shops and making a full circuit of the running track, occasionally stopping and pointing at nothing. John smiles to himself when the men following stop where they have just been, and stand and look all around to try and figure out what the two have seen and what they have found so interesting. By the end of the day, Ted isn't a happy bunny as he finally realises that they have been on a wild goose chase the entire day. Ted sits near to them in the park area and scowls, pure hate filling his eyes.

John stands looking out of the apartment window late at night. He stares at Tom, the gardener, as he skulks in the shadows, watching their apartment. John makes a decision to wind them up even further. He takes his torch and creeps from the apartment building, but making sure that the gardener sees him. He walks slowly around the perimeter wall, stopping occasionally, and touches the wall, moving his hands in a circular motion, he then moves a few paces further on and repeats the circular hand waving. John makes a full circuit of the Dome, and then walks back into his apartment. He pushes a chair under the door handle again and climbs into bed next to his more than willing, olive skinned lover.

CHAPTER 13

John is up, dressed and ready very early the next morning. With torch and warm coat at the ready, he looks out of the window, checking in all directions to make sure that the trio are not already in position outside the apartment. He makes his way cautiously to the stone building. After a final look around he makes his way inside, and down to the cold carpark. He doesn't switch the lights on, but checks he is on his own as best he can. Cautiously, he makes his way to Colin's Rothe's van. He shines his torch through the windows but can see nothing because the windows have been designed so that they can be seen through but only from the inside. John tries every door but finds that they are all locked. He shines his torch under every wheel arch.

He finally finds the van's keys hidden under the front right-hand wheel arch, the keys are tucked into a specially created slot, he unlocks the side door, and taking a final look around pulls the door open. He steps into the van and drops onto the black seat that has been set in the centre of the interior floor. He then shines his torch all around the interior to see a large piece of paper leaning against the main computer screen in front of him.

He looks closer at the A4 piece of paper, and reads:

Hi,

My name is Colin Rothe. I have left this note to let you know that there is a way to escape from this bloody awful place, which you will discover when you have seen every disc that I have left for you. But to play those discs, you will need electricity. If you look on the side of the door behind you, you will see a roll of cable, which has been connected at the van end. Take the cable and go to the front of the van, then walk to the left, unrolling the cable as you go. When you get to the end of the cable, look in the wall. You will see a small finger sized hole about a foot from the ground. When you place your finger into the hole, you will feel a button. Press this button and a panel will drop open.

There you will find your electrical socket. But remember, you must always unplug the cable and stow it back in the van when you have finished with it, making sure that the van is always securely locked and please leave the key where you found it because if you take the key up top and someone else finds it, you will have lost it forever. Finally, only when you have fully closed the door can you switch the computer monitors on. The red switch on the top right-hand corner of the panel is the on/off switch. Finally, when you switch on the power, everything will suddenly become very clear.

Good luck,
Colin

John runs the cable to where he has been told and easily finds the socket. When he returns to the van, he locates the switch and flicks it on, his world suddenly becomes illuminated, as the bright roof light comes on. A bank of screens flash into life. A heater slowly fills the van with much welcomed warmth. He looks over the rest of the van to see that every available space is taken up with storage boxes. John looks back to the screen and can see every area of the Dome, he looks at each screen in turn, he can see Elsa sitting on a bench drinking coffee, the three crooks closely watching her. A short message is printed on the lowest screen, it simply reads:

I tried too tell Andrews what I had discovered but he just laughed at me. Let me give you a word of warning, as you are allowed access to the car-park then you must be on the trail of our diamond thieves. There are bodies hidden in various car boots down here, each body is minus its right thumb. This small fact will answer many of your unanswered questions.

I have left a wooden box of discs on the top shelf to your right and I would suggest that you take the time to view each of these in turn, and when you do decide to follow me out of here, please take the discs with you, as you may be a lot more intelligent than myself and know the best thing to do with them. If in the future you require me to back up your story, then you are obviously intelligent enough to find me. We will require a password for the time when we do eventually meet 'Chile' will do. Remember this word because when you turn the screen off, the password will automatically delete itself.

Good luck,

Colin.

John, having found the wooden box, picks up the first disc and pushes it into the machine. A picture of an empty Dome comes up on the screen, there isn't a single person in sight and John suspects that it has to be night time. For some unknown reason John hadn't even thought to consider what happens at night while they are asleep, but it looks as if he is about to find out. A white light appears on the ground, which is on the left side of the screen, it travels all over the roof of the Dome and disappears into the ground on the opposite side from where it originally began. Nothing happens for a while then a lone Army officer in full military dress uniform, walks into the middle of the main square, he looks all around the grounds of the facility and then talks into a hand-held radio.

A few minutes later there is a loud click and the Dome's outer shell begins to slowly split open just wide enough to allow three green Army vans to enter and draw up in the main square. He watches as men and women, some in Army uniforms and some in civilian clothing, take trays of different stock into the various shops and bring out unused or out of date stock and place these into the vehicles. Another van comes into sight and a team of men remove every bit of rubbish from the bins. When the trucks and personnel leave the compound, the same Army officer again looks all around the Dome's interior, satisfied he talks into his radio and the Domes outer shell begins to close up again. Once this operation is complete everything falls silent, the light dims and the facility is in complete darkness.

John ejects the first disc and places the second into the machine, a long white unoccupied office comes into view, it is mainly empty, but for the far end of the room, where lying in a row on the bare floor is a line of clear empty plastic tubes. The tubes are around ten feet in length and four feet across. Nothing immediate happens so he fast-forwards the disc and stops it when he sees a flash of movement. He finds the place where the action begins, a tall thin man has been sucked up into the first tube, he scratches at the wall of the tube and by the look on his face he is screaming in silent terror. A round disc slide over the end of the tube and turns clockwise, until the disc is locked into place, with a loud click it seals itself over the end of the tube. The air is then sucked out of the tube, he watches as the man slowly suffocates to death. When he is finally dead, the tube with the man's body still inside moves to one side and another empty tube moves into place, to wait for the next victim of the Dome's lethal justice system.

When nothing else seems to happen, he fast-forwards the disc again, he is about to give up when some alien looking shapes appear on the screen. He stops and rewinds the disc to the appropriate place, four Army personnel walk into the room, they stand and look down at the corpse. They remove it from the tube and place it in a black body bag, once inside the bag they roll the tube back into position ready for use again. They pick up the body bag by handles that have been sewn into each corner, then carry the body from the room.

John is about to pick up the next disc when he hears a sound outside the van. He stops what he is doing and closes everything down as his eyes peer into the darkness of the car-park, a flash of a torchlight catches his attention. He watches as a man does something furtive underneath the bonnet of a small black van, which is at most ten yards away from where he is sitting unseen. Whoever it is seems to know what they are doing, the man finishes what he is doing and closes the bonnet down, he then stands and shines his torch all around the rows of cars, confident that he hasn't been seen, the man leaves to return to the surface.

John decides that he has seen enough for one day. So he rolls up the electricity cable and hangs it on the back of the door. He locks the van and replaces the key in it's hiding place. He is about to leave the car-park but stops when he reaches the van that the man has been doing something to. He searches for the bonnet catch, flicks it and opens the bonnet and props it up. He shines his torch around the old engine, it is when the touch light moves past the old van's plastic water bottle, that the base sparkles. He shines his torch light into the bottle, he can see that the bottom of the bottle is completely covered by diamonds, hundreds of different sized sparkling diamonds. He has found their stash of stolen gems. He replaces everything exactly how he had found it and with a smile on his face leaves the car-park a very happy man.

He finds Elsa relaxing on the bed in their apartment; not being sure whether Ted has bugged their apartment or not, he places his finger onto his lips telling her not to speak. He takes her hand in his and leads her outside. They walk silently to the benches and sit down, he looks all around before he tells her quietly what he has found in the car park. Well, almost everything, he neglects to tell her about the diamonds. Elsa's face has shock written all over it and she has great difficulty believing him. He tells her about the other discs in the van and she says that she wants to be there when he views them. It is then that he realises that they are being watched again. Ted is sitting at the next table staring at John, when John looks back at him, Ted asks in a vicious voice.

'Are you a copper? If you are, you had better keep your nose out of my business, understand that copper?' With that, he stares menacingly at John for a few seconds longer and then, standing up, he puffs out his chest and walks away.

CHAPTER 14

Sarah is getting very close to full term and she seems to be getting bigger by the day, and has begun to get all sorts of twinges and strange feelings. She is experiencing a mixture of unusual cravings, the latest for pickled onions, which, she would not normally eat, even if her life depended upon it. Molly is on speed dial and ready to drop everything at a moments notice, Joan has the car packed, full of fuel and ready, the nursery is ready, and all they are waiting for now is the arrival of the baby. Sarah is now in the habit of praying every night for her husband's speedy return. She prays and crosses herself each night before she climbs into bed, she desperately wants him to come home before the birth because, secretly, she is terrified at the thought of giving birth and needs him to be there for reassurance, if nothing else.

John and Elsa search the shadows for their watchers, but after half an hour, not a single movement has been seen. Elsa had felt the need for sleep at one point but managed to stay awake with a bit of encouragement from John. It is late when they move out of the apartment block and make their way down to the underground car park. Once there John takes the key from its hiding place and unlocks the van. He sets up the electric cable, closes the van's door and switches the power on, which in turn turns the screens on. Nothing moves anywhere on any of the screens, they sit and wait patiently for something to happen. They eventually see a white light move from one side of the Dome to the other, it reminds John of one of those zip up food bags being unzipped. They wait another ten minutes and then the same Army officer goes through the same routine as before. The same vans are driven into the Dome and do the same thing, a large green water tanker comes into view and waters every blade of grass.

They watch as the inside surface of the roof is cleaned by a team of men. When everything is done, the officer speaks into his radio again and the Dome's shell closes up and becomes eerily still once more, as darkness descends. Elsa is about to speak but John holds his finger up to quieten her and says, 'There's more, just wait and see, we'll discuss it back at the apartment.' She nods and sits watching the screen, waiting to see what will happen next.

John picks up the next disc and pushes it into the machine, initially all they can see is darkness. Thinking that it is a blank disc John fast forwards it, when lights suddenly appear on the screen, he presses play, the car park that they are sat in suddenly lights up on the screen. Nothing happens at first then the side of the Dome seems to split in two, opening like a chocolate Easter egg. A large red crane slowly enters the car park, the driver then maneuvers the crane into position and extends its long arm so that the crane reaches over the top of the rows of cars. A group of men in green Army fatigues walk into the car park, the leading soldier carrying a clip board. The men locate the car that they require, straps lower down from the crane until, the soldiers can reach them, they watch as the soldiers place the straps around the wheels of the car which is then raised up and withdrawn from the car park.

They sit and watch as the cars battery is charged using a booster charger, they start the car and one of the soldiers drives it away. Then when the crane has reversed out of the car park, the wall of the Dome closes back up, the lights go out and the car park returns to its eerily quiet self. They sit and look at each other in total disbelief, simply not believing what they have seen. John says, 'And that is how he must have made his escape, when they were messing about with the car, he slips out behind them and disappears into the night.'

They slip the next disc into the machine, a picture of Ted's workshop appears on the screen, John presses fast forward and the disc whisks on. He stops the disc when Ted comes into view, he is working with a long strip of metal on the workbench, when Tom aka Ponytail comes into view with his arm around the shoulder of a much older thinner man, the older man stands looking at what Ted is doing, when Tom strikes the older man on the back of the head with a metal bar. He slumps down onto the floor, Tom wraps a length of cord around the old mans neck, and pulls on the cord with all his might, throttling him. Ted takes a pair of wire cutters out of his tool box and cuts off the dead man's right thumb which he places into a jar of clear liquid. The two men stand and look at the thumb and shake hands, obviously happy with their day's work, they then stuff the victims dead body into the maintenance cart and close the door. Ted writes something on a label that has been pasted onto the side of the jar, then places the it inside the workbench. John can only imagine that he is locking the jar away inside the homemade safe. They then see Ted push the cart out of view and that's where the disc ends.

They look at one another in shocked amazement, John says, 'Well, that explains how they can use an inmate's thumbprint after that person has gone missing, and it explains how they can keep buying those diamonds.'

John selects the next disc and pushes it into the machine. A picture of the wall of the Dome appears, nothing happens for a while. They then see Joe walking towards the blank wall. He stops short of the wall and waits patiently. A panel opens in the wall and a man is standing there motionless. The man opens his eyes and simply steps forward and the panel closes behind him. Joe holds out his hand, the other man shakes it, and is led into the heart of the Dome. John realises that if Joe knows what is going on here, then so does the fat bank manager.

They close everything down, lock the van, and make their way back to the surface, walk silently to their favourite bench and sit down. Elsa walks to the shops to fetch coffees, they sit next to each other and discuss what they have just seen. The three killers stroll up to the next bench, sit down and stare at them again, Ted, the leader says, 'I don't like you copper and what's more I think that you are messing in my business, I won't tell you again, stay out of it.' The trio sit staring at them for a few minutes longer before getting up and walking away.

John looks at Elsa and says, 'We are going to have to be very careful from now on, maybe we should stay away from each other for a while, until it is time for us to make our escape.'

She reaches forward and placing her hand over his says, 'Where you go, I go, we have to stay together John, maybe we can even up the odds a bit, what if we were to tell Andrews that baldy has been up to no good, it won't exactly be a lie, will it?'

John considers this, and thinks that maybe he should wind them up a little bit more first, which might force the killers into taking some sort of action, that way he can justify going to Andrews about one or all of them.

CHAPTER 15

Sarah calls out in the darkness for her mother-in-law, her waters have broken, she is crawling around on the bedroom floor on her hands and knees, breathing hard. When her mother-in-law comes rushing in. Sarah whispers, 'Please, call Molly and tell her to get to the hospital quickly.' Joan phones Molly and tells her that the baby is on the way. Joan manages to get her daughter-in-law into the car and heads to the hospital. Joan has rung ahead and they are waiting for her at the main entrance, with a wheelchair. The nurses take Sarah straight to the maternity ward, the midwife gives her gas and air and tell her that the babies head is crowning and it won't be very long. Sarah lies on the bed doing her breathing exercises, all the time holding onto Joan's hand. They are just about to take her into the delivery room when Molly comes rushing in. Joan lets the two friends go off to the delivery room together, slightly disappointed to have been left out, but understands. When she sits and thinks about it, she realises that she wouldn't have wanted her mother-in-law present at her own son's birth.'

In the delivery room Sarah looks, and is, terrified. 'I wish John was here Molly, I need him so much' another fierce contraction hits her and the sheer force of it makes her call out at the top of her voice and take deep gulps of gas and air. The midwife places Sarah's feet into the leather stirrups, the next hour is very fraught, but Sarah gives birth to a healthy baby girl of six pounds, eleven ounces, who is perfect in every way. Sarah is suddenly inconsolable because she misses John so much and he hasn't been with her at this very special time, a time that they should have shared together. When her new born baby is placed in her arms, all thoughts of John leave her for the moment, as she falls in love with her beautiful daughter.

Joan listens to Sarah screaming out for her son one minute, the next minute she is calling him all the names under the sun. Joan smiles when she hears the baby cry for the very first time, a sound that tugs at her heart strings, and a single tear makes its way slowly down her right cheek. She clasps her hands together in front of her and says a silent prayer and hopes that the prayers will somehow reach her son.

John makes a very serious, almost deadly mistake, when he goes down into the car park, removes the stash of diamonds and decides to hide them in Colin's van. He gasps out loud as he tips the diamonds onto a clip board in Colin's van, there are many different sizes and shapes, he counts them and all together there are four hundred and ninety-eight stones. He spends hours making many different patterns out of the sparkling stones, a dog, fish, boat and a house, he has no idea of the value of the stones but that it will be substantial.

John and Elsa act normally, as they dress and go out to supper at the Bell, and at the end of the evening they take a bottle if wine back to the apartment, they hadn't seen the band of three for at least a couple of hours which is a little worrying. The couple fall into bed and make passionate love, they are in a deep sleep when all hell breaks loose. John screams out in agony as he is repeatedly beaten with a baseball bat. He is beaten over and over, on every part of his body. The sound of the bat pounding on human flesh is sickening to hear. Finally the beating stops, and Ted asks menacingly, 'Where are they copper?' John looks up at him through his good left eye, his other already swollen shut. Ted has hold of a naked, groaning Elsa by a handful of hair, his free hand is squeezing her left breast so hard that John can't see his thumb or fingers.

The pressure of his grip is making Elsa moan with pain, again Ted asks, 'Tell me where they are copper or your little lady here will suffer' When John says nothing, Ted nods to Baldy who begins hitting him again, John feels his ribs crack and his right arm go completely numb as the blows land, he looks at Ted again, who snarls, 'Tell me where they are copper or I will kill your slag, but I'll make sure that she has a real man before she dies.'

With that, he forces his hand between her legs and begins rubbing her. Elsa squirms as she tries to move away from his fingers but he just yanks her hair back harder, which forces her head even further back and makes her open her legs, when John again says nothing, Ted again nods at Baldy who hits John hard on the side of the head, driving him instantly into a state of deep unconsciousness.

When John finally comes around he moans out loud in pain. Joe is sitting on his bed waiting for John to open his one good eye. John seems to hurt everywhere, he knows that he has broken bones from the dull ache in his ribs and his left arm. He feels as though he has been wrapped in bandages from head to toe. Sweat instantly begins to run down his face as nausea washes over him. He lifts his head up enough to see that his left arm is in plaster, and his ribs are strapped up. His one good eye finally regains full focus as he looks at a concerned looking Joe. John whispers, 'Elsa?'

Joe shakes his head and says, 'Ted has taken her down below into the car park, that was three days ago, we have the lift under guard so he won't be able to escape that way, and we have taken care of Tom. And we have some volunteers out looking for Eric as we speak. They are searching everywhere for him, each is carrying a side arm, it is only a matter of time until we find him and then we will take care of him as well. We're going to leave Ted until tomorrow and then we are going down there mob handed to search the car park for him.'

John whispers, 'But you have to go now and rescue Elsa, I want to come with you Joe, because you can't possibly leave her down there with that animal. Please take me with you, I have to find her.'

Joe smiles at the bravado shown by John and says, 'You'd better leave this to us John, you're in no fit state to move from the bed, let alone go down there, we'll take care of Ted, as for Elsa, if she is still okay, then we will do our best to bring her back to you.'

First thing the following morning Joe and six big burly men go down in the lift to search for Ted, and Elsa. Once in the car park the armed men split into pairs, it doesn't take long for them to find Elsa, she has been tied to the bed of a large white van, her arms and legs are secured so that she looks as though she is doing a star jump. When they shine their torches onto her naked body. They can see that her wide open eyes are glazed over, her lips are a deep blue and purple red bruises cover her torso where she has been badly beaten. It is obvious that Elsa is dead and they are sickened by the sight of a metal bar, which has been pushed up inside her body. They untie her and Joe pulls her eyelids down to cover her staring dead eyes. Two of the men search cars and vans until they find a blanket, in which to wrap her battered body. With this done they carry her to the lift. Joe stands and shouts for Ted to give himself up as there is nowhere for him to go, because when they leave they will deactivate the lift. He calls out one last time, waits a short while and shouts out finally, 'fair enough Ted, we'll see you in about a week's time.'

Joe tells John about what has happened to Elsa and leaves him alone with his guilty thoughts. Silent tears run freely down his face as he knows full well, that his selfishness and greed has been the cause of her sad unnecessary death, a death that will haunt him forever. A man from the surgery arrives at his apartment with a wheelchair, he is wearing a white coat, he also has nurse Ellen with him to help get John into the chair. When John asks where they are going, he is told that it is a surprise. John is taken down into the courtroom, where he sits with a few of the other inmates. Andrews comes into the courtroom dressed in his wig and gown. Two big burly men drag a squirming Eric into the room, they stand there and hold him by the dock, he stares at John, hate filling his eyes as he begins shouting at the top of his voice, 'You should have told him you bastard, then none of this would have had to happen.'

Andrews ignores the outburst and begins talking.

Are you Eric of Apartment 21, block B?'

The prisoner glares at the fat man and shouts, 'You know I am, you fat bastard, and I will be waiting for you in hell.'

Andrews ignores the ranting and reads through Eric's catalogue of crimes. He asks the prisoner what he has to say in his defence? Not waiting for a reply, he looks at the men who are holding Eric and then nods his head at the tube. They drag him kicking and screaming to the base of the tube, stand him on the silver base, as the tube slowly lowers down. They let go just as the tube encases him. Eric stands motionless as he stares hatefully at John. When he feels himself lifted off his feet, his eyes never leave John as he thumps the inside of the tube with all his might, in a final act of defiance. Finally the jewel thief disappears upward and then out of sight. John closes his eyes and visualises what is happening to the killer at this moment, as he knows from what he has seen on the discs, that the very life is being sucked out of him.

They take John back to his apartment and help him back into bed, where he lies alone for days on end plotting his escape. He will have to figure out what he can do with the information that he now has in his possession. He tries to sort out in his mind who he can really trust on the outside, with the information that he now has. As he lays there, now in complete darkness a lot of thoughts come to him, he has to figure out the actual purpose of the Dome. Why has it been built at all, how have they built it, and with what futuristic material?

A week later, he is finally able to get up and about, it is slow at first but he has a beautiful Indian nurse named Sasha looking after him. Sasha spends most of her days helping with his rehabilitation, her closeness as she holds him and the smell of her rose scent begins to drive him mad with desire. He spends most of his time with his arm around the nurses waist as she helps him to become more mobile. John is having to be very careful about what he says, because he is becoming suspicious of Sasha who has been asking him a few questions that he thinks are a bit to inquisitive. The more he thinks about the questions she has been asking, he thinks that she is pumping him for information, she is trying to find out exactly what he knows about the running of the Dome.

When Joe and his men decide it is time to go back down to the car park and look for Ted, they ask John if he would like to go with them. Naturally he says yes and when the time comes to go, he is again placed in a wheelchair. They take him down in the lift, and once they are in the cold car park, the men split up. It doesn't take them long to find Ted's stiff, lifeless body, he is hanging from the same van they had found Elsa's body in. He had tied a rope around the front bumper of the van, taken the rope over the roof of the van and hung himself at the rear. His face and neck are purple, his swollen black tongue is sticking out from a black lipped mouth, as with Elsa his bulging eyes are glazed over and staring at nothing.

They cut him down and lay him out in the rear of the van, Joe sends up for a body bag, John stops him and says, 'You had better get a lot more bags, because I think that you will find all your missing inmates down here. They have been hidden in the boots of some of these cars, you will need to search every car in the whole car park' The group of men split up and search each row of cars in turn, they eventually find all eight bodies, each one missing its right thumb.

The stiff black, partly decomposed bodies are eventually taken up in the lift and laid out in the courtroom. The searchers are all sitting silently, as if guarding the bodies laid out in a row in front of them. Andrews again enters the courtroom in his wig and gown, all the searchers rise. The tall man from the jeweller's shop is flanked by two large men as he walks into the courtroom, head bowed. He stands with a stiff back as he bravely takes up his position at the dock, his eyes search each face of those present. There are two big men standing directly behind him, blocking any attempt of escape.

The jeweller eventually looks at the row of black body bags that are laid out in front of him, he shakes his head from side to side as his eyes flicker from the body bags to the tube and back again. He shakes his head again as he realises that everything has gone wrong, he takes great gulps of air before lowering his chin onto his chest, as he silently wishes that he had never got involved with Ted and his men in the first place. Andrews looks at him and asks. 'Are you Anthony the jeweller from Apartment 13, Block B?' The slightest of nods comes from the tall man.

'You have been charged with assisting in the death of these eight people for personal gain, with the help of your associates Ted, Eric and Tom. Have you anything to say in your defence?' asks Andrews, the tall man shakes his head. Andrews then nods his head to the two men who are standing behind the jeweller. The tube lifts as the trio of men walk slowly towards it. They stand the tall man on the raised platform, and hold onto him as the clear tube, slowly lowers over his tall thin body.

The sound of rushing air fills the courtroom as the tube nears the platform on which stands the condemned man. Everyone in the room watches as the jeweller begins to rise upwards. When Anthony is finally gone. John closes his eyes again visualising what is happening to the man in the plastic tube, as the life giving air is being sucked out of the tube, his terribly thin body twisting and turning as it enters the final spasm of death.

CHAPTER 16

Sarah arrives home with her new born baby daughter, she sits on the couch and looks at the two women who have been there for her and without whose help, she knows that she would never have managed, she says, 'I would like to thank you both for helping me through to this wonderful moment, I couldn't have managed without both of you, and because of that I am naming her Molly Joan Stratton.'

The three women all hug one another. Joan retreats into the kitchen and returns with three flutes of chilled champagne, she passes them each a glass, she raises her own glass and says.

'To Miss Molly Joan Stratton.' They all touch glasses and then empty the flutes in salute to baby Molly, then smile broadly at one-another.

Joan hands Sarah a small pile of envelopes, each one containing a congratulations card. When Sarah opens them she smiles broadly as some are from work colleagues, some from John's office and most are from nearby neighbours. Some of the neighbours cards even offering to baby sit if need be, other cards contain offers of coffee and cake or even hot meals.

As time goes on, Molly eventually returns to work, so Sarah and Joan happily settle into a routine of new parenthood. As the weeks pass slowly by all thoughts of John returning home become less and less frequent, and after a while, any hope of his return begins to fade even further.

John is finally up and about, although he still has his left arm in a sling and has a slight limp, he spends most of his time walking around the running track, all the time thinking about and planning his escape. He has to try and find out when the Army will be opening the Dome to remove another car. He has a plan for the dark clothing that he will need but before any of that, he will need to go back down into the car park and look through the rest of the discs. He decides that if he goes down there late at night, he can stay down there at his leisure and look at every disc to see whether he has missed anything.

In the evening, he has a gentle stroll around the buildings just to make sure he isn't being watched. He then slips into the stone building, and rides silently down in the lift, in a now well-practiced routine he soon has the power on in the van. He takes his seat and switches everything on. He soon feels the warmth from the heater and smiles at the screens that are displaying different areas of the Dome. John watches the empty screens and waits patiently for the Army officer to appear and do his thing. Again he watches the whole operation as it unfolds before his eyes. When he is sure that there will be nothing more of importance happening, he settles down to watch the rest of the discs. The two things that he most needs to know are, how often do they open the car-park and when will they be opening the Dome again, because that is when escape will be possible.

He falls asleep in the warm van while watching the discs, and wakes with a start.

When he looks at the screens, life in the Dome as he has come to know it, is in full swing. He thinks that he ought to be up there doing something useful, but what? It suddenly occurs to him that he has nothing at all to do, no useful purpose and no way to fill his time, because now that the diamond thieves have been dealt with, there are no longer any serious criminals to be caught, maybe now they will finally let him go. He will need to change the way in which he is thinking because if they do decide to let him go, from what Joe had told him on his arrival at the facility, he will remember nothing of what has happened to him during his incarceration. He picks up a pen and pad that happen to be in the van, and sets about writing himself a letter.

Some two hours later, he has every detail about his incarceration, that he can remember, written down, he takes the wooden box that holds the discs, and adds the diamonds and the letter. He then sets about hiding the box in the boot of his own car, he wraps the box with an old walking coat and stores the whole bundle, deep in the tyre well. He then puts the cable away and locks the van, placing the key in its hiding place he makes his way up to the surface. He sits in the warmth of the artificial sunlight and drinks coffee. He watches people going about their everyday business, he can see Joe as he walks towards the bank. The more that he thinks about his situation, the more he convinces himself that they no longer have any reason to keep him here, that he will most likely be released.

John decides that he can do nothing more but sit and wait, although he decides to continue with his escape plan and thinking that maybe he will return down below later that night mainly because he likes the solitude there. He watches as the fat bank manager leaves the bank and heads to the square for his lunch. He follows him to the Bell, and watches as he walks inside and sits down in a reserved window seat, his normal order is placed in front of him. John stands in the shadows of one of the shops opposite and watches the man as he devours his food. He then drinks a large glass of beer, before eating desert. A couple of beers later, he leaves the pub and strolls back towards his office, the whole event takes just over an hour. He follows him as he waddles back to the bank, stopping to chat with a couple of people on his way. By the time he finally reaches the bank, he has been away from his office for just under one and a half hours. John sits and wonders how this information can be useful to him, it comes to him in a flash. If he can find out when the next person is due to leave the facility, then they will be opening the Dome to get that person's car out, then just maybe, he can simply sneak out as Colin had done, out to freedom and back to Sarah.

The next twenty-four hours are nerve racking, John nervously sits at his usual bench waiting for the fat man to go for lunch. Andrews finally leaves his office and heads for the square and as soon as he is out of sight, John walks across to the bank. He enters the bank calling out the banker's name, just in case. Once he is in Andrew's private office, he picks up the remote and aims it at the large screen, he flicks through the menu, and when it comes to departures, he clicks onto the word. A large Enter Password prompt appears on the screen, in large white letters.

'Shit,' he exclaims out loud and thumps the desk in frustration. With that plan now out of the window, he turns the screen off and disappointedly leaves the office, he sits in his usual seat drinking more coffee, totally and utterly deflated.

His mind for some reason turns to his dead lover, he hadn't really missed her at all until now and he suddenly wishes that she were there because he needs someone to hold him, to reassure him, to tell him that everything will be okay. He blocks out the thought that he caused her death because of his greed and bloody-mindedness.

He watches the fat man return to his office. Totally pissed off, he stands and walks towards the bank. He knocks on the door and walks in. Andrews is seated behind his desk with his hands folded across his huge belly. He has a contented look on his face, and his eyes are drooping, he is close to falling asleep.

'Ah, John, how may I help you?' he asks with a smile, John sits down in a chair opposite him and asks, 'Have you got anything useful for me to do, only I feel like a spare part sitting around all day doing nothing.'

Andrews looks at him for a few seconds before saying, 'You must take plenty of time to recover from the beating that you took but if you really are feeling restless, there is one thing that you can do if you feel up to it. The powers that be would like you to locate and retrieve the missing diamonds, they have to be here somewhere, don't you agree?'

John nods his head and makes out that he is thinking about the problem, 'How many diamonds are we talking about here?'

Andrews shrugs his shoulders, 'We are not exactly sure, but they have been collecting them for nearly two years, we can't see how they could have possibly managed to get the stones out of the Dome, but we can never be certain can we?'

John says, 'But there is a way of getting the stones out of this place if you think about it, let's just say for example that you are in Ted's position and like me have access to all departments, let's say that he looks on your screen here and finds out who is being released. He then makes sure the he has that person's details. He then hides the diamonds in their car, somewhere obscure knowing that they will never be found, then when he finally gets out of here, he will simply go to that person's home and retrieve the diamonds.'

The fat man sits there nodding his head and says, 'Yes, I can see how that could work, but how do we know if it was done that way or not?'

It is John's turn to shrug his shoulders and say, 'I guess we will never know for certain, but there is always that element of doubt, isn't there?' John convinces the bank manager that a look around Ted's workshop and apartment will be a worthwhile exercise and if they do happen to turn up something, then it will be a bonus. John carried out the searches himself and just as he knew he would, found nothing except the amputated thumbs, which he presented to the bank manager, who sat there looking at the thumbs with distaste and nodding his big head until John put the thumbs away.

John sits in front of the fat man and asks, 'What shall I do next then, Mr Andrews?'

Andrews looks at John spreads his arms wide and says, 'That I am afraid depends on the powers that be, but I am sure that they will let you know, one way or another' That evening when John came out of the shower, he had thought of another problem that he had to solve. He needs to find a way of reminding himself about the box in the boot of the car, it needs to be something permanent but not visibly obvious.

He goes over to the dresser and takes out his pack of pens, one of them is a black permanent marker, he looks for a place that will not be seen, he chooses the bottom his right foot, and draws a cross, 'No-one will possibly look there, will they?' he asks himself.

CHAPTER 17

Sarah has now given up hope of John ever returning home. He has been missing for just over a year and she's now planning to return to work. Joan is more or less living with Sarah and has agreed to look after baby Molly while she's at work. She is even thinking about selling her own home and moving in with Sarah permanently. Sarah couldn't argue with her logic and if she were honest, she couldn't see any other way that she can possibly manage without her mother-in-law being there. She knows that if Joan does move in permanently, then at least baby Molly will always be bathed and fed. She also knows that when she returns home from work, there will be a hot meal waiting for her. So, she makes the decision to ask Joan to move in with her, as a sort of live-in nanny.

The decision now made, they drive to Joan's house and put the property on the market, they stay there for three days and sell whatever furniture they can. The rest is packed into storage boxes, and taken to Sarah's house.

The sale of Joan's house goes through very quickly as it is in a desirable area, she puts the money in the bank, just in case her son does eventually turn up. If so she could always buy a small flat close by so she would always be on hand to help out with baby sitting.

With Joan living with her, Sarah decides it's time to take control of her life, so calls Molly and tells her that she is going to return to work full time. Molly says that she doesn't blame her one little bit; Sarah then makes a telephone call to her old boss and asks him if her old job is still available. He reassures her that he never breaks a promise and that she can return to work whenever she feels that the time is right for her and for as many day's a week as she needs. They chat about John and baby Molly for a while, and decide she will return to work the following Monday.

John is bored stiff doing nothing all day, he spends most days lying on the settee watching TV. He has been back down to the van to watch the discs again, just for something to do more that anything else. He is now playing with the pile of diamonds on a regular basis, making more and more obscure shapes with them as he tries to think of a way that he can turn the diamonds into hard cash, without arousing suspicion. How could he explain how he acquired so many diamonds? He has added even more information to the letter that he has written to himself. He then replaces everything back into the boot of his car before returning to the complex. He is beginning to put on weight due to his inactivity. After lying in bed all afternoon he will wake up and go and sit in one of the pubs until closing time, where he will eat and drink to excess, he realises that he is not only slowly going mad but is quickly turning into an alcoholic.

He opens his eyes the next morning and instantly feels like throwing up, he sits up, puts his head over the side of the bed and is just about to dump last night's drink onto the floor, when he senses that there is someone in the room watching him. He manages to swallow his vomit back down and forces his eyes to focus. He is shocked when he sees a pair of feet standing by the side of his bed, he slowly lifts his eyes up the long body to see Joe standing there looking down at him, who says.

'You are a bloody mess John and you're getting worse by the day' he stands looking into the bloodshot eyes of his only friend, John holds his shaking hand up, the palm side facing Joe which helps him to focus, 'Then' why don't you let me go home?' he asks.

Joe asks him, 'Can you be ready in one hour?'

John forces his eyes open again and asks, 'What for, have you found something for me to do, at last?'

Joe shakes his head in disgust as the fumes of vomit waft towards him. 'No John, you are going home, I'll come back for you in one hour.'

It takes a few minutes for the information to register. He suddenly jumps up and down on the bed and does a little dance, when he begins laughing he suddenly realises his mistake and has to sit down on the bed to let his brain refocus his whole body. When he does finally manage to stand up without wanting to fall over, he strips his smelly clothes off and runs into the bathroom. He has a long shower, dresses and sits on his unmade bed, waiting for Joe to return.

Joe leads John up the pathway that takes them towards the outside wall of the Dome, they stop by the outer wall, Joe turns to his friend and holds his hand out. John grips the hand and looks into the other man's eyes, Joe says, 'We would like thank you for everything that you have done for us, we are sorry for the inconvenience that we have caused you, now you do remember what I told you when you first arrived here, that when you leave this place, you will remember nothing of your time here. But I can honestly say that we will never forget you John, it has been my pleasure to have known you, I only wish that we could have met under different circumstances, good luck.'

John turns towards the outer-wall, he just stands there motionless until Joe says, 'Just take a step forward, John.'

John takes the step to his much welcome freedom.

CHAPTER 18

John opens his eyes to find himself sitting in the services on the M40 facing northbound, he starts the car and heads home. When he pulls into the driveway he is surprised to see his mother's car there, she hadn't said that she was paying them a visit. He puts the key in the lock, opens the door, walks in and calls out, 'Hi Sarah, I'm home.'

He drops his briefcase onto a chair as he always does and looks at his wife, standing there with a young baby in her arms. His mother is standing by his wife's side with her mouth wide open. The three of them stand looking at one-another, no one says a word but silent tears ran down both of Sarah's cheeks. John walks up to Sarah and looks at the baby and asks, 'Who's is this little darling then?'

Sarah pulls Molly closer to her chest as if protecting her from a stranger and finally says, 'This is your daughter John, this is Molly.'

He looks startled and confused. Joan stands up and walks over to her son, strokes his cheek lovingly and whispers, 'Welcome home John. Come and sit down, dear.'

She then looks at Sarah and says, 'I'll call Molly.'

Sarah remains standing, just staring at her long lost husband, who becomes slightly annoyed and says, 'I don't understand Sarah, what do you mean she's my daughter, you didn't have her this morning when I left for work?'

She sits down in a chair completely stunned, her eyes staring intently at her husband before saying, 'You have been missing for almost two years John, where have you been all this time?'

He frowns and sits down, looking up at his beautiful young wife, he stammers, 'I don't understand any of this Sarah, what the bloody hell is going on here?'

Joan comes back from the kitchen, sits down and stares at her long lost son and says, 'Molly is on her way, she says that she won't be long and to do nothing until she gets here.'
He looks from one woman to the other and asks, 'Who's Molly? We don't know any Molly.'

Sarah replies, 'Molly is a police officer and a friend. She has been helping us while you have been gone. She has been trying to find you. Everyone has been searching high and low for you, where have you been John?'

Molly arrives with a tall, solidly built, man in his late fifties, he has short grey hair and a pock marked face but his eyes are a sparkling royal blue, alert and full of intelligence. The newcomers stand looking at John, Molly says, 'This is Chief inspector Eric Morris of the serious crime unit, and I'm DC Molly Wright. Well, hello John, we're glad to finally meet you, and we need to ask you some questions. Do you feel up to it? We can do it here or at the police station, whichever you prefer, it is entirely up to you.'

He looks in turn at each face in the room, each pair of eyes staring back at him, his eyes finally resting on his wife eyes and spreads his arms wide, and demands, 'What the bloody hell is happening here Sarah? For Christ's sake tell me what is going on.'

Molly takes Joan to one side and asks her to call John's doctor and ask them to come out immediately. Eric Morris sits down next to John and quietly tells him everything that he knows, but nothing that the policeman says makes any sense to John. He keeps looking at his wife who is sitting there with a young child in her arms. He looks at the child and then into his wife eyes and asks. 'Is she mine then, Sarah?'

At that point, Sarah bursts into tears and runs hysterically from the room. John looks at his wife's retreating back and wonders what he has said that is so wrong.

Doctor Lisa Chong arrives and speaks quietly to Molly for a while, she clears the kitchen of people, so that she can examine her confused patient. After a thorough examination, she decides to put John to bed and sedate him. When she returns, she speaks to the whole room saying, 'Understandably, John is in a very confused state, I've sedated him for the moment, but he will need to be admitted to somewhere where we can access him more thoroughly and give him all the help that he needs. I don't know where or when but John has had a very severe beating, in which he has sustained some long lasting injuries.

He will need a full body scan to see if any permanent damage has been done, but I suspect that there have been broken bones. You might ask, how do we get John back to normal? Well, that I don't know the answer to that question, but he will certainly need a lot of professional help in his recovery. There is one strange thing, and that is that John has a large black cross on the bottom of his right foot, what its significance is, I don't know, and if John, himself, knows, I will be very surprised indeed.'

John is taken by ambulance to a private hospital in the Cotswolds, where he will be get plenty of rest, so as to take on board what people are trying to tell him. He will need time to comprehend the changes that have occurred in his family during the time that he has been missing. Sarah is allowed to visit him for only an hour a day, she isn't allowed to take baby Molly, as this still irritates him, because in his continuing state of confusion, John still can't understand how she can have conceived, given birth and indeed have a baby, all in one day. It just doesn't make any sense to him, even though everything that has taken place has been explained to him repeatedly.

Molly has an idea and runs it past the doctors and they all agree that it is worth a try. Molly leaves the hospital and says that she will ring back later if her plan can be put into action. She rings first thing the following morning and asks Sarah if they can meet her at the hospital at lunch time, as she has a surprise for her. Molly arrives at the hospital, with an elderly couple who Sarah can't quite place at first, Moly has to remind Sarah who they are, she explains that she has told Mr Norman all about John and she thinks that if he talked to him about his own experience, then it could possibly help.

The four visitors enter John's room. He looks at the old couple quizzically and then at Sarah. Sarah sits by his bed and holds his hand to reassure him, Molly then begins talking, and says, 'John, this is Andy and Mary Norman, Andy has been through exactly the same experience that you have. He walked down to his allotment one day as normal and wasn't seen again for fourteen months, until one day he walked back into his house as if nothing had happened, exactly as you have done. Mary almost had a heart attack when he turned up after all that time, and just like you, he can't remember a single thing about where he had been or what he had been doing, and there are many others, just like you two, many others.'

John looks at the old man and says, 'All that I can remember is the colour blue and that is it.'

'That's a lot more than I can remember, my minds a total blank.' The old man says. 'I only knows that it was the truth, cause of the state of my allotment, what a royal mess it was, took me weeks to get it back to right.'

John seems somewhat reassured by the old man and his tale, and from that moment on, begins to slowly recover, over time all his deep wounds have been treated. He is told that at some point in the future that he will most likely have to have his arm re-broken and reset.

John returns home a week later, his first night in bed with Sarah is just like the first time that they ever slept together, with both of them feeling nervous, neither of them have any thought of sex. They lie as far apart as they possibly can, each trembling and that is how they sleep, but they wake in each others arms. John holds a trembling Sarah in his arms and begins to talk quietly to her, apologising and trying his best to reassure her. He explains his confusion about baby Molly, about how everything seems so impossibly different, how everyone looked at him accusingly. He felt as though it was he who had somehow done something wrong. He whispers that slowly things are beginning to make a lot more sense to him. He kisses her tenderly on the forehead 'I'm so sorry, Sarah. I'm sorry that I doubted you. I had no right to do that, I hope that one day you will forgive me?'

She looks deep into his eyes, reaches up and pulls his lips to her own, after a first kiss she pulls her lips away and whispers, 'Please make love to me, John. Just like you used to.'

They make urgent passionate love and that simple act alone changes everything, they laugh at breakfast for the first time since his return. Joan suggests that she look after little Molly and perhaps take her out for the day, leaving them to get to know each other again.

Things improve even further when John's friend and work partner DI Dan Rogers arranges to visit him. Dan is a very big man, single, thirty-six years old with short slightly greying hair, He spends most of his spare time in the gym. They sit together in the garden, drink a beer or two and chat for hours.

John tells his friend what little he knows about what has happened to him and what he has been through, Dan promises that he will be there when he is ready to sort out the missing months and if he needs anything in the meantime, he will always be just a phone call away.

CHAPTER 19

John is slowly getting his life back to normal. He has begun playing with baby Molly, which brightens Sarah's heart no end. He's beginning to drive again, if only locally so far, Joan and policewoman Molly have been flat hunting but John suggests that they build a granny flat on the side of the house, that way it will solve all their problems. They all agree and a builder is chosen, plans are drawn up, planning applications are submitted to the, all is underway.

Reading the daily paper in the living room on a bright summers day, John plans on having a lazy day. Sarah is busying herself dressing baby Molly, when Joan walks in with the push chair as if they are going out somewhere, 'Off somewhere?' he asks.

Sarah places Molly in the pushchair and turns towards the front door, Sarah stops, turns to her husband and passes him a CD in a case, John take the CD and looks at Sarah questioningly, she says simply, 'We will be back in an hour or so, I think that it is only fair that you watch the disc on your own and we can discuss it later, that is if you want to.'

He is about ask her what's on the disc, when she quietens him with her hand and tells him to just watch the it.

The women leave the house and John slips the disc into the side of the television, nothing happens for a second or two then a nervous looking picture of Sarah appears on the screen, she is wearing a red dressing gown, she moves around restlessly until she settles and then looks at the camera and saying, 'John, I am not sure that you will ever watch this disc but I feel that it is the right thing to do. You have been missing for seven months now, as you can see I am carrying our child. There are some things that a married couple must always share and the sight of my swollen body is one of them. She stands and after undoing the belt, opens the dressing gown, takes it off and throws it onto the settee, to reveal her almost naked body. She stands facing the camera wearing a pair of white pants and nothing else, she turns sideways to show him her bump, then turns back to face the camera and lifts a swollen breast in each hand. You would have loved these John {She rubs her hands over her huge stomach and says} this is our baby in here John, this is your baby, I don't know if it is a boy or girl because I don't want to know. I wish you were here John to share this wonderful time with me, I have to admit that I am struggling at times and if it hadn't been for your mother and Molly, I am not so sure that I could have coped' He then sees Sarah reach forward and switch the camera off, the next picture takes John by surprise. Sarah is lay on a hospital bed is a surgical gown, she is red faced as she turns and to look at the camera.

'Where the fuck are you John Stratton? This is all your fault' she shouts at the top of her voice before she groans in pain as another contraction hits her.

'Push, that's it dear' he hears someone say, the camera turns and he sees that

Sarah's feet are in stirrups, her naked legs are wide open, the midwife and two nurses are waiting to help Sarah give birth. Another contraction hits Sarah and she groans at first and then the groan turns into an ear piercing scream.

'That's, it dear, I can see the head now, one more push and the baby will be here' says the calm midwife.'

Sarah looks at whoever is holding the camera and shouts at the top of her voice, 'Film the baby coming out for John, he would have wanted to be at the birth.'

A few seconds later, he can plainly see the top of the baby's head as it prepares to leave his wife's body. The next ten minutes are amazing as he witnesses the birth of his baby daughter, he is slightly shocked by the language used by Sarah as she gives a final push, but he can forgive her. He will never forget the look in Sarah's eyes when the midwife placed his daughter in her arms. All the pain, worry and embarrassment is already forgotten. The next sequence of pictures are of Sarah breast feeding her daughter and there is that look again, that special look that the two women in his life share. The next footage makes John cringe as Sarah changes her daughters nappy for the first time, he knows that it is his imagination but he convinces himself that he can actually smell his daughter first runny motion.

The next scene is the one that he will never forget where Sarah is bathing her daughter in a small white plastic bath, she is holding Molly's head in her right hand to keep it above water as she splashes soapy water over the tiny body, all the time they deepen their love for each other as they stare into each others eyes, Sarah is singing a soft lullaby. Next there are a lot of still pictures of different people holding the new born baby, he felt very proud when a picture of his mother holding Molly appeared on the screen. Next is a picture of Sarah whispering into the camera, she has her finger to her lips as she refocuses the camera so that it is shows Molly lying on her back in her cot, covered up to her chin in a soft white blanket. The soft tinkling sound of her butterfly mobile is the only sound heard as she drifts off to sleep. The next picture shows Sarah in the bathroom, standing in her dressing gown with her left arm outstretched as she adjusts the camera. She looks into the camera and opens her dressing gown and reveals her flabby body, she lifts her stomach and shows him her pink stretch marks, turns to the side and shows him the size of her flabby stretched stomach before she lifts her right breast and moves towards the camera, she holds the nipple towards the lens and squeezes some thick grey baby milk out of the nipple and says, 'I promised myself that I would share everything with you John and I know that this will have been of particular interest to you.'

The next forty-five minutes is filled with short films of Sarah spoon feeding Molly, Molly on the swing, Molly swimming, Molly crawling for the first time, Molly standing for the first time and her first steps. It is only when he has seen the whole disc, that he realises that he has been crying all the way through. Watching the disc has made him realise just how hard it must have been for his wife, to have gone through everything on her own.

When his little family return from their walk and Sarah walks into the room, John rushes to her and holds her as tight as he dares whispering 'sorry' into her ear. When Joan sees that they are sharing a very private moment she takes Molly into the garden. John and Sarah hold onto each other as tears of love run down both their faces.

John lies on the bed in his boxers having just come out of the shower, holding a giggling baby Molly in the air at arm's length, both laughing as he thrusts her up and down, Molly screams with delight. Sarah walks into the bedroom and says to her husband 'I thought that you were going to have a shower?'

He looks at her and says. 'Thanks a bunch love, I have just come out of the shower.'

She says, 'Well, you missed a bit,' and points to the bottom of his right foot. John pulls his foot around so that he can see the heel, a look of confusion appears on his face, as he looks at the black cross. He looks at Sarah and shrugs his shoulders and says,

'I don't know where that came from or what it means but it must be there for a reason. He lies awake in the early hours of the morning thinking about the black mark on the bottom of his foot, there is something buried deep in the back of his mind but he just can't seem to be able to bring it forward. He eventually falls into a deep sleep, when he wakes he doesn't know why, but he just knows that he has to check the boot of his car. He climbs out of bed and pulls on his dressing gown, runs down the stairs two steps at a time, grabbing his car keys on the way, he runs to the car and opens the boot. He stands there looking at the contents, seeing nothing obvious he begins removing everything in there, searching every item as he goes. When the boot is empty he stands leaning on the back of the car with both hands, somewhat disappointed. He has been through everything to no avail, he looks at the empty boot thinking that there must be something in there. Seeing two small black rings that are set in the carpet, he pulls it up to reveal his old green coat stuffed in the centre of the spare wheel. Removing the rolled-up coat he replaces the carpet and then places the coat down, and unrolls the coat to reveal a foot-long, brown, wooden box.

He takes the box into the house and sits down at the kitchen table, lifting the lid he sees a long brown envelope and opens it, inside is what appears to be a letter addressed to himself, written in his own handwriting. He reads the letter and can't believe what is written, he picks up the box of discs and looks at them, he picks up another smaller box and gasps, the bottom of the box is covered with different sized diamonds, hundreds of them. He checks that he is on his own and hides the smaller box underneath the sink. He thinks to himself that he will have to find a more suitable place to hide them, because he doesn't want Sarah knowing about them just yet, not until he himself knows what is going on. He calls Sarah and asks if she will send his mother to the shops and take Molly with her. When Joan has gone, he passes his wife the letter that he has found in his car, she finishes reading the letter and looks into his face with a confused look and says, 'My god John, what does it all mean?'

He shrugs his shoulders and says, 'We had better watch the discs, and see what they tell us, we may need some professional help with this, Sarah.'

They watch each of the discs in turn, and sit in complete silence, neither of them understanding what they are seeing. They have no clue as to what to do with the information that they have in their possession, Sarah suggests that they call Eric and Molly, but first they must swear them to secrecy. John isn't sure what to do, normally he will have gone straight to his boss but he hasn't seen him for almost two years, so doesn't know his personal situation any more. They decide to talk to Molly, Sarah makes the call and says that she is inviting herself and John to her house for a takeaway and asks Molly if she trusts Eric, when she says that she would trust him with her life. Sarah then suggests that she invite him as well.

John spends the next day hiding the diamonds in the garage, he removes a breeze block from the top of the garage wall in which to hide the diamonds. Having gone through Sarah's jewellery box he finds a small empty purple velvet bag, he hides the stones inside one of the block's holes and then seals the hole up, he replaces the block back into the wall. He takes his time and cements the block back into position. He checks the drying process every two hours.

Finally, he is happy with his work, as when he stands back and looks at the grey breeze block, he can't tell the difference from any of the other grey blocks in the wall.

On their way to London the next evening they to collect the food on the way, and take it to Molly's flat. They eat the food and only when the plates are cleared away, does Eric ask, 'This is all very mysterious, can you tell us what's up? You aren't pregnant again are you, Sarah?'

Sarah shakes her head and says, 'What we have to share with you two, doesn't make much sense to us, but before we show you, we must have your word that it goes no further than this room, until we know what to do with the information.'

Molly looks at Eric and when he nods his head, she agrees as well, John passes them the letter which tells of his time in the Dome. The letter gives the complete story, except him sleeping with Elsa and finding the diamonds. When they have both read the letter, Eric says, 'This is a little farfetched isn't it, John, very futuristic. Flight of fancy, maybe?'

John smiles and says, 'Maybe these will convince you that what I have written down there is, in fact, the truth.' He asks Molly and Eric to watch each of the discs before passing any further comment.

When the last disc ends, Eric exclaims, 'my fucking God!'

Molly asks, 'What does it all mean?'

John says, 'That's why we wanted to show you what we have, we thought that you may have an idea as to what we can do with the information?'

Eric sits deep in thought, eventually he says, 'We need someone high up in government or the law that we can trust, but first we 0need an insurance policy of sorts, we need someone to see this and become our banker, so to speak, because I can assure you that the military will not want this little lot getting out, under any circumstances. It seems they have murdered civilians, have kidnapped hundreds of innocent people and held them against their will, the government must know about this, there's no way that they can't know. But what's the reason for such a place to be created the first place, what does it achieve?'

Molly coughs politely and says, 'I do know someone that we can trust. I went to university with her. Her father owns a few of the daily newspapers including the Tribute, her name is Melissa Kelvin, her father is Sir David Kelvin, the newspaper Baron.'

Her boss asks, 'Do you think that a newspaper man is the right person for this?'

They all look at one another until John says, 'At least a newspaper man will have the right connections and they won't be able to keep him quiet, and he will know exactly where to hide this information.'

Eric says, 'The first thing that we need to do is copy these discs and hide them somewhere, give them to someone who will know what to do with them. Just in case anything should happen to any one of us.'

Molly gasps, 'Do you really think that it could come to that, one of us getting hurt, even killed?'

Eric adds, slightly worriedly, 'Well I can tell you this much, the military won't want this little lot getting out.'

John says forcefully, 'But, we can't just let them get away with this, they have murdered civilians, kidnapped people, ruined many lives, it's just not right, is it?'

Nothing is said for a few minutes, John eventually says, 'I don't think we have a choice, we have to go with Molly's idea.'

Eric says, 'I have to agree, but first we must copy everything and place it somewhere safe, I could always send it to my brother, he's a bank manger. He can place it in his vault, unopened, that way we know it will be safe' With the decision made they all agree to meet up the next evening, to copy, then pack the original discs and the original letter, ready for delivery to Eric's brother and hopefully by the time that this is done, Molly will have arranged a meeting with the Kelvins

The discs and letters have been copied, all four of them have signed a statement that they agree with the course of action being taken. The package is sent by courier to Eric's brother, with instructions that the letter is only to be opened on the death of everyone on the list provided. Eric has called his brother and the bank manager understands that in his difficult job as a senior police officer, Eric sometimes needs a secure safety net.

A meeting with the Kelvins has been set up by Molly for the following morning at the newspaper man's country house. The Kelvin's sixteenth century house is hidden away in the Dorset countryside. It is a huge white house, set in the middle of a large country estate. When they drive through the grounds they see herds of deer on either side of the road, some are lying down, others are grazing without a care in the world. The house demonstrates the wealth of the Kelvins, when they draw up outside the recently refurbished property and climb out of their car, they stand in a group overawed by the sheer size. They are met and welcomed by Melissa who is stunningly beautiful and wears a white summer dress, her long blond hair and tanned body make her look like a fashion model. As they walk up the white marble steps that lead to a pair of large oak door, she introduces herself by saying,

'Hello, I'm Melissa Kelvin welcome to our home, if you need anything at all during your time with us, please ask'

With introductions made, they are shown into a large ornate office. Sir David gets to his feet and shakes everyone's hand as they are introduced to him. He is an intelligent looking man, casually turned out in a white open-necked silk shirt and blue jeans. He is tall, very good-looking, and it is obvious to everyone that he works out a lot. He takes a seat behind a huge, highly polished oak desk. His daughter is standing by his side. He looks at John, holds his hands out wide, and says, 'Well?'

John passes him a copy of the letter that he wrote to himself, David Kelvin reads it and places it face up on the desk and looks at John, he asks, 'And, do you have any proof of this?'

John passes Melissa the box of discs, they play each in turn. When they have all sat silently through the viewing, the newspaperman looks squarely at John and asks, 'Is all this for real, John?'

It is Molly who answers, 'Yes, it is very real, we have other people who we can bring forward, people that have been through the exact same experience, but they, like John here, can't remember anything about their time in the Dome. The military must have used some sort of mind altering drug.'

David sits quietly and for a full minute thinks about what he has just witnessed, before saying, 'This is potentially a very dangerous problem and will need an awful lot of serious thought. The government won't want this little lot getting out. I am a hundred percent certain of that, but on the other hand I can see that they can't be allowed to get away with any of this' He rocks back and forth in his chair, eyes closed, deep in thought, he finally asks, 'Have you made copies of all this information?'

Eric nods his head, Kelvin tells his daughter to get everyone drinks while he makes a phone call. He leaves the room for a few minutes and when he re-enters, announces, 'My MP friend and golf buddy, Sam, will be here in a few minutes. He lives just down the road from here, and will know exactly what to do with this information.'

While they wait for the man's arrival Melissa takes Molly and Sarah on a guided tour of the large house, which is complete with a swimming pool, gym and snooker room. Eventually the doorbell rings, Melissa lets her father's friend in. He is short but fit, his thinning brown hair is long and he wears an expensive pin-striped suit, he has a ruddy face and half-rimmed glasses. Introductions are made and Melissa passes the bright-eyed man a tumbler half full of scotch, which he receives with a smile. They all sit silently and watch the discs again, Sam sits and reads the letter a second time.

Sam turns his head and looking at John and asks, 'And, you don't remember any of this?'

John shakes his head, and then says, 'No, not a thing, not a single thing.'

Sam sits and rubs his chin finally saying, 'You do know that this information, if it gets out will most likely bring the government down, don't you? On one hand, I agree that the government can't be allowed to get away with this. But, on the other, this will need a great deal of thought because not only will we have to handle things correctly, we will also have to be very careful indeed because I sense danger here.'

Major Jerry Keen, Professor Raymond Stanley, Mary Gardener and the prime minister's personal secretary have been summoned to Downing street on a matter of some urgency, they all stand outside the prime minister's office, like a band of naughty schoolchildren. When the PM's secretary waves them all into the Prime Minister Thatchmore's office, the PM looks grave and from his face, it's obvious he isn't a very happy man. He waits until they are all sitting down, then looks from face to face, he nods to the major and says, 'Please introduce yourselves.'

The major says. 'My name is Major Jerry Keen, and I'm in charge of security at a top-secret government installation.'

He then looks at the man sitting next to him, who says, 'I'm Professor Raymond Stanley, and I am Director of Morton Laboratories and an underground bunker, again at a top-secret installation.'

He looks to the woman sitting next to him, who says in a very high, trembling voice, 'My name is Mary Gardener. I am the minister for science responsible for the same top-secret installation as the professor.'

She glances at the man sitting next to her who says, 'My name is Robert Hutchins, personal secretary to the prime minister.'

'Right, you may not all know each-other personally, but now that we all know who we are, I can tell you that you all have some sort of involvement with the top secret project known as 'The Dome', and before we get to the problem at hand, Mary here will explain why the Dome was created in the first place and it's intended future use, Mary?'

The minister for science clears her throat and begins speaking, 'The concept of the Dome is a simple one really, it is a futuristically constructed facility that was initially intended to house the royal family and members of this government in the event of a third world war. The Dome facility is controlled from Morton Laboratories which are run by Raymond Stanley and from the underground bunker we can control every aspect of life in the Dome, from thoughts, actions, birth control and almost every other aspect of life. I could go into how we do all of these things but it is a very complex system, one which uses satellite dishes and top secret mind altering gasses that have been developed with the Americans. I am not even going to try and explain the technology involved in the creation of these gases. After three years in operation, we as a team decided that the Dome was running perfectly and everything we wanted to achieve, had been achieved.

It was at this point that we decided to use the facility as a sort of research facility, because we were confident that we could control people in almost everything that they do, we decided to try the system out on a few criminals, so we introduced a different mix of inmates, people such as stalkers, thieves, and murderers but we decided that there would be no police. We took this course of action because we believed that as we could control an individual's thoughts, we could suppress their deepest thoughts and desires meaning we could theoretically stop them committing crimes. Just think about it for moment, if this system worked we could eventually use it the real world, no more repeat offenders of rape, murder, drink driving, stalking, the list is endless.

We added oestrogen to the water supply which controlled the birth rate, in-fact in the three years of the facility's existence there hasn't been a single child conceived or born in the Dome, just imagine how this could work world-wide, no more poverty in third world countries, we could even control how many children each family would be allowed to have by a single injection. We could in fact control how many people were living on the planet, how many people in each town or city in every country in the world. This information would be worth a fortune to this country but more importantly, it would save the planet from its inevitable self-destruction. Think about security, we can control security in the Dome without having a police force, simply by controlling a person's thought process. Everything went wrong though, when we brought in a team of London Jewel thieves and gave the leader of the gang the job of maintenance man, this job allowed him access to all departments, twenty-four hours a day. And once he was underground, working, well to be honest we lost control of him. This particular man is very intelligent and soon realised that once he was underground we had no control over him and he used this information to his benefit as it wasn't until very recently that we realised that we had lost control over him and his two friends above ground as well. We still haven't got to the bottom of why or how this is happening but we need to find out. This small group soon realised that if they kept their heads really close together, then we couldn't fully control them, although personally, I think that these men had discovered a way to deflect the messages that we were sending to them. Don't ask me how, because I don't know. But this ability allowed them to carry on committing crimes without us realising what was going on. We hadn't even considered the need for the use of underground mind control because we thought we had control of those trusted personnel we allowed to go underground. One of us made the mistake of giving a jewel thief the ability to roam freely around the facility, and that is where we are at this point in time.'

Everyone just sat open mouthed at this, it was the PM who spoke next and said, 'But we have a problem, information has been passed on to me that this supposedly secure information has somehow leaked out. The information is now in the hands of a well-known newspaperman and we can't let this go any further, can we, Major?' The Army man shook his head. 'What we have to decide today is, firstly, can we close the operation down completely, or secondly, can we suppress the information that has somehow leaked out of a supposedly secure unit. I was personally assured that this couldn't happen, any ideas?'

It is Mary Gardener who speaks first, saying, 'If we decide to close the Dome down, sir, we will have to suddenly release five hundred or so people back into the general population and can we do that without further information concerning the construction technicalities and the top secret materials that we used, being leaked?'

The professor speaks next and says, 'I can guarantee that the people that are still incarcerated in the Dome, can be released without any memory whatsoever.'

The prime minister speaks next, asking, 'Tell me professor, how can you make that guarantee after what has happened here today? You have in the past assured me personally that the gas you use, is foolproof, but the information has somehow still leaked out, so what the bloody hell went wrong?'

Having been firmly put in his place and somewhat embarrassed the professor lowers his head and stares at the highly polished table top, the PM's secretary speaks next and says, 'I will ask the question that obviously has to be asked! Can we dispose of five hundred bodies and get away with it?'

Each person in the room sits and shakes their head at the very thought of murdering so many innocent people, no-one wants to comment on such a drastic suggestion.

The PM says, 'Right then, this is what we will do, the major will do his best to suppress the leaked information and retrieve these discs that are so incriminating,' he looks accusingly at the minister of science. We will then want to know how these discs have been made without you knowing anything about it? And finally, I want to know how someone managed to get the discs out of such a secure facility. When, you yourself, Minister, assured me that it was impossible'

The minister sits with her head lowered and mumbles that she didn't know that it had happened, but at the time she honestly believed it to be completely impossible. With a wave of his hand the PM dismisses everyone, except the major. When it is just the two of them, the PM sits and looks at the Army man, who is also a very good personal friend and says, 'You have to sort this mess out, Major, but you must do it in such a way as to not cause us any more embarrassment, we have to get these discs back at any cost and the people involved must be dissuaded from taking things any further. You do realise that this whole bloody fiasco could do this government irreparable damage.'

The major promises to do whatever it takes to retrieve the situation and to use whatever force is deemed necessary.

CHAPTER 21

Email addresses and phone numbers have been exchanged, warnings given by Molly to be very careful, the discs are copied yet again, the letter is copied yet again. Nothing happens for a few days and then things change one morning, when John realises he is being followed. A grey Ford estate car is keeping pace with him, he says nothing to Sarah but calls Molly and quietly asks her advice. She asks if he is certain he is being followed, because she honestly can't believe it. He assures her that he is. She goes immediately to her boss and tells him what is going on. Eric Morris decides to give it a couple of days and see what, if anything, develops.

The next day, John decides to take the whole family to Brighton for the day. Within minutes of them leaving home, the same grey car is following them again but this time the car turns off as the Stratton family join the M25. They spend a pleasant day out in Brighton, but when they arrive home late in the evening, Sarah opens the front door to find a scene of total devastation, the house has been literally trashed, every room has been turned upside down, even the baby's mattress has been ripped apart. Sarah, and John's mother hold each other and cry. John calls Molly who says not to touch anything and that she and a team will be there shortly.

Molly and Eric arrive at the Stratton household and can't believe what they see; Eric says that it will be best if they book into a hotel, somewhere busy with plenty of people, while they get the forensic people in to dust for prints. John goes into the garage and checks on his hidden safe place and is relieved to find place it as he had left it. And, so it begins, already someone that they have spoken to, has spread the word and it looks like they will stop at nothing to get the discs and letter back. They spent two nights in a local four-star hotel, while they spend their days tidying the house and putting it back into some sort of order. Sarah wants to take baby Molly away somewhere safe but John argues the point, saying that he wants to keep the family together.

What happens next changes everything, Molly rings John early the next morning; and tells him that she needs to see him at the Kelvin's house, as soon as they can get there. He jumps into his car and drives to Kelvin's country home. When he arrives, there are police cars parked everywhere, their flashing blue lights make the large white house, look like something out of horror film. Molly walks out to meet John on the steps, she warns him that the house has been turned upside down but the searchers have upped the stakes. When they enter the house, again it is total devastation but in the middle of the floor is standing a large wooden chair that has lengths of cut rope laying around it and small pools of drying blood. There are blood splatters all over nearby walls and furniture. Molly says, 'David Kelvin has been badly beaten, so badly that he couldn't see or speak, and has been taken straight to intensive care. Where two fully armed police officers are standing guard outside his room.'

John phones Sarah and tells her to pack some things and leave the house, as quickly as possible; He doesn't want to know where they are going, not because he doesn't care, but this way he couldn't tell anyone where they are, if he was asked by someone none to friendly. Sarah starts crying on the phone because she doesn't want to lose him again so soon. But when she tells her mother-in-law the situation, she hurriedly begins packing and within the hour they are in the car and heading north on the M1. Joan spends the first hour of the journey looking out of the rear window of the car, for any following vehicles. But, luckily they have made good their escape unseen, where are they going? Only Joan knows the answer to that.

John calls his police friend, Dan and asks him to join them, John, Dan and Melissa sit patiently in the hospital waiting room, desperately waiting for news of Kelvin's condition. They draw up a short-list of who can have possibly spread the word. Molly vouches for her boss, which only leaves one person, David's friend, the MP, Samuel Grantham. John and Dan leave Melissa with instructions to ring the minute that they hear anything. They intend to have a quiet word with the MP. Melissa has given them directions to the man's house. When they arrive they knock on the door, for it to be answered by a young, oriental maid. She tells them politely that Mr Grantham isn't at home and that he will be out of the country for the foreseeable future. Knowing that there is no point in trying to argue with her, they leave not only angry but also very disappointed. Heading back towards John's house, Dan notices that they have a large camouflaged Range Rover bearing down on them and the driver makes his intentions obvious by continually flashing his headlights at them.

Sam suggests that John lead them out into the open countryside and use their superior speed to lose them. When they are out of the bright lights of the built up area, John puts his foot down and initially pulls away from the big heavy car. Within seconds the rear view mirror is filled with a bank of glaring head lights. John tries his best to outrun the car but it is right on his tail, the threatening noise of the big engine filling their ears. They are forced to swerve all over the road as the Range Rover rams into the rear of their car, with a sound of breaking glass and twisting metal. Again and again they are rammed, the more the driver runs into the back of John's car, the more the back of the car begins to disintegrate, it begins to slow down as the damage begins to take it's toll. They drive as fast as the damaged car will allow into the bright lights of the next town and the Range Rover drops back slightly. Sam who is watching the aggressors closely in the nearside wing mirror takes his seat belt off and shouts to John to take a side road and lead them around a back street to somewhere quiet, and if he sees a narrow gap, then to stop, so that they can confront their tormentors.

Unfortunately, the followers aren't that gullible, they immediately see through the ruse, turn off and disappear into the distance. The two trembling men stare at one another at what has just occurred, it's John who asks his friend, 'Do you think they were actually trying to kill us?'

Sam shakes his head and says, 'No, mate, they were just trying to scare us, or they would have driven us off the road back there in the countryside where it was nice and quiet, then they would have taken us both out, lets face it they had the perfect vehicle to do the job' After a few minutes they think it best to dump the car and report it stolen, they take everything that is of any value out of the car and walk to the main road and look for a taxi. It is in the darkness of the taxi that John suggests that they keep the evenings events to themselves, that way it won't worry Sarah.

The next morning, Melissa rings John and says that her father is out of danger, but they are keeping him in an induced coma for a while yet, until they can give him a complete MRI scan. John says that he has to pick up a hire car and then they will swing by and pick her up, and that he will give her a ring when they are outside the hospitals main entrance.

With Melissa now safely sitting in John's car, they are heading back to her house when the newspaperman's daughter says, 'Dad told me that he called an old friend of his, a man named Joe Everall, who is the minister of human rights, but he is away on business and isn't due back into the country until today. Dad has left a message for him to call me at his earliest convenience. I have his number in my phone if you want to ring him first, and then maybe we can all go and meet him at the airport, we can tell him everything that has taken place so far.'

Sam speaks next, saying, 'Tell me Melissa, do we know we can trust him, any more than Grantham? But on the other hand we desperately need someone in authority on our side, someone that we can really trust, someone friendly to help us sort this mess out'

John asks Melissa, 'Do you know this Everall chap personally?'

She shakes her head and says, 'I have met him at dinner a couple of times, he's a very pompous man but he always seems to speak for the ordinary man, so I guess that he must be okay. At the end of the day we do have to put our trust in someone, don't we?'

The men look at each other and nod their agreement. Melissa rings Joe Everall, and has a one sided conversation with the man, at the end of which she is given a post code. The grumpy sounding minister didn't seem to be very happy about being dragged into a fight against the government, but tells them that he well be expecting them first thing the following morning.

Early the next morning Melissa gives John the post code to put into the sat-nav, she and Sam have stopped at John's house to pick up John, the discs and letter. They then head west to Marlow, to see Everall. They arrive at the large country house, situated high on Marlow Hill surrounded on three sides by tall trees. They sit looking through the black painted electric gates at the impressive looking house in the distance. Melissa speaks into the intercom and the large iron gates swing open, they follow the long tree-lined driveway to the front of a very impressive house. A confident looking man in a blue silk dressing gown and a gold cravat, is waiting for them, he stands at the top of the stone steps next to a round pillar smoking a large cigar. He smiles and shakes hands with each of them in turn as they walk past him and enter the fifteenth century house.

They are shown into a very impressive, book-filled library, where Everall, a tall, youngish, obviously gay man drops into a deep brown leather chair. He waves them all to seats and begins reading John's letter, he rereads it twice more before he studies John for a few seconds, 'And you say that you remember nothing of this, nothing at all?' he asks.

John shakes his head and says, 'No sir, I don't remember anything, but when you see the discs, everything will become clear' they all sit in front of a screen and watch the discs yet again. When the last disc has finally come to an end, Everall stands and walks towards the window, where he stands with his hands clasped behind his back, rocking back and forth on his heels. He finally nods to himself as if he has come to an important decision. He claps his hands together in front of him and rubs them vigorously together before he sits back down, his eyes are now sparkling as if he is relishing the upcoming battle. 'Melissa,' he asks, 'you say that these people have badly beaten your father?'

She nods her head and says, 'Yes, they beat him so badly that he is in intensive care.'

Everall smiles and says, 'I think it best if we try and smoke them out, that way they will be too frightened to take any further violent action. I can maybe even raise it in the house tomorrow, that will definitely put the cat amongst the pigeons,' he chuckles to himself at the prospect.

After a short discussion, the decision is made that if it his actions put an end to the violence, then the risk will be well worth taking.

As an MP, Everall is duty bound to inform the Speaker of the House of the matter he intends to raise in the house. The moment that he does, the Speaker is shocked by the news, and hurriedly leaves the room telling Everall to sit tight until he returns. Unknown to Everall, a security man is positioned outside the door, to ensure that he doesn't leave until the Speaker has taken advice on this Dome matter, something that he knows nothing about.

There is a forceful knock on the door, which bursts open and a very large, black-haired, middle aged woman enters. She storms into the room and drops a large green folder onto the table, so violently that its contents almost spill out. She stands and looks him up and down before sitting down opposite him, looking him straight in the eye. She says confidently, 'Hello Joe, we've not met before but you'll know my name, Mary Gardener, minister for science. About this question that you wish to raise, I would like to know where you obtained your information, and where it is now. I would also like you to hand it over to us immediately, as it is a matter of national security. This information that you say you have, is very delicate and cannot under any circumstances be allowed to become general knowledge, you do understand that, don't you Joe?'

Everall sits still, looking at this large, Scottish, woman and with an ironic smile says, 'It's a bit late for that, don't you think Mary? If I know about it, then I can assure you a lot more people know about it, and when you start beating up prominent citizens and putting them in hospital, ransacking people's homes and terrorising women and tiny children, I can assure you things will not go away. I will do whatever I can to keep the story out of the papers, but when you beat up a newspaper baron, well, you can't really expect him to say nothing when he comes out of hospital, can you minister?'

She glares at him, and blusters, 'But this a matter of national security Joe, and we must protect the Dome at all costs, with that being the case, you will immediately be taken from here to a place of safe keeping, mainly for your own safety, I might add.'

He stands up making her jump as he thumps the table as hard as he can, before whispering menacingly, 'Who the fuck do you think you are talking to, you stuck up cow? You can't just lock me up for no reason, you just try and see what happens. If I don't return home by this evening then this whole affair will be headline news by tomorrow morning.'

She stands up and stares at him belligerently, then bangs the file on its end in an attempt to straighten the spilled papers, saying angrily, 'Please wait here,' she stops and glares at him and with that, turns away and slams the door behind her, as she storms out of the room.

The head of Parliament House Security is next to enter the room where Joe Everall is quietly waiting, and says, 'Please come with me, sir' he turns and walks away without waiting for Joe, who stands and follows. They walk along the corridors until he is asked to wait outside the deputy prime minister's office. The heavy oak door eventually opens and he is shown inside the plush office by a young male secretary. The deputy prime minister, Robert Hutchins, is sitting behind a large oak desk writing, he hasn't the courtesy to look up at Joe, just says, 'Sit.'

Hutchins finally looks up at Everall and says, 'It seems that we have a problem here Joe. We would prefer that this delicate matter would not become common knowledge, it could be most damaging to the government.'

Joe looks at Hutchins and asks, 'Do you even know what this delicate information is, Minister?'

Hutchins looks down at the papers that he has been working on and says, 'Well no, not really, but that isn't the point, is it Joe, you have been asked to do something to benefit our country, so you must do it.'

Everall looks completely stunned by what the Minster has just said, and says, 'Even when hundreds of people have been kidnapped and held for years against their will, even when people have been murdered and their bodies have been dumped on waste ground?'

Hutchins looks Everall, scoffs and says, 'You must be over-exaggerating Joe, the government wouldn't knowingly be involved with something like that, it is just not possible.'

Joe stands up abruptly and says, 'I suggest, minister, that you check your facts before you begin to doubt me, because I have seen the evidence myself, which is very damning indeed. And I can assure you that what I say is the truth.' With that, he stands, and walks, stiff backed, out of the office and out of the Houses of Parliament. When he returns home to report to a waiting John, Sam, Molly and Melissa, Joe tells them exactly what has been said and by whom. They are not only stunned but also shocked at the attitude of the government.

The small gathering sits around a table and regroup. Joe says, 'I think that we definitely need to take some legal advice now and get some form of security; we need somewhere, other than the bank, to store a copy of the letter and discs as I'm pretty sure that once a lawyer has these items in his possession, the government can't legally touch them.

I will ring my man Geoffrey and have a word, to see what he advises, I trust him because he has worked for my family for well over twenty years' He leaves the room and make a phone call. He re-enters, smiling and says, 'We now have legal advice. Geoffrey will be here first thing in the morning. You are all welcome to stay here tonight and join me for supper or you can travel home and come back again first thing in the morning, it is entirely up to you.' Naturally, at the mention of good food and comfort, they all choose to spend the night in such lavish surroundings.

CHAPTER 22

The major, a sergeant and two burly men are sitting in a grey car watching Joe Everall's house. The sergeant, sitting in the driving seat says, 'We could always go down there and take them all out, then set fire to the house, that would solve the problem.'

The major shakes his head, saying, 'They aren't that stupid, just imagine if you were in their position, wouldn't you have a back up plan, just in case anything like that should happen?'

The sergeant asks, 'So what are we going to do, we can't just sit here all night and do nothing, there must be something we can do?'

The major sighs and says with the sound of defeat in his voice, 'It might already be to late to do anything, we could all be out of work by this time next week, we could even be in prison for a very long time.'

The sergeant sighs deeply and says, 'Well, if that's the case, I'm going home to the missus.' With that, he starts the car and drives away.

The deputy prime minister is sitting stiff-backed in front of the prime minister. He crosses his long thin legs and asks, 'It's this problem with the Dome, Prime Minister, is it something to worry about and should I not have been informed of its existence?'

The PM sits back and steeples his fingers on his ample stomach, looking long and hard at his deputy. He flicks an imaginary speck of dust from his trouser leg to give himself more thinking time before saying, 'Look Robert, we have been good friends for a long time, I made the decision not to involve you in this at the very beginning, in case something like this should happen. You do know that this business could lead to my downfall, which in turn will mean that you Robert, will have to step up to the plate and sit in this very chair.'

Robert says, 'Would it be prudent for you to tell me about it now Sir, otherwise I am trying to defend something that I know absolutely nothing about, can you imagine just how difficult that is?'

The PM considers this and, finally, says, 'The creation of the Dome was suggested to me some seven years ago. The structure has been built from a newly discovered material that has been developed in a joint enterprise between ourselves and the Americans. It has been developed in a top secret laboratory based in the east of England. The Americans are, as we speak, erecting a similar structure, only theirs will be situated in the desert. They intended to use the same means as us to populate the project, but now that all this has taken place, well, I am sure that they will look at what has happened here, and find a more suitable alternative. The original idea behind the Dome was simply this, in the event of an epidemic, nuclear attack, world war, threat to the royal family or the government, all vital personnel would be placed in the safety of a facility such as the Dome. The Dome and its residents would then be regulated from a sealed underground bunker called Morton 2, currently run and overseen by Morton Laboratories, who developed the futuristic materials used to construct the Dome. They have, at the same laboratories, also developed a mind-altering gas that the inmates breathe in twenty four hours a day, and the gas can control every aspect of their lives. The lab uses a space station to take control of the inmates, when I saw this particular part of the operation in action, I must say that I couldn't quite believe what I was seeing. They can somehow direct an invisible beam from the space station onto any individual inmate. The operator then whispers into a small, round, dish-shaped object and any message that the operator wishes to relay, is then by some invisible force, implanted into the mind of the chosen subject.

Then the inmate does exactly what he is told and carries out the instruction without any argument. The instruction that has been directed at the inmate, is received as a suggestion, but in actual fact, it is a command that has been given. The inmate can't tell the difference between a suggestion and a direct instruction when under the influence of the gas. As I understand it, this method was successful in ninety-nine point nine percent of the inmate population, with the final prediction that it will eventually be one hundred percent. Also, each inmate subconsciously reacts to a silent signal which is passed to them through a beam of bright light, which tells the inmate's brain that it is time to go to sleep. The inmates simply return to their apartments and go to bed.

Again this notion has been implanted into the subconscious, its all very clever, don't you agree?'

Robert nods his head in agreement, and the PM continues, 'There is sex in the facility, obviously, but no pregnancies as yet, that is simply achieved by adding oestrogen to the water supply, the plan being, that in the very near future, the oestrogen will be reduced, because the scientists want to find out if they can control the health and education of the inmate's children. They can already control the common cold, flu and many other contagious diseases. As you can no doubt see, the whole enterprise is very exciting, but in order to test the Dome to its fullest potential, we took the inmates from the general population, admittedly against their will, but they are very well treated and want for nothing. I only wish that life could be truly like that, don't you agree?

'New inmates can be selected using the space station, but they only take certain people who's skills are required to the benefit the Dome, such as police officers, bakers, nurses and chefs. We did take some of the worst criminals off the streets, to test their need to continue to commit crimes, and to see if we could succeed in altering their behaviour. In some cases it worked very well and the individual completely changed and became a decent, respected member of society. But, for those for whom the technology failed and they continued to act in the same manner, well, they can have an appointment with what the controllers call the tube. It is only used when an inmate commits three crimes, and I can assure you, the tube puts a permanent and deadly end to any further criminals activities, it is so final that the inmate disappears, never to be seen again.

The controllers would then research, select and bring in new law breakers, and the experiments would begin all over again. There is one problem that has recently come to light and has the scientists slightly baffled, and that is: if a group of inmates are sitting really close together, and they are sent an instruction to go to the main square, the group can apparently recognise the thought as an instruction and choose to ignore it, whereas an individual would automatically act on the instruction. Also, it has been suggested that a person with a very high IQ can also differentiate between a thought and an instruction and therefore that person can also ignore the instruction. So there are still a few minor issues for the scientists to correct.

Their thinking is, if they can find a way of controlling these criminals and changing their behaviour for the better, the technology could in theory be sold to governments all over the world, to be used, for example, in prisons as a tool for rehabilitation, which, would make the world a much better place. The technology exists to enable us in the future to control individual vehicles, so in theory, there will be no more police car chases, it could even come about that the space station can in the future eventually control all aspects of our transport needs. There is a strict yet severe justice system in the Dome, it's simple but effective, three strikes and you are out, the Tube which I have already touched upon briefly, always ends in a pain free execution and humane execution. The important point here is that every inmate knows the rules, so in effect there is very little crime. Why can't we have a tube in every prison, every police station? It's the type of deterrent needed to control violent offenders, not like the current system, which is no deterrent at all.

Having said all that, I still have every confidence in the major and his men to come up with a suitable solution and hopefully solve all our problems. As I see it the main one being, do we have enough time for the major to do his thing before this all becomes public knowledge and is beyond our control?'

Robert sits still digesting what he has just been told. Suddenly he looks very worried and asks, 'And what can I do to help, Prime Minister?'

The prime minister shakes his head and says, 'Stay well out of it Robert, that way I'll know the right man will be there to step into my shoes, if things go so badly that I am forced to step aside.'

A long silence follows, taking this as meaning that the meeting is over. Robert stands to leave, the two men smile at one another, shake hands and part company. Robert decides that it would be prudent to take some much needed annual leave, and disappear for a while.

CHAPTER 23

Joe Everall sits opposite his family solicitor, Geoffrey Yates, watching him read John's letter. Geoffrey shakes his head in disbelief as he reads, looks up and asks, 'Is this the ravings of a lunatic, Joe?'

Joe places the box of discs on the desk, pushes it across the towards Yates, and says, 'These discs will convince you that the letter is genuine, and when you have seen each one, I think it best if you place both the letter and the discs somewhere very safe, and if, for any reason, you don't hear from me every three days, pass everything you have onto the leader of the opposition, Ronnie Compwell. He will know exactly what to do with the information.'

Once back in his office the solicitor sits quietly and views each disc in turn, when he has seen the final disc, he closes his eyes and with a deep sigh calls his friend and says, 'As you are a close family friend Joe, I will reluctantly get involved, but that is the only reason, had you not been such a good friend, I wouldn't have touched this with a very large barge pole. I think you ought to be very careful Joe, there is the possibility of real danger here. I take it you have already hidden copies of these things somewhere safe?'

Joe confirms that he does indeed have copies hidden away. 'Then I will keep these safe for you as well. I will have to inform my partner of the existence of the letter and the discs, but I will not put him in any danger by telling him the contents of either.' And that is how things were left between the two old friends.

Melissa needed some clean clothes and other items from home, so she jumps into her car to drive herself there. It is just getting dark and the route she has chosen to take edges past the local high rise council estate. It is an area local residents know better than to venture out into after dark, because of the gangs and a growing drug problem. Flashing blue lights in her mirrors force her to pull over to the side of the road, a large man in a police uniform opens her driver's door, looks down at her and says. 'Good evening, Miss, this is only a routine stop, will you take a seat in the back of our car for a moment, please?'

'Have I done something wrong?' she asks. The policeman reaches into the car and removes the car keys and smiles politely as she climbs out of the car. He walks with her to the rear of the unmarked police car and opens the back door. As she slides into the car, huge muscular arms grab her and force her head down onto the back seat, a big hairy hand holds a smelly cloth, which is forced around her mouth and nose, she struggles as best she can but is held tightly, until she slips into unconsciousness. The sergeant walks back to Melissa's car and places the keys back into the ignition and opens all the windows. He then walks back to the major's car and folds himself happily into the passenger seat, knowing full well that the local youths will have the abandoned car away in ten minutes flat. He also knows that when they have caused untold havoc with it, they will set fire to it down some obscure country lane, thus solving the problem of what to do with Melissa's car.

The major and the sergeant drive up to the barrier of Morton 2 underground bunker. The security guard looks into the car and on recognising the two Army men, waves them through. The major then drives into the compound and parks in front of the bunker, they carry Melissa's limp body into the private rooms and lay her down on a single bed. The sergeant walks off in search of a doctor to examine her. When they are happy that she is okay they post an armed guard outside her room. The major sits in one of the many offices in the laboratory and takes out his mobile phone. He smiles smugly as he dials John Stratton's mobile phone. When John answers, he says, 'If you want to see the lovely Melissa alive again, stop what you are doing, I want every bit of evidence that you have involving the Dome. I also want everything sooner rather than later.' Before he gives Stratton a chance to speak, he ends the call and smiles to himself, very happy indeed with his night's work.

John looks up at his friends Sam, Molly and Joe and says, 'They have Melissa, they want everything that we have on the Dome, if we ever want to see her alive again.'

Joe and Sam sit and shake their heads, Sam asks, 'So what do we do now?' All of them remain silent until John says, 'We need to find Colin Rothe, just as quickly as we can. He is the only one that knows where the Dome is, and you can bet your life that is where they are holding Melissa.'

Sam asks who Colin Rothe is, and John explains about Colin's escape from the Dome and that he is the person who left him the written clues and discs. Sam asks, 'But how do we find him?'

John sits and thinks about this problem for a long time before he says, 'We know that he is a surveillance expert, so you can bet your life he has gone back into the same business, let's Google him.'

Molly opens her laptop and searches through the list of security experts, but none of them has the name Colin Rothe. They try all things related to the surveillance industry, with no luck. John lays awake in bed that night and thinks about what Colin had written, saying that if he is intelligent enough to find his van, then he is intelligent enough to find him on the outside, which means that Colin will have left him a clue. Unable to sleep he goes downstairs and switches on the laptop and sits looking down the list of surveillance experts. He begins at the top of the list and writes down the letters of each company name, to see if he can somehow come up with the name Colin Rothe. It is almost five o'clock when he realises that he has made a fundamental mistake. He has been trying to find the name hidden in amongst other long names, instead of trying to find the name hidden in a name, a name with the same number of letters that are in his name, ten letters.

He trawls through the list of experts yet again and writes down each name that contains ten letters, there are twenty-three in total. He sits there until the sun comes up and the dawn chorus begins. Still writing out variations of different names, with itching eyes it is ten to seven in the morning when the name 'Linco Thore, Surveillance Installations', catches his attention. It doesn't take long for him to change the letters of the first two words around to come up with Colin Rothe. John has finally found him, and celebrates by jumping up and dancing around the kitchen, waving his arms in the air excitedly. He calms down and writes Colin an email, saying simply:

Thanks for your letter, the information that you left behind is proving to be very useful, but we have a very urgent problem that may need your most urgent input. Chile.

All John can do now is wait for a reply, Sam walks into the kitchen to see John sitting at the table, staring intently at the computer screen.

'You look bloody awful.' Says Sam as he stands there in a pair of blue striped pyjamas, scratching himself all over. John smiles at his friend and says, 'I may look awful, but I have found our missing Colin Rothe, I am now waiting for a reply as we speak.'

John takes great pleasure in showing Sam the list of names. Eventually the computer pings with an incoming email. John opens the email to find this note:

I see that I was right about your intelligence, I will meet you outside the Market Cafe in Soho Square at ten o'clock this morning. I will observe you first, so carry a copy of the Sun newspaper in your right hand, if I am happy that you are on your own, I will make contact with you.
Good luck,
Colin.

Joe, Molly and Sam want to go with John to the meeting with Colin but he knows that he has to go on his own, because if Colin sees a group of people waiting outside the cafe, he may think that it is some sort of trap.

John stands outside the Market Cafe waiting for Colin Rothe. People walk in and out of the cafe but no-one even glances at him, let alone makes any contact. He looks at his watch one more time and sees it is almost eleven o'clock, he has one final look around and then decides to leave. He turns around and has one final look in the cafe. A man is sitting in the widow seat, smiling at him, he winks at John and waves him inside. John sits down at the table and holds his hand out to Colin Rothe. Colin shakes his hand and John says, 'I have been standing out there waiting for you to contact me, what took you so long?'

Colin just smiles at John and says, 'Just making sure that you were on your own and I suggest that you stop smiling at strange men as they walk past you. You may get arrested or worse. The two men smile at each other, shake hands again and formally introduce themselves.

John leans over the sticky table and tells Colin, everything that has happened to him in the last few weeks, and about the kidnapping of Melissa. Colin rubs his chin and asks, 'And, what is it that you want from me, exactly?'

John studies the man sitting opposite him. He looks to be around thirty, well built, fit, and good looking. John can tell that from his demeanour that he has had some form of military training. 'I want to know where the Dome is because I think that's where they will be holding Melissa.'

Colin studies the other customers within earshot, then leans closer to John and asks, 'Did you watch all the discs that I left for you?'

John nods his head, 'then you know that the Dome is a military operation,' again John nods, 'The night that I escaped, I was sitting in my van watching what was going on up top, that is when they opened the outer shell to get a car out of the car park, I just walked out when they weren't looking. I made it as far as the outer fence and climbed into the back of an Army lorry as it slowed down to go over a speed hump. That's when I found out that the whole place is surrounded by high hedges and patrolled roads to keep the public away. I sat on a hilltop and watched the whole operation unfold, and from what I could see the Dome is controlled from some sort of underground compound housed close by. At most the control centre is a quarter of a mile away from the Dome.

When everyone is asleep, the Dome's shell opens up just like parting a chocolate egg, it is then that the Army trucks begin to move from the compound to the Dome, dropping off supplies to various shops, emptying bins, washing paths, the whole operation is well thought out and run to military precision. As I see it the best time to rescue your friend is when they are restocking the Dome. It takes the best part of three hours so all that we have to do, is figure out a way to get in to the compound. Can I ask is it just the two of us or have you some friends involved?

John says, 'Well, I have my best friend Sam and Molly, I can count on them.'

Colin looks at John for a full minute, before he says, 'I think it will take more that the four of us. Let me make a few calls and I'll get back to you in a couple of days but don't worry, we will get your friend back.'

The two men exchange phone numbers. Then spend time talking about what they can remember of their time and experiences in the Dome. John reports back to Sam, Molly and Joe. They are sitting around the kitchen table, talking about Melissa's kidnapping when John's phone rings, a menacing voice says, 'You have just thirty-six hours to deliver everything to us, if you fail to do this, we will kill your beautiful little friend.' Before John can answer, the caller, again, hangs up.

'Shit,' says John He tells the others what has just been said and calls Colin. Colin tells him that he has been in touch with a few friends, who are more than willing to get involved. An emergency meeting is arranged for that same evening, to be held in the back room of the Flying Fox pub in Harlow at eight.

When John, Molly and Sam enter the pub Colin is waiting for them, introduction are made and he takes them into the back room where six men are sitting quietly around a table.

The first thing that John notices is their eyes, they each have a look that tells him they have seen some bad things that normal people will never see or even want to. Colin looks at the men in the room and says, 'Let me introduce you to John, Molly, and Sam,' the seated men all nod their closely shaved heads in welcome.

Colin says, 'My friends will not speak to you unless it is to give you instructions, and you will not try and communicate with any of them, unless it is a life or death situation, is that understood?'

John and his friends look at one another and nod their heads in agreement. Colin stands in the centre of the small room looking around the room at each face in turn, and says, 'I have explained to my friends here the problem and they are more than willing to lend a hand, on one condition, and that condition is simply this. We are all militarily trained, so we will give the orders, which must be obeyed without question. Clear?'

John, Molly and Sam nod their heads in agreement.

'Right,' Colin continues, 'then, this is what will happen. Tonight my friends and I will take a look at the target and decide the best way to get into the control centre and rescue your friend. We will meet here tomorrow morning at noon to formulate a plan, another thing we will need is somewhere quiet to work out of, a unit on an industrial estate, or a big lock up.'

Sam says they can leave that with them to sort out, then asks, 'Why can't we come with you tonight?'

Colin smiles and answers, 'we as a team are all trained for these situations and do things automatically. If you are along, then we will have to look out for you and one of us might miss something vitally important. So it's best to do it our way.'

With that, he nods to his friends and without a word being spoken, all six men change into camouflage clothing, cover their faces in brown and green face paints. The result is that they all look simply terrifying.

They then all clip utility belts around their waists, which hold all sorts of military equipment and each has a black hand gun strapped to their sides. They take their guns out and check they are ready for use before leaving through the rear of the pub. They climb into the back of a windowless Transit. With Colin driving they join the fast-moving traffic. The three left behind, stand and watch until the van is out of sight.

John turns to his friends and asks, 'What have we started, those were real guns you know, and we are all supposed to be serving police officers?'

Sam says, 'I think that they are SAS, so entitled to carry guns, but going up against their own government forces. I don't quite know how they will come of if what they are doing should end up in a court case. But then again, if they free Melissa, I don't really care.'

The three friends make their way back to Joe's house but choose not to tell him what is going on, in order to protect his reputation.

CHAPTER 24

Colin and his small army are lying on top of a rocky ridge. They have cut their way through a tall outer wire fence. They will have to use all their training to bypass the security measures put in place to protect the facility. They move slowly forward until they are looking down into a dark unlit valley that holds the Dome facility. They have to wait until darkness falls before they can formulate a final plan. Colin has already sent three men to the other side of the ridge. When they are in position they will radio Colin to let him know. At one twenty-four precisely, the valley suddenly changes from darkness to almost full daylight, temporarily blinding the watchers for a few seconds. The light becomes even brighter, and spreads even further with the silent opening of two large hangar doors that have been built into the sides of the rocky hillside, the lights are so bright that they block out every star in the clear night skies above.

Colin says, 'My God, just look at that.' They can now see right into the underground hangar, and can hardly believe their eyes as trucks and land rovers are loaded with soldiers and civilian personnel. There is a loud click that echoes through the darkness. They watch in astonishment as the Dome begins to slowly split open like a freshly sliced orange. When fully open the entire facility looks like a large clear ball, that has suddenly split in two, covering an area so large that they wonder why no-one has ever discovered it. Perhaps they have, but maybe they have not lived to tell the tale.

They can now see each of the white buildings, and the full layout of the Dome, they have to admit to themselves that the whole operation, is really quite impressive. They watch an Army Officer as he marches into the centre of the facility, stands still for a few seconds and then slowly turns around making certain he is on his own. They watch as he lifts his radio to his mouth, seconds later the waiting trucks and land rovers head across open ground, towards the Dome. The vehicles drive to their designated positions and stop, men and women disembark and begin their various tasks.

Colin speaks into his radio, saying, 'I'm going in to have a closer look the rest of you make your way closer to the entrance of the underground bunker, and be ready just in case.' As one, they all rise out of the undergrowth and move off cautiously towards the entrance.

Colin cleans his face of camouflage paint, then moves up behind a stationary lorry, from where he watches proceedings with great interest. He takes his chance and steps out from behind the lorry, lifts a wooden box out of the rear, and waits as a few soldiers walk past him on their way into the bunker. He joins the end of the line and following them confidently, enters the nerve centre of the Dome. He is amazed at the sight that greets him. On the right hand, as he enters, is what looks like a large office, with banks of computer screens. Each workstation is fitted with different coloured levers and keyboards, men and women are sitting at each terminal, silent fingers crawl over black keys as numbers and rows of letters flash across screens. Each person has a set of headphones on and stares intently at the brightly lit screens. Colin walks deeper into the bunker, no-one challenges him even though the odd person glances at him. He notices that each soldier has on a plastic identity pass, complete with their photograph, he knows that he will have to acquire one of those before he leaves the bunker

He turns down a passageway and makes his way slowly forward, comes to a sharp right hand bend. He stops and takes a quick look around the bend. He sees a row of single occupant, fully fitted rooms all, except one in near darkness. That room is brightly lit and standing outside are two armed soldiers both with their backs to the room. Colin has found what he is looking for, now he has to make good his escape. He turns to go back the way that he has come from but is made to stop abruptly, as blocking his way is a group of soldiers, listening to a huge brute of a man as he passes on instructions. The officer is wearing the golden crowns of a major on his shoulders. He is obviously telling, what are evidently new recruits, the rules of the Dome, Colin has to wait in the shadows until the group move away until he can make good his escape.

Keeping his head down, he is forced to wait until the coast is clear before he can walk out of the bunker without being challenged. He gives a huge sigh of relief as he makes his way to the rear of the parked lorry, he used for cover on his arrival. He puts the box back in the lorry, but as starts to step around the vehicle, he hears someone quietly humming to themselves. He takes a quick glance around the side of the lorry and sees a soldier having a crafty smoke.

He removes his gun from its holster and stepping confidently around the back the lorry places the barrel against the soldier's back, the soldier instantly stiffens, cigarette half way to his mouth. Colin whispers in the man's ear, 'One sound and you are dead, understand?'

The soldier gives a nod of his head. Colin nudges the man in the back, the soldier raises his arms and they move off into the darkness. After about fifty yards three dark shapes rise out of the undergrowth, like ghosts. The prisoner gasps and jumps back with fright, he is just about to call out when Colin prods him in the back, again to silence him. The three men turn and lead the way back to the top of the ridge. They wait silently until their three comrades join them. They lay in the darkness and watch as a red car is brought out of the Dome and loaded onto the back of a low-loader lorry, once the car has been made secure, the lorry is driven away. Someone who appears to be unconscious is then carried out of the Dome on a stretcher and placed in the back of a private unmarked ambulance. It is obvious to Colin that someone is being released from their incarceration.

They stay perfectly still and watch the whole operation as it unfolds. It is three hours later when everything is finally closed down and the Dome moves back into it's original position, it is only then that the valley returns to an eerily silent darkness. It is a few minutes later when their eyes have readjusted to the darkness, that the deathly silence of the valley makes them wonder, if what they have just witnessed, is really true, and if the Dome is really down there. They bundle their prisoner into the back of the blue van and head back to the recently rented lockup where John, Molly and Sam will be waiting for them.

The blue metal doors are wide open when they arrive at the lockup, Colin drives the van inside and John closes the doors behind it. When the van has finally come to a stop and the engine has been turned off, the soldiers pour out of the back. Molly pours them all a cup of steaming hot coffee and uncovers a tray of sandwiches. Colin drags the bound prisoner out of the back of the van and drops him unceremoniously onto the hard concrete floor, where he is told to keep his eyes closed. The team take a few minutes to congratulate each other on a job well done, shaking hands and slapping each other on the back. John asks about the prisoner.

Colin looks down at the prone man and says, 'He will tell us what we want to know, then we'll kill him and dump his body somewhere nice and quiet.' He says this loud enough for the prisoner to hear but winks at John, who smiles and says, 'I know just the place, deep and very lonely!'

Leaving the shaking man lying on the cold dirty floor, the group move to the work bench on which lies a long strip of white paper, at least four feet long and two feet wide, it looks similar to a roll of wall paper. Colin picks up a black marker pen and draws a rough plan of the inside of the bunker. He draws a route to what he believes to be the medical centre and with a black cross, marks the room where, he is certain, they hold Melissa. He explains the sketch to the other men, then moves to the prone man and removes his security pass. He places the pass face up on the bench and says that they will each need one of these, and he knows a man who will sort it out at the right price.'

Before Colin can continue, John says, 'Just get them done, I'm sure Melissa's father will be more than happy to cover all expenses.'

Colin nods and continues, saying that, 'This man will get the passes done in a day. He walks over to the prisoner and lifts him bodily from the floor to stands him upright, then drags the trembling figure to the work bench where he looks from face to face. Colin points to the sketch and indicates the marked room where he thinks Melissa is being held, the prisoner confirms his suspicions with a nod of his head. He is then bound to a chair and placed in the far corner of the lockup.

Colin continues talking to the whole group, 'Right, as I see it, we'll get the passes done tomorrow and go in tomorrow night. The only problem I can foresee is the two armed guards outside Melissa's room, but if we walk towards them as if we haven't got a care in the world, we may just get away with it.' Colin uses his smart phone to take photographs of his friends, when this is done, each of them rolls out a sleeping bag and climb into their makeshift beds and go to sleep. The four that are still awake stand at the workbench and look at the sketch again. Colin talks them through exactly what he had seen earlier in the underground bunker.

He then goes on to explain that, the two men will be going with them the following night but their job is to stay on top the ridge and film everything that they can see, as it happens. And looking at a disappointed Molly, Collin says that the reason that he has left her out is because he wants her to remain at the lockup with a medical kit, just in case of any injuries. That way, if he and his men are taken prisoner,

John and Sam might still be able to escape with enough evidence to take to someone who can do something useful with it.

Melissa stands with her arms folded and looks at the stiff backs of the two armed guards, there is no way for her to escape from the room, she is certain of that. She has tried to sweet talk her way out of this situation but the big man in charge just smirked at her and said nothing. Her only hope is that she will be rescued, but how will her friends rescue her, when they don't even know where she is being held.

But what really worries her is that she has now seen the control room, with all its computers and gadgetry, and having seen it all, she wonders if they will ever let her go having seen to much, or will they have no choice but to kill her. She is very worried and knows deep down she is in big, big, trouble and that she will be very lucky to get out of this place alive.

CHAPTER 25

Sarah is holding a sleeping baby Molly in her arms, silent tears run freely down her cheeks as she thinks about her yet again absent husband. Where is he? What is he doing? Is he in any danger? Is he dead or alive? No sooner has she got him back, but he is gone from her life again. She wills the phone to ring but knows he won't call until it is safe to do so. John wouldn't put his little family at risk, she knows and understands that, and also the reasons behind his thinking, but that doesn't mean that she doesn't miss him terribly. Joan, John's mother is Sarah's rock at the moment; and she knows that if it were not for the older woman, she would have fallen apart days ago. And on top of all that she thinks that she may be pregnant again. She is only a few days late but she feels the same as she did before, just as she had felt when she was expecting Molly.

The would-be rescuers are preparing for their night's activities, no-one feels the need to speak as each goes through his own well practiced routine. John and Sam both hold video cameras, Sam films the men as they cover their faces in camouflage paint and prepare their equipment. The van is outside the lock up, its tank full and ready to go. Colin hands out the security passes and each man clips his into place. To make it feel as though she hasn't been left out, Molly has been asked to buy a full medical kit and have it laid out and ready for use, just in case. She is also in charge of the prisoner and the preparation of food when they return with Melissa. At the agreed time the men all climb into the rear of the waiting van, Molly waves as the van moves off but no-one waves back, she guesses, rightly, that they are preparing themselves mentally for whatever is about to be thrown at them. When she walks back into the lock up the prisoner begins to talk to her, trying to gain her confidence but she is having none of it and tapes his mouth shut. But his eyes still follow her every step. So she walks over to him and turns his chair around, forcing him to face the wall. She stands leaning against the workbench, chewing her lips nervously as she stares at her mobile phone, willing it to ring, but knowing it is much to soon.

Colin and his men lie on top of the ridge, they wait in the darkness for the bunker doors to open; John and Sam begin filming, as if on some silent signal the men rise as one and begin to move forward. Within seconds they are out of sight, disappearing into the darkness like ghosts. Sam can't believe what he sees as the bunker doors open fully, and the Dome clicks and begins splitting in two. The two watchers film every movement, eventually they see Colin and his men walk confidently into the bunker, they keep their fingers crossed as all they can do is wait and hope that everything ends well.

Colin confidently leads his group into the bunker, they chat amongst themselves to create the illusion of belonging there but he knows that his men are taking in everything and everyone around them and are ready to meet any threat head on. As a group they head into the passageway that leads to Melissa's room, still talking and joking between themselves. The two guards look up, but dismiss them as any kind of threat. The men draw level with the guards and at an invisible signal the surprised guards are silently grabbed and rendered unconscious. Colin opens the door to Melissa's room, she jumps up about to scream, when he holds his finger to his lips and says urgently, 'John and Sam have sent us for you.'

The guards are gagged, bound and hidden in the shower room out of sight. Colin passes Melissa a bag and tells her to hurry up and put the clothes on. Now dressed in a small Army uniform, they place the woman in the middle of the group and tell her to keep her head down and not to look at anyone. They hurry down the passageway towards the outside of the bunker. It is as they are walking towards the outer doors that a large sergeant and two tough looking soldiers walk past in the opposite direction, the two groups glance at one another. The sergeant makes a point of glancing at their passes and seems to be quite happy that they are genuine.

Colin feels certain that they have just seconds to make good their escape before the alarm sounds So he picks up the pace and the moment that they are out of the bunker, they turn right and disappear into the night. Seconds later, the sound of screaming alarms fill the valley, lights come on everywhere, searchlights scour the surrounding hillside, fully armed soldiers run in all directions. The big sergeant walks out into the front of the bunker and stands with his hands on his hips amidst all the confusion, he looks all around and shakes his head at the chaos. He takes out his mobile phone and dials John's number, when John answers the phone, the man says, 'Very fucking clever, how did you find us? This isn't the end of this you know, we know where you are, and you will be seeing us sooner than you think.' This time it is John who laughs into the phone and ends the call.

When Melissa sees John and Sam, she runs into their arms and begins sobbing uncontrollably as all of her pent up tension is suddenly released, they hold her for a second before Colin guides them silently to the hidden van, he ushers them into the vehicle saying they need to get out of there very quickly. Once in the van John holds onto Melissa as she is visibly shaking from either the cold or the release of adrenalin, he isn't sure which. Colin drives the van without using any lights at breakneck speed. Sam, sitting next to him closes his eyes and says a silent prayer. Colin seeing his discomfort, reaches out and grabs his passengers knee, making him jump, saying, 'It's OK mate, I had carrots for my tea last night' and bursts out laughing. They finally join the main road, slow down and turn the lights on, at which, everyone in the van visibly relaxes

When they arrive back at the lock up, Melissa hugs Molly and both women cry with sheer relief at seeing each other again. Molly takes her friend into the far corner of the lock up, they sit down and then Molly talks quietly to her friend, she holds the freed woman to her and strokes her back as she reassures her and tells her she is now perfectly safe. It takes a bit of time but Molly eventually begins to calm her down by saying that Colin and his friends, will take care of them all. When Melissa asks who Colin and his friends are, it takes Molly a while to explain what has been happening whilst she has been held prisoner.

The men all sit around and talk about what they had seen earlier at the bunker, look at the recordings on the cameras and wonder at the sheer size of the Dome operation. They begin wondering what steps to take next, when Colin says, 'The first thing to remember is that someone is going to be mightily pissed off about tonight, and I doubt they will let it rest.'

The two women approach the table, and the men all turn to look at them. Melissa tells them about how a police car had stopped her, and about how she had been knocked out with a foul smelling rag. She then goes on to tell them about the Army Sergeant and his two friends.

Colin nods his head and says, 'We saw him on the way out of the bunker. His sheer size makes him look really scary but don't worry, I will find out about him and then we will decide what to do about it.'

John asks, 'So, what do we do now?'

With a nod from Colin, and without a word being spoken, two of his friends, untie the prisoner and lead him out to the van. When the two men return an hour or so later, they are on their own. No-one says a word or asks about the absent man.

John stands and introduces Melissa to Colin and his nameless friends, then tells her everything that has happened since her kidnap. There seems to be an instant connection between Colin and Melissa as she takes his hand in hers and thanks him for his help in rescuing her and saving her life. They lock eyes for just that tiny bit too long until he stammers nervously, 'It was my pleasure, I'm sure.' It is Melissa who blushes first.

They break eye contact and she turns, red faced to John and says, 'I would like to see my father as soon as possible, please.'

Before John can even open his mouth to answer her, Collin stutters, 'I can take you if you like?' Melissa blushes deeply and smiles agreement, which brings a few sly comments from Colin's mates. He turns and looks at his friends saying, 'Maybe a couple of you ought to come with us, just to make sure that Melissa is safe?'

The two biggest men instantly stand up, ready as ever to support their friend. John and Sam stand outside the lockup and watch the van as it speeds away. John says, 'Our friend Colin seems to have taken quite a liking to our pretty young paper girl?' Sam nods, smiles and agrees.

Melissa leads the way into the hospital and to her father's room, where two armed police, who are standing outside, stop them. After checking their identities, they all enter the observation suite. David Kelvin looks at his daughter through his one good eye and tries his best to smile. The other eye is still very swollen, and like the bruises on the rest of his battered body, a deep purple colour. They hug carefully but he still winces at the bodily contact. Colin stands watching father and daughter as they lovingly hold hands and Kelvin listens intently to his daughter, as she tells him everything that has been happening whilst he has been in hospital.

She obviously says something about Colin because, David turns his bruised face towards him and nods his head in thanks. Colin nods back and smiles although what he really wants to do is march into the room and say that he would happily lay down his life to protect the Kelvin's beautiful daughter. They are leaving the hospital and heading towards the van, when without a word Colin places his arm around Melissa's shoulder and guides her toward a late night cafe. He ushers her to a corner table and orders them both coffee and cakes, she looks hard at him and says angrily, 'What the bloody hell is going on, Colin?' He tries to fob her off with some cock and bull story about his friends going for a paper, but she isn't that stupid.

'Don't give me that crap,' she snaps at him, he just shrugs, and says 'One of our nasty army friends is watching us, so the lads have gone for a quiet word.' The two men eventually return to the cafe. One of them has a bruise on his right cheek and his right eye is bloodshot, they nod to Colin and stand waiting. Colin pays the bill and they all walk out to the van. Melissa looks into the back of the van from the passenger seat and sees a bound man wearing a blindfold, lying face down and unmoving between the feet of the two men. She glances at Colin who smiles and shrugs his shoulders and says, 'The lads have brought us a little friend to play with.'

They drag the bound man across the lock up floor and sit him down in a chair at the back. They take their time tying their prisoner to the chair. Then they erect purpose bought thick plastic sheeting all around him, so that when they are finished working, he is confined in a small room, around eight feet square, made out of floor to ceiling plastic sheets. They pull a large metal table into the room, and lay out a number of very intimidating looking work tools which could double as instruments of torture. Colin carries in a set of aluminium step ladders, which he climbs to remove a light bulb, which he replaces with a light fitting connected to a long lead that hangs limply. The wire with a plug like connector on the end hangs down far enough to reach the table, he then connects it to a red box that has three glass dials on the front. Also, coming out of the front of the box are two leads about four feet long, one red and one black, each of the leads has a shiny copper coloured metal clip on its end, the kind used for charging a battery.

With everything set out and at the ready, Colin removes the blindfold from the prisoner, who's eyes go straight to the table and take in each of the painful looking tools. He looks at the red box and his eyes follow the wire all the way up to the light socket. He swallows deeply as if he knows what is coming, he turns his eyes back to Colin who stands smiling at him. Colin leaves the soldier on his own for two hours in the shrouded room, giving him plenty of time to look at the table and the tools, until he walks confidently back in. He is followed by one of his friends now dressed in a green operating gown, with over his mouth and nose, a surgical face mask.

The man in green pulls on long black surgical gloves as he walks towards the prisoner. Walking over to the bound man he takes hold of his wrist as if taking his pulse. Seemingly happy, he smiles at the prisoner and then nods to Colin, indicating it is safe to carry on. The doctor then walks over to the table and picks up one tool and then another, as if examining them, then walks over to the light switch, after flicking the switch on and off a few times to test that everything is working correctly, he looks at the trembling man and flicks the switch on, this time he leaves it on, which brings a loud and constant humming from the red box.

All three men look at the glass dials to check that the box is set for maximum voltage. The doctor checks each dial in turn, when he is happy that everything is working, he picks up the two metal clips protruding from the red box and touches them quickly against each other. There is an instant loud crackling sound and an array of spectacular sparks which makes the prisoner jump. The doctor stands, holding a clip in each hand, as he looks down at the terrified man. Finally ready, he turns his head and nods to Colin.

Colin then looks down at the now shaking prisoner and pulls the tape from his mouth, which makes the man instantly lick his dry lips. Colin asks, 'What's your name?'

The prisoner looks from Colin to the doctor and then back to Colin and says, 'Corporal Brad Johns.'

Colin says, 'Well, Brad, we want to ask you a few questions about your friends, we want to know who and what we are dealing with, and what their plans are. Now you know that you will tell us in the end, one way or another, but before we get to that, you must be punished for beating up an innocent man, wrecking two houses, kidnapping the newspaper man's daughter and scaring her half to death, and threatening a defenceless baby.' The prisoner immediately begins to claim his innocence. To silence him, Colin reaches forward and replaces the tape over his mouth. He then steps back and lets his friend move forward towards the prisoner, who's eyes go wide when he sees a silver scalpel in the man's gloved hand.

The doctor bends down and looks deeply into Brad's eyes before reaching forward and cutting a long gash in both legs of the bound mans trousers, just above the knees. Brad watches carefully as he then places the scalpel back on the table, turns back to the prisoner and rips the mans jeans wide open, exposing white hairless skin. Next he picks up a wet sponge and wets the bare skin of both naked thighs, the prisoner is visibly trembling as he watches every move made by the man dressed in green. Finally done, he picks up both clips, one in each hand, looks at Colin, and then stands there waiting for instructions. The prisoner is now visibly squirming because he knows what is coming next, his eyes begin to bulge as he screams in terror behind the silver tape that covers his mouth.

The doctor steps towards his victim and bending forward, smiles from behind his surgical mask. He stares straight into the other man's terrified eyes, then looks down at the bare pale skin. He places one metal clip onto the prisoners left thigh and holds the other clip just above his right knee. He turns to look at Colin for approval, Colin nods for him to carry on. At the touch of the clip on his skin, 240 volts of electricity enters the prisoners body, Brad screams as loudly as he can from behind the tape as his body goes into a muscle tensing spasm. After only a few seconds the metal clip is lifted from the victims bare skin, leaving the man breathing very hard and his eyes bulging in their sockets.

Colin says, 'Again,' and the metal clips are placed upon the naked skin and again the prisoner screams out from behind the tape, as his jerking body, goes into another spasm.

They wait for a few minutes for Brad to calm down. At the first sign of recovery, Colin says, 'Again,' only this time the clips are held against the prisoners skin for a lot longer, leaving red burns on his thighs, this time when the clips are removed the victim's head falls forward until his chin rests on his chest, as if he has been rendered unconscious. Colin pours some cold water from a large jug over the prisoner's head which revives him slightly. He waits until the prisoner's eyes are back in focus before he leans forwards and tears the tape from the man's mouth and asks, 'Are you ready to talk yet?'

The prisoner looks into Colin's eyes and whispers, 'You know that I can't talk to you, it is more than my life is worth.'

Colin smiles at him and shakes his head, 'Pity,' is all that he says.

An empty chair is placed it in front of Brad, and Colin sits down and crossing his legs, stares at Brad as his friend drops to his knees in front of the prisoner and begins to remove his socks and shoes. He then stands up and makes a point of selecting a pair of pliers from the tools on the table. He shows the pliers to Brad before kneeling down again, and taking a firm grip of the prisoners left foot with his right hand, he lightly grips the man's little toe with the teeth of the pliers. He grips Brad's foot tighter so that he can't pull away, then stops and looks up at Colin for permission to carry on.

Colin looks at Brad and asks, 'Well, are you ready to talk?' Brad shakes his head and takes a deep breath, then closes his eyes tightly; Colin nods to his friend who squeezes the plies as hard as he can around the soldiers little toe, Brad's screams fill the lockup, to such an extent that Melissa and Molly cover their ears in an effort to block out the man's desperate cries.

Colin raises his eyebrows questioningly at Brad in the vague hope that he will speak, but the man's response is to shake his head, so Colin nods to his friend who removes the pliers from the now flat little toe and places the pliers on the little toe of the other foot, without waiting for permission he begins squeezing as hard as he can, and again terrifying high pitched screams fill the lockup.

Colin waits patiently until Brad lifts his tear filled eyes to look at him before asking, 'Well, are you ready to talk?' Brad shakes his head defiantly, then closes his eyes and lowers his head awaiting whatever pain is to come next. Colin kneels down and lifting the prisoner's head, looks deeply into Brad's pain-filled eyes and says, 'I appreciate that you have been trained not to talk, the same as we all have, but we need to know exactly what we are up against. Now as you can see, we are quite prepared to break the rules to get what we want, this is your last chance to tell us what we want to know.' Again the prisoner shakes his head and Colin shakes his in disappointment.

Colin sighs deeply and stands up, walks over to the wall and turns off the light switch. He then turns and walks back to the table where he picks up two six-inch steel nails, both of which have been ground to a sharp point. With a nail in each hand he kneels in front of Brad and holds the nails out so that Brad can see them and asks, 'Are you going to talk?'

Brad shakes his head defiantly even though he has a fair idea what is about to happen to him. Colin lifts his right hand and holds the nail in front of Brad's eyes so he can see the sharp point of the nail and without hesitation, plunges the nail deep into Brads thigh muscle, the needle sharp point sinks easily through the flesh so deeply that the tip reaches all the way to the bone, bringing another high pitched, ear-piercing scream from Brad. Then Colin plunges the second nail deep into his left thigh muscle, again until the point of the nail touches the bone. Brad's teeth begin to shatter as he screams out at the top of his voice, the tortured man's screams fill every corner of the lock up. They wait until he finally stops shaking before Colin's friend moves forward and attaches a clip from the red box, onto each nail, he then smiles at the prisoner before standing up. Colin walks over to the light switch on the wall, and places his finger on the switch, he turns his head and looks at Brad questioningly, Brad's tear filled eyes lift from the nails, he looks back at his torturer with blood shot eyes, closes them and shakes his head.

Colin flicks the light switch to the 'on' position, which sends high voltage electricity surging through the prisoner's already tortured body. Brad grimaces with the excruciating pain as his once perfect teeth begin to shatter from being clamped together to hard, and his body goes as stiff as his bonds allow, bringing forth even more ear-shattering screams. The sound is so bad that Molly has to run from the lockup with her hands clasped firmly over her ears, in an effort to block out the screaming. Colin switches the power off and walks casually over to the empty chair and sits down in front of Brad, who is now trembling and has big fat tears running freely down his pale cheeks. He also has white froth and bright red blood oozing from beneath the tape that is covering his mouth, and also from both nostrils.

'Well?' asks Colin, the prisoner shakes his head but when Colin stands up and turns towards the light switch, Brad whispers something that Colin cannot understand. When the tape is torn away from his mouth, Brad whispers, 'Please don't.'

Colin sits back and asks, 'Are you going to tell us everything that we want to know?'

Brad shakes his head, 'You know that I can't tell you,' he whispers. Colin shakes his head, stands up again and walks over to the light switch. He places his finger on the switch and looks at Brad who looks pleadingly back at him, resigns himself to what is coming, closes his eyes and lowers his chin onto his heaving chest.

Colin flicks the switch and Brads head is forced back so hard that every sinew stands out in his neck, his eyes are clenched together and the sound of his teeth shattering can be heard. His mouth is a wide ugly looking snarl, his ruined teeth clearly on show as his body is wracked with further excruciating pain, this time it is a deep guttural groan rather than a scream that comes from his mouth, as his remaining few teeth crumble, the low pitched groan seems to rumble through the lockup.

Brad, now openly crying, shakes his head slowly from side to side, blood is running freely down his chin from his bruised gums. Colin removes the tape from his mouth and the broken man spits broken teeth all over the concrete floor. Finally, Brad nods his head and lowers his chin onto his chest.

Colin lifts the prisoner's head up by his hair and looks deep into his tear-filled eyes, after a few seconds, Brad whispers, 'Enough, I will tell you everything,' and finally begins to talk.

'Major Jerry Keen is the man in charge and he takes his orders from the PM himself. He has his own way of doing things and I promise you that when he catches up with you, he will take you all out and your bodies will never be found. You can still put a stop to all this, it's not to late, all you have to do is just give him what he wants. You can give the information to me and I will pass it to him and do my best to talk him into letting you all go free.'

Brad looks at Colin hopefully but Colin shakes his head, smiles and says, 'Nice try Brad, but do you honestly think that we are that stupid? If need be, with one phone call, we can get enough bodies here within twenty-four hours to completely wipe the Dome and bunker from the face of the earth. We can blow the whole lot sky high, but make sure that the major and his men are sitting right in the middle of the lot, then we will start on the people in charge.'

Brad nods his head in understanding and asks quietly, 'What will happen to me?'

Colin looks hard at the prisoner and says, 'We will keep you here for as long as it takes, but if you try to escape or cause trouble, you will disappear without trace, do you understand?'

Brad nods and lowers his head so that his chin rests on his chest, he is a beaten man and knows that the man in front of him has just lied to him, he now knows that his days on this earth are numbered.

CHAPTER 26

The prime minister calls an emergency meeting. In the room are the major, his sergeant, Professor Raymond Stanley and Mary Gardener. A worried PM looks from face to face before asking, 'Will, someone please tell me that we can survive this situation and how much these people actually know?'

No-one seems willing to speak, so the PM looks directly at the major and asks, 'Well, Major?'

The major shuffles about in his seat before saying, 'It seems that we have lost some control, Prime Minister, it appears that they know almost everything, even where the Dome and the bunker are situated, and they know that you are in ultimate charge of the whole operation. I would imagine that they have enough information by now to bring the whole lot down.'

The sergeant coughs and says, 'Well, we can go in hard and take them all out, and hope that the information stays buried.'

Raymond Stanley then speaks, 'Is there really any need for that sort of thing? Surely we can sort this out without resorting to violence, I mean can't we ask these people to join us and be part of the whole operation?'

The major chuckles and says, 'It's a bit late for that, don't you think, Raymond?'

Mary Gardener, furiously red in the face asks, 'Tell me, who's fault that is, Major? If we had discussed the situation before you went off beating up newspaper men and threatening defenceless children, we may well have come up with a more peaceful solution. But now it seems that all our work has been for nothing. We will have to let everyone go, I can't see any other option.'

The room is deadly quiet for a full two minutes before a very concerned PM speaks again, looking at the minister for science, he asks, 'Is it not possible to set up a meeting with these people, somewhere neutral, somewhere where they know it isn't a trap?

The major brushes a none existent piece of dust from his trousers and says, 'I can ring them and ask but I doubt that they will want a meeting, we will have to think of another way to sort this mess out.'

After a few minutes silence, the PM says, 'The very least that we can do is try and talk to these people, let me talk to Joe Everall and see what I can sort out. If it achieves nothing, well, then we will have no option but to try the major's way.'

The major nods his head but Mary Gardener stands up and says angrily, 'I want nothing to do with any sort of violence, we will have to find a peaceful solution'

The major chuckles and says, 'My way will be quick and clean, we will just have to hope that my actions will scare everyone else involved into complete silence.'

The PM asks, 'Do you know where and who these people are?'

The major answers by saying, 'From what I can gather they are just a couple of junior police officers, I have a man following them as we speak.' The major had conveniently forgotten to mention the group of soldiers that had raided the underground bunker and rescued Melissa, so with this reassuring comment the PM concludes the meeting.

Brad spends a pain-filled night in the cold dark lockup, trussed up like a chicken in his tiny silent plastic enclosure he cries because not only has he been beaten physically and broken mentally, he has soiled and wet himself, he is very sore and smells so bad that he is embarrassed. He has sworn that if he does ever make his way out of this place alive, he will make them all pay for what they have done to him. He looks down to where the nails are still embedded into his thigh muscles, a red ring has begun to spread around each nail. The sound of a car pulling up outside the lockup makes his heart race a little faster because he doesn't know what the future holds for him. Colin enters Brad's plastic world, looks at the man, and says, 'I have a question for you Brad, and it is, where can I find these friends of yours?'

Brad smiles and says bravely, 'They will rip you to pieces when they get hold of you, and you will get nothing more out of me and call yourself a soldier, you piece of fucking shit.'

With that Colin looks at the red rings around the nails and says, 'That looks nasty, Brad.' He smiles broadly. With that, he reaches out and grips the top of the nails and moves them both in circles, pressing down hard so that both tips of the nails are scraping against the infected bone, which brings a sharp intake of breath from the bound man but he still refuses to talk.

Colin smiles and says, 'You are a very proud man Brad, but a very stupid one. I'll be back, and then you'll tell me what I want to know.'

With everyone gathered at the lockup, Colin leans back against the table, looks from face to face and says, 'Me and the lads have had a chat and, think the major and his friends have not many options left to them because, we hold all the cards. We think it will come down to the major trying to kill us all and then hope everyone else involved will be too afraid to take any further action. So what you four have to do now is decide amongst yourselves, just how involved you want to get from here on in. Me and the lads are more than willing to take care of things and are in the position that if we do need more help, we only have to pick up the phone and ask for it. So if you want to go to a hotel and leave us to it until it's all over, I can assure you, we won't take offence.'

John looks at each of his friends and gets a nod from each in turn, telling him that they are with him one hundred percent, he then looks at Colin and says, 'We are all with you to the bitter end.'

Colin replies, 'Right, if that is the case, this is what we'll do, we'll meet the threat head on and do what we can to we to find the major and his friends. I know just the man who can tell us exactly where to find them' He steps away from the table and walks towards the plastic prison.

Standing in front of Brad he actually feels sorry for the man, who has obviously pissed himself more than once during in the night, he smells bloody awful and looks like he has given up on life. Brad looks at his captor, trying to look tough but Colin can see that he's trembling, either from the cold or terror, he doesn't know which.

He asks him, 'Tell us where we can find your friends Brad, a time and place when they're all together?'

Brad shakes his head so Colin reaches out and touches the top of the nail embedded in his right thigh. Brad takes a sharp intake of breath at the pain that shoots through his body makes him grimace. Colin smiles and walks over to the table and takes one of the electrical clips in each hand, he clips the clips around the nails again, the slightest touch on the nails makes Brad gasp, Colin stands up and looks down at a terrified Brad and says, 'We don't have to go through all this again Brad, all you have to do is tell me what I want to know, none of your friends will ever know the difference.'

Brad looks at Colin and says, 'I will know.'

Colin shrugs and walks over to the light switch, places his finger onto the switch and says, 'Last chance?'

When Brad doesn't answer, Colin flicks the switch, the screams that comes from Brad make the two women cover their ears, in an attempt to block out the sound. Colin repeats this three times before moving to the bound man who has fresh blood dripping from his chin having opened up the old wounds in his mouth, he is now openly crying.

'Are you going to tell me where I can find your friends?' Colin asks. Brad shakes his head in defiance, so Colin removes the clips from the nails and places them back on the table. He moves back to Brad who has soiled himself again and kneels in front of him. He reaches out and rests a finger on top of both nails, making Brad gasp. Beads of sweat appear on Brad's forehead, when Colin moves both nails around in small circles, the points of the nails grate against the now badly infected bone. The prisoner clenches what teeth he has left and groans deeply.

'Tell me,' urges Colin. Brad defies him again, so Colin grips the nails and pushes down on them as hard as he can, which sends the nails deep against the bone. Brad is now screaming out at the top of his voice as he grinds his toothless gums together. Colin begins to press harder and then moves the nails in a circular motion, this is all to much for Brad and he thankfully descends into unconsciousness.

Colin tips a bucket of cold water over Brad's head, he slowly opens his eyes and shakes his head before lifting it and looking at Colin through bloodshot eyes. Colin asks Brad if he's enough, Brad is close to giving in, Colin can tell by his eyes, so he changes tactics, saying quietly, 'You may as well tell me Brad, because you know that you will in the end, so why put yourself through any more unnecessary pain?'

Brad takes a deep breath and shakes his head defiantly, one final time, Colin grips the nails and Brad gasps and whispers, 'Enough.'

Colin lets the tortured man settle down and waits for him to begin talking, his soft voice is barely more than a whisper, 'We all meet on Friday evenings at the Black Ball snooker hall on Church Street, that's when we get paid and then get pissed.'

Having said his piece Brad lowers his head and closes his eyes in defeat and hopes that he will soon die. He now knows that his time on this earth is nearly up but is proud of how he has held out, and if his comrades in arms knew what he has been put through, then they too would be very proud of him.

CHAPTER 27

It's Friday evening, Colin and one of his larger friends walk up the steps into the Black Ball Snooker Club. They sit at the bar and have a beer. They've already seen Major Jerry Keen, the big sergeant and two other men playing snooker at a table in the back of the room. Colin chooses the table that is nearest the exit and they begin to play snooker. They aren't very good but that doesn't really matter, as they don't plan on being there long. Colin is waiting for one of the four men to go to the toilets to put his plan into action, and the way that the major and his men are drinking, it won't be too long. Sure enough, a few minutes later, one of the major's friends walks out of the room and into the toilets. Colin and his friend follow him and stand either side of him at the urinal as he goes about his business.

Colin looks across at his friend and says, 'That Brad sure could scream' his friend answers, 'Cried like a baby, didn't he?' And they both laugh out loud. The man between them looks at them, finishes his business and hurries out. Colin and his friend walk back into the snooker room to see the major and his friends rushing towards them, as if by a signal the pair turn and run down the steps with the big sergeant's heavy steps close behind. The huge man is shouting all sorts of violent threats, as he bounds after them.

Colin and his friend burst out of the front door of the snooker hall and immediately turn to the left, they can hear the big man breathing hard, as he follows them. They run between two high metal gates that lead to the back of the hall, as they pass through the gates the big sergeant shouts, 'Got you now you fuckers, there ain't no way out of here.'

The other men run into the almost empty yard, Colin and his friend stop and turn to confront them, only now Colin and his friend are standing between two more of Colin's comrades. The major and his group stop and look at the four men standing in front of them, the major looks along the row of men and shouts angrily, 'And who the fuck are you lot then, are you on a fucking death wish? And, what's all the fucking crap about Brad?'

Colin smiles and says, 'Brad's still alive for the minute but he isn't very well, you see we had to hurt him a little bit to find out where you were hiding out, but let's just say that he is in better shape than you lot are going to be in a few minutes. As you can see we aren't defenceless women or tiny children, we will fight back.'

The major places his hands on his hips and burst out laughing saying, 'One on one you four ain't got a fucking chance against us, we are fucking Army for fuck's sake.'

Colin smiles and nods his head. The major and his men all turn when they hear the big metal gates behind them being dragged together by Colin's two remaining friends. When the gates are locked into position the two men pick up brand new baseball bats and walk towards the major and his men. When the major turns back to look at Colin and his friends, they to, now hold shiny new bats. The major knows that he is in serious trouble and decides to try and talk his way out of the situation.

But before he can even open his mouth to speak, the sergeant standing by his side growls out loud and charges head on at Colin. The big man is cut down in seconds as he is hit once in the face, once on the top of his head and once in the chest, as he goes down the major and his other two friends charge towards Colin and his friends, baseball bats flash and make strange muffled sounds as they meet flesh and bone.

Soon all of the major's group are laid out on the cold concrete floor, the only person moaning is the major himself. The whole thing is over in seconds, the sergeant's head is literally split in two, the warm grey brain clearly on view, the other motionless men lying by his side will never breathe again.

The badly injured major is dragged to his feet and held upright between two of Colin's friends. He is thrown unceremoniously into the back of the blue van. Colin sits in the back and keeps a close eye on the injured man, who is now lying on his back with his eyes closed, breathing heavily, a strange gurgling sound coming from his chest. He is for the present, incapable of any movement.

The van drives into the lockup, the back doors are thrown wide and the major is dragged out. He is dropped unceremoniously onto the cold concrete floor where he lies moaning until he is lifted up. He is then seated on a wooden chair and securely bound with masking tape. When they are happy with their work, they pick him and the chair up as one and carry the whole thing into the plastic prison and sit him down, so that he his facing a sorry looking Brad. Brad looks at the badly beaten major who has thick red blood oozing from a deep gash on top of his head and is slowly making its way down the side of his face. Even though his injured boss is showing some sign of consciousness, Brad doesn't speak to him, instead he turns away, shakes his head and lowers his chin onto his chest, utterly defeated. Suddenly, he begins to cry like a baby.

Melissa kneels in front of the major and tends his wounds as best she can, when she is done, she stands up and turns to Colin and asks, 'Did you have to beat him so badly? He really needs to be in hospital.'

Colin smiles his best smile and answers, 'If it had been the other way around, do you really think that they would have treated us any differently?'

Melissa nods her head in understanding. John and his friends are now sitting in the lockup trying to decide what to do next. It is Colin who speaks first when he says, 'What we need first is a full confession from the major about his and his mens' part in the whole operation, but you can leave that to me, I will take great pleasure in sorting it out.

Then you will have to decide what your next course of action is going to be. When it comes to dealing with the government, personally I think it best if me and my friends aren't part of those particular negotiations. At that point I think it best that we wait here, just in case you need us for anything further.' At that last remark Colin smiles at Melissa who blushes a deep crimson colour before she turns away.

Melissa suggests that they all go to her house for a meal to try and formulate a plan of action. As they file out of the lockup Colin places his hand in the small of Melissa's back and smiles affectionately at her, Melissa smiles at him and then blushes deeply, because she can feel the heat from his hand burning into the small of her back.

He stands and watches her walk away from him, when she turns around to see if he is still looking at her, he smiles broadly and happily punches the air, shouting, yes!'

CHAPTER 28

The group of friends sit around a table and eat a Chinese takeaway, chat excitedly amongst themselves and relax for the first time in what has been a very long and exhausting week. On the way to the house John made a call to both Joe Everall and Geoffrey Yates to ask them if they can come over to the house for a meeting. When the two men arrive, they all sit around the same large table and it is John who takes charge. He sits and tells the newcomers most of what has taken place over the last few days. Joe asks if anyone has been injured, John instantly changes the subject but Joe asks the question again. This time John tells him the truth, at which Joe sits and shakes his head before saying, 'But that just makes us the same as them, don't you think?'

John does change Joe's mind somewhat when he tells him of the death threats that had been made against all of them, including Joe himself.

Joe then asks about the major, are they certain they can obtain a full confession from him?'

Melissa instantly speaks up and feels herself blushing a deep scarlet colour as she says, 'I'm sure that Colin will do whatever is needed to get what we want from him, I have every confidence in him.'

John glances at Sam and smiles knowingly. When everyone has had their say, they sit looking at Joe because it is obvious that the next move is up to him, so he stands and taps Geoffrey on the shoulder and beckons him to follow. The two men stand in the corner of the room and talk animatedly for a few minutes. When they return Joe says, 'Geoffrey and I will try and arrange an urgent meeting with the PM. We'll try and sort out this problem, you've done what you needed to do, now let us do our part.' Joe stands, takes his mobile phone from his pocket and calls the PM's private secretary.

The major looks at his battered friend and feels the colour drain out of his own face as he can see what they have done to him, how he has been tortured and the state he is in now. His legs where the nails remain are an angry purple colour, swollen badly and the smell is awful. When the major looks at the tools laid out on and the table, he can instantly tell that his friend wouldn't have given them what they wanted unless he had suffered terribly. He also knows that he will be going through the very same experience soon enough and he isn't sure that he will be able to hold out for so long. He knows deep down, he is not a brave man at all, in fact he knows he is a coward, which is why he has always surrounded himself with real hard men. He eventually falls into a fitful sleep but is woken some hours later when two men are untying a very weak Brad. They try to lift him, but the nails are still buried deep in his legs and tear the putrefied flesh, making him cry out in agony.

Without any warning, one of the SAS men kneels down and yanks both nails out of Brad's legs, causing him to scream again. A pale green puss begins to ooze out of both holes and make its way slowly down his legs, the smell of rotting flesh is repulsive. As the two men begin to carry a moaning Brad out of the lockup, the major asks where they are taking him. The men ignore him completely as they drag the dying man out of the plastic room. There is no need to shackle him as he is too weak to try and escape. The major hears the shutter door open and the van's engine start up and that is the last he sees of Brad. The major now sits on his own and begins to shake uncontrollably.

Colin walks into the plastic room early the next morning and stands looking at the officer who has a dark stain on the front of his trousers where he has wet himself more than once. He glares up at the SAS man and asks, 'What have you done with Brad?'

Colin ignores the trussed up man and continues to set up a video camera on a tripod, he makes sure the major is in frame and then switches the recorder on. He turns to the table and picks up the two puss covered nails. He stands smiling in front of the major and says, 'We want to know all about your involvement with the Dome and also what the government's plans are. I promise that you will tell us exactly what we want to know, one way or the other, painfully or painlessly, it is entirely your choice. Oh and by the way,' he holds up the puss covered nails, 'your friend Brad seems to have become very attached to these. I'm sure that he would have wanted to share them with you.'

With that, Colin begins to rub the points of the nails all over the majors trembling body, he then lays them back down on the table, picks up the scalpel and turns back to the major, whose wide bulging eyes can't leave the silver, razor-sharp scalpel. Colin bends over and cuts the officer's neatly pressed trousers wide open, just above the knees, the same way that he had Brad's trousers. He stares into the man's deep black eyes as he rubs the blade of the sharp scalpel back and forth over the naked hairy skin of the man's trembling thigh.

119

Sarah tries her best to put a brave face on in front of her daughter but deep down she knows that she is a mess. She has taken a test confirming her pregnancy, but doesn't think that she can go through it again, not on her own. She doesn't ask for much out of life, why can't she have a normal family, a husband who is there at the birth of his child? A husband who goes to work in the morning and comes home in the evening, when they sit, eat and talk about their day, then sit and watch the telly together. But not her husband, oh no, he has to be a hero out there fighting the villains and trying to save the world.

She has told Joan of the pregnancy and the older woman is really happy about the news, whereas Sarah has seriously thought about getting shot of the baby. But then thinks to herself, if only I had John here to help and support me, I know everything would be okay. At that moment, little Molly crawls towards her, Sarah her scoops her up and sits her on her knee, exposes her right breast and begins feeding her. Mother and daughter gaze into each other's eyes as the baby receives the food of life. Sarah seems to draw strength and will to carry for her sake, someone she loves more than life itself.

Joan stands at the door and watches her daughter-in-law, who is so depressingly lonely. The old woman knows that from this day on, she will have to keep a close eye on Sarah, because she has seen depression before and knows that Sarah is fast heading in that direction. She closes her eyes and tries to use telepathy to reach her son and tell him to come home soon, as they all need him so much.

Melissa is at the hospital collecting her much improved father. She has to push him out to the car in a wheelchair, but she doesn't mind, she is just glad to get him home. She has made arrangements for a private nurse to look after him while he recuperates. Nurse Bridges is a retired Matron of advancing years and Melissa has made sure that her father knows that the she will stand no nonsense. She has been given her instructions by the family doctor and Melissa knows she, will follow those instructions to the letter, no matter what her father says or does.

Joe and Geoffrey are patiently waiting outside the PM's office early the following morning, they have been pacing the corridors for over an hour, the only sign of life, the occasional raised voice that is coming from the other side of the highly polished door. It is an hour later that the door finally opens and they are shown into the well-furnished room, which is stiflingly hot to the point of being oppressive.

The pale looking PM casually waves them to seats and they sit down. He begins to speak and says, 'I would like to introduce you to Professor Raymond Stanley and Mary Gardener, both have had a great deal to do with the creation of the Dome. Talking of which, let me ask you how much you think you actually know about the Dome?'

It is Geoffrey that answers, saying, 'We know enough, Prime Minister, to cause you some serious damage but there is no need for that, not if you were to choose to close the facility right away, release everyone held captive and personally apologise for the lives that have not only been lost but also ruined whilst the Dome has been in operation'

The prime minister smiles broadly, holds his hands up and says, 'Slow down a bit Geoffrey, lets not be to hasty, there is a lot to be taken into consideration before we get to that stage. First let me explain about the Dome and it's purpose' the PM tells them of the need for the enterprise and the reason for its creation

He begins, 'The idea for the Dome was originally conceived in case of a nuclear attack, the need for somewhere the royal family could be taken out of harms way, that sort of thing. The facility is big enough to house all the royals, in any kind of national emergency. Even some government officials could be housed there, should the need arise. You do see that they was no other option but to use humans as inmates, it's the only way the whole enterprise could have possibly been made to work,' he ended with, 'they weren't that badly treated you know.'

The professor shakes his head at the PM's defence of the project and says, 'I honestly think that if you had asked for volunteers from the armed forces, you would have had plenty of people come forward, if not you could have asked for volunteers from the general public. I'm sure that plenty of people would have been more than willing to help out with the experiment, especially if they thought that they could live freely for a few years, and not having to worry where their next meal was coming from.'

Thatchmore leans back in his deep leather chair and steeps his fingers on his ample stomach, looking from one man to the other, he says dismissively, 'We will require more time to consider our options, now, if that is everything gentlemen, can we meet again in say a week's time?'

Joe coughs and speaks for the first time saying, 'Excuse me sir, but I don't think that you fully appreciate your position, we have more that enough information on this to go public. We also have a friend of yours staying with us, who I am sure, will tell us everything that we need to know to end your political career, so as I see it, you have two choices:. first, you either, close the whole enterprise down completely and release everyone involved, or second, we will go public and force you to close the facility down and find a way to release everyone ourselves.'

Joe and Geoffrey sit and look at the PM, waiting expectantly as he mulls the proposals over, he finally closes his eyes and waves his hand at the door, and says, 'Please leave us, we will need to talk about this, one of us will contact you later on today.'

With that he swings the chair so as he has his back to them As a passing shot, Joe says, 'Until the end of business today then. James?'

With no answer forthcoming the pair walk out of the office. Not only pleased with the outcome of the meeting but happy with the way they made the PM squirm.

Back at Melissa's house, Geoffrey proudly informs everyone, of what has just taken place in the PM's office. They are all sitting quietly when Melissa glances round at her father and asks him, 'What do you think, dad?'

Her father looks around the table at the expectant faces and says, 'I have had quite a few dealings with Thatchmore over the years, he will not do anything in a hurry, he will just hope that all this will somehow go away. So I suggest we get Vince Page over here and sort out a front page spread for tomorrow, so if Thatchmore does not call, at least we will be ready to go to print.'

Melissa turns to the other people in the room saying, 'Vince Page is our editor in chief, he's not only a good friend but also a very intelligent man. When Vince arrives at the house it takes David Kelvin a good hour to fill his editor in on the Dome and what they intend to do if the PM doesn't contact them. Page takes out his note pad and begins roughing out his front page spread ready for the next day's edition. The headline read, 'Government hold 500 UK citizens against their will!'

David sits quietly and reads through the quickly written piece, smiles and nods his head in approval, which pleases his editor and friend no end. All they can do now is wait and see what happens next.

John holds a quiet conversation with Colin and they agree that any imminent threat of violence is now over. He asks his friend if he thinks it will be okay if his family return home. When Colin says that he can't see any reason why not. John takes out his phone and with shaking hands calls his wife, having had more time in the last day or so to realise just how much he is missing her. Sarah answers after the first ring, and when she hears John's voice, bursts into tears. He asks her how long it will take them to return home, she asks if he is sure that it is now safe, he reassures her and says that he will be at home waiting for them. He has to admit that he can't wait to take Sarah in his arms and tell her that he loves her, and make love to her.

John stands looking out of the bay window in his living room, he is patiently waiting for family to return home for good. When he sees his mother's car turn into the driveway his heart leaps. He runs out to the car and as soon as Sarah climbs out, they fall into each other's arms and hug, as if they have been apart for years.

Joan sits in the car, holding her hands over her eyes and openly weeps as she now knows that her daughter-in-law will be fine, and baby Molly will finally have a loving family around her. It is still early in the day but everyone is absolutely worn out from the strain and stress of the last few weeks, so when John suggests that it will do them all good to catch up on some much needed sleep. Joan smiles knowingly at her son and agrees to an early night. After everyone has gone to bed and John and Sarah have made passionate love, Sarah chooses that moment to tell him she is pregnant again. John sits up and looks down at his smiling wife, he places his hand tenderly on her stomach, for once in his life he is lost for words, as tears of joy and happiness run freely down his cheeks.

CHAPTER 30

A much refreshed John is standing in the living room in his dressing gown; it is just after six in the evening. He is not surprised that there has been no contact from Thatchmore. He checks that nobody else has heard anything, then phones David Kelvin. When David answers, John tells him that nobody has heard anything and asks if he is ready to take the next step. David reassures John that he has considered all his options very carefully and mulled over the problem from every angle. Where necessary he has taken advice. So yes, he is ready to take things further. He tells John that all he has to do is to ring his editor to check everything is ready to go and give the go ahead.

David asks John, 'If we go ahead with this, you do know that we will need a full and frank interview with you for the next day's edition?'

John doesn't hesitate for a second before agreeing to the interview. Knowing that he can do no-more, he goes back upstairs and checks on baby Molly, he knows that he is standing there with a stupid lop-sided smile on his face He stands by the bedroom door watching his first born as she sleeps peacefully, but can't help himself because after recent events, he just wants to spend some quality time with her. Finally happy with life, he climbs back into bed with his sleeping wife and for the first time in what feels like a lifetime, sleeps the sleep of the dead.

The smell of bacon cooking wakes him early the following morning; he walks down stairs in his dressing gown to find his wife sitting at the kitchen table, feeding Molly. They smile at each another, and he sits down next to her and starts to eat his breakfast. Before he has eaten much, his mobile phone buzzes, he picks it and answers, 'Hello?'

A reporter from one of the broadsheets asks him if he is willing to give them an exclusive interview about the Dome. He mumbles some sort of answer saying that he will have to think about it and hangs up. The phone instantly begins to buzz again, in the end he has no option but to turn it off. It is then that Sarah's phone begins to ring, and she is forced to turn hers off too. She looks at him accusingly, and asks him what has he done to warrant the papers hounding them, especially this early in the morning.

He tells her everything starting from the beginning, she sits and shakes her head in total disbelief, but agrees in principle with what he has done, and that was the right thing to do and that she will support him one hundred percent. The doorbell chimes. When John looks out of the window he is shocked to see a BBC television van outside the house and a man with a huge camera on his shoulder, already filming.

On seeing John, he instantly turns the camera to face him. John hadn't thought that the press would find out about him so quickly, but obviously they had. He will have to think of a way to protect his family if he can, he will have to try and keep them away from the press and everything that comes with that. He opens the door a fraction and as soon as he does, a black microphone is thrust at his face, and a young blonde woman begins firing questions at him.

He holds his hand up and says, 'I have promised that I will give a full interview to the Tribute and until I have done that, I cannot say another word on the subject.' With that, he closes the door, but the doorbell instantly chimes again.

John dresses in his best suit and nervously prepares for his day, from his bedroom window he sees that the usually quiet street is full of newspaper crews. Reporters are standing three deep outside his house, he groans inwardly as Sarah walks into the bedroom carrying baby Molly.

'What are we going to do about these reporters, John?' she asks, irritably.

He shrugs his shoulders and admits that he doesn't have an answer but says, 'Give me a minute, I'll speak to David, he'll know what to do'

When John explains to David what is going on, David laughs out loud and says, 'What did you expect, John, you're front page news, but don't worry. Is there any way of getting out of the house without them seeing you?'

John looks out of the window to the rear of the house and sees that it is clear for the moment, so he says, 'Well, at the moment we can get out the back way.'

David says, 'Stay put for now and pack a few things for your immediate needs, and I will send Melissa. She'll come to the back door as quickly as she can, you can all come and stay here, as my guests, that way you will all be safe.

John smiles and gives Sarah the thumbs up and says, 'We'll be ready, thanks David.' He hangs up and tells Sarah of the plan. She rushes around the house, picking up toys, nappies, baby clothes and baby food and throwing everything into bags.

Melissa eventually arrives and parks a rented white mini bus, with tinted windows near the rear gate of John's house. She calls John on his mobile to say that the coast is clear. John and his family dart out of the back of the house and climb into the mini bus. Melissa is dressed like a farm worker with a wide brimmed hat and blue dungarees. When they are all in the bus, she tells them to get down as low as they can, out of sight if possible. Melissa turns around in her driving seat to check that they can't be seen, then drives out of the road and away from the house, luckily without being seen. Some of the reporters do glance at her, but on seeing how she looks, dismiss her as a local farmer or grower.

When they arrive at David's house, Joe, Geoffrey, Sam and Molly are already there and sitting watching television, on the screen is a picture of the front page of the Tribute, under the headline 'Escape from the Dome.' There is a full page picture of John, the story begins:

John Stratton (pictured above) made good his escape from a futuristic prison like facility known as the Dome The facility has been created and controlled secretly by the government, a full and frank interview with Stratton will be printed in the Tribute tomorrow.

Which isn't exactly true, but close enough to get the desired affect. The TV screen then shows pictures of the, now empty, Stratton house before switching over to 10 Downing Street, where a well known male reporter is saying that they are expecting a statement from the prime minister. And that an emergency cabinet meeting has been called, the cameras then show different members of the cabinet rushing tight lipped into number ten.

It is the minister for science who eventually walks stiff backed out of the famous black door, she is dressed in a sombre black dress and black shoes. She walks confidently to the bank of microphones, shuffles a few sheets of paper before glancing at the gathering press..

Taking a deep breath and looking directly at the camera, she says confidently, 'My name is Mary Gardener, minister for science. I would like to confirm that the government and my department have been working closely together. In partnership we have been trying to develop a super structure, that in the future if ever necessary, would in case of emergency, safely house the royal family and all essential government personnel. This futuristic building is in-fact a top secret facility and it is still the government's main aim, that it will stay that way. Thank you.'

Reporters call out all sorts of questions but the she turns and with a stiff back, walks purposely and silently, back into Number 10. The meeting inside continues in earnest, the PM has asked for suggestions from his Ministers but almost all of them are suitably shocked by the disturbing news, and sit silently looking down at the polished table top, as if trying to distance themselves from the PM and his terminal problem. At this point the PM realises that he is on his own and certainly in real trouble, maybe so serious that he may not survive. He also knows that as he is in ultimate control of the Dome, the buck stops at his door, and he will be lucky to stay out of prison. At best he knows that he will have no option but to resign.

He walks to the window, looks out at the hoard of reporters, takes out his mobile phone, and dials the major's number. For the hundredth time his call goes directly to voice mail, which tells him to leave a message. It seems that even the major who he took to be his closest friend and confidant, is another who has deserted him.

The disgraced prime minister pulls on his suit jacket and checks his appearance in the mirror. He takes a deep breath, walks out of his office and heads towards the front door. The doorman stands with his hand on the handle, as he waits for the nod to open the door. Another deep breath a nod and the black door opens, The PM steps towards the bank of microphones to deliver his resignation speech.

Melissa sits across the table from a nervous John, formally interviewing him for the Tribute, the interview has been planned for hours because they need to be certain they have all the relevant facts on the Dome. Melissa reads through her notes and checks the most important points with John to make sure that she has the facts right. When the interview is finally over, Melissa sits quietly in her father's office and writes the article for the Tribute. Happy with her morning's work she passes the piece to the editor, who reads through it very carefully. Melissa is given a nod of appreciation from the editor, she then stands and reads the statement in front of everyone in the room, giving everyone involved, the opportunity to add their own thoughts as they see fit.

Having listened to the proposed article it is Joe Everall who breaks the silence, saying, 'It does all sound so bloody impossible doesn't it, I mean who ever thought up such an awful place?'

Nobody answers him but some of the listeners shake their heads at the thought of being caught up in something as unlikely as the Dome. Sam speaks next from the police perspective and says, 'You do all realise that there will be charges laid against the PM and the minister for science, Mary Gardener. It is most likely they will both end up in prison because of this little fiasco.'

There is the muffled sound of a phone ringing and Joe Everall removes his phone from his pocket and looks at the caller ID, he then asks to be excused. He walks to the window and stands looking into the darkness of the surrounding countryside, as he holds a private conversation. When he sits back down at the table he has a huge smile on his face, when he realises that everyone is looking at him, he coughs politely and says, 'I have just received a very interesting phone call from Ronnie Campbell, the Leader of the Opposition, offering to give us any help required. I told him that at the moment we have everything under control, but out of politeness I thanked him anyway and made a promise to keep him informed of any changes in the situation.'

DCI Molly Wright is next to receive a phone call, but she answers the call while sitting at the table, all she seems to be saying is, 'Yes, sir,' every few seconds. She ends the call by saying, 'Yes, sir, right away, sir.'

With that, she stands up and says, 'I have just received a phone from my boss Eric Morris, he wants me to meet him at Scotland Yard immediately, he says that there is going to be an investigation at the highest level into the Dome, it seems that we have stirred up a right hornet's nest.'

John suddenly realises that his heart is pounding, at the thought that all this is his doing and he is responsible for all the trouble that he has caused everyone. He looks across the table at his wife and standing up, walks over, stands behind her and reassuringly rests his hands on her shoulders. Whether to reassure her or himself, he isn't really sure. Sarah reaches up and places her trembling hand onto her husband's, both of them wish they had never become involved in mess in the first place.

Eric Morris stands outside Scotland Yard waiting for Molly to arrive, when he sees her walking towards him, he rushes up to her and gently taking her by the arm, eases her into a shop doorway. He uses his huge body to shield her from prying eyes and ears, when he is happy that no-one can hear them, he looks down and stares deep into her green eyes and says quietly, 'I have to warn you before we go inside that the shit is about to hit the fan, big time. Rumour has it that the prime minister has been forced to resign in a bid to distance himself from this damn business, so I need you to tell me everything, and I mean everything that has happened over this last week or so, and make sure that you leave nothing out.' Molly stands there and tells him everything, even down to their holding the major.

Eric says, 'I know all about the major and his reputation for dishing out punishment, especially with his little crew of helpers, it's about time he was brought down a peg or two. I know about his band of hard men and of their demise, I take it that little incident is something to do with this bloody Dome thing?'

Molly looks into his eyes and nods admitting that Colin and his friends are responsible. When he says nothing, she watches him closely as he stares silently at her with unseeing eyes, he in thought, he finally says, 'I think that you ought to ring John and tell him to bring the major down here for questioning, that just might isolate the PM even further, now, if we can get hold of Mary Gardener as well, that will leave our distinguished leader just where he deserves to be, all on his lonesome.'

Molly says, 'I can give Colin a ring and see what he can do about Mary?'

Eric smiles at her and says, 'Let's get the major down here under lock and key first, then we will question him, see what he has to say and we can deal with Mary Gardener after that.'

Having spoken to her boss at length, Molly rings John and tells him what her boss has suggested regarding the major. He hesitates for a few seconds before answering her and then says, 'I'll have go to the lockup and make sure he is fit to travel before we agree to bring him down there, you know what Colin is like when the mood takes him' He agrees to call her back as soon as he knows the situation at the lockup.

John walks into the chilly, almost empty, industrial unit, to find some of Colin's friends fast asleep in sleeping bags on the hard concrete floor, the others are sitting at the table paying cards. He looks at the plastic room and can see a ghostly figure moving around inside and the eerie sound of muffled voices, made indistinguishable by the wall of plastic sheeting. All of a sudden there is a deep groan of pain from within the cell like space, John enters the major's prison to see Colin on his knees in front of the still trussed up officer, who has his face screwed up in agony, the major already has one puss encrusted nail plunged deep into his right leg, the nail has gone in so deep that the sharp point has easily pierced the bone. Colin holds the second nail at shoulder height and is just about to plunge it into the major's other thigh, when a raised eyebrow and stern look from John stops him.

The major opens his eyes and looks at John pleadingly, from the way that the officer's eyes are screwed up and bloodshot, John can tell that he is in an awful lot of pain. He indicates with a nod to Colin that he stand up and move away from the prisoner. Colin stares down at the major before he steps away from the obviously relieved man. John kneels down in front of the major and looks closely at the nail embedded deeply in his thigh. John looks into his eyes sees pleading there, so says, 'I have a one time offer for you, Major, it seems that Scotland Yard want to have a little chat with you, and they want you down there, as soon as is feasibly possible. Now I can take you there immediately and let them deal with you or you can stay here and play with my friend Colin, the choice as they say, is yours?'

The major tries his best to speak but the gag won't allow him to, so John lowers the dirty tea towel, at which the relieved man licks his dry lips and swallows deeply, when he can eventually speak, the cowardly major begs to be taken to London.

Colin seems a little bit disappointed and asks, 'Can't you leave him with me until tomorrow morning and let me have a little bit of fun first?' He is standing there looking down at the major, menacingly twisting the long dirty nail around in his fingers. The cowardly officer is, by now, almost begging John to take him to London, as quickly as he possibly can.

John looks at Colin and says, 'You had better remove that nail before we start our journey.'

Colin smiles and says, 'With pleasure'

He kneels down in front of the major and says in a stern voice, 'Do you remember when you beat up my friend and threatened a tiny child, and completely wrecked their house?' The major is about to speak but Colin lifts a finger to his lips to shush him. He then grips the nail which makes the major grimace, and with his free hand replaces the gag in the major's mouth. He then looks into the major's eyes and smiles a wicked smile.

Then with great pleasure he pushes the nail deeper into the man's thigh bone and begins to move the nail in a slow but deliberate circular motion. This action makes the major scream as loudly as the gag will allow him to. His eyes are wide open and filled with terror as the pain in his is almost unbearable, tiny drops of sweat break out on his forehead and big fat tears run from both bloodshot eyes and soak into the dirty tea towel tied around his mouth.

CHAPTER 31

Early the next morning when John turns on the radio, the news is fully taken up with talk that James Thatchmore the ex-prime minister has been arrested and is being held at Scotland Yard, pending an investigation into suspected multiple kidnappings and involvement in multiple murders. John turns on the TV and the minister for science, Mary Gardener is being grilled by a BBC News reporter. When the journalist asks when the inmates of the Dome will be released she becomes flustered and begins blurting out things like, 'It is not as easy as that, there are many things to be taken into consideration, you just can't release five hundred institutionalised people back into the general populace, it would become chaotic. Some of the inmates have been away from their homes for up to three years, they will all have to be fully debriefed and properly reintegrated, which will take time to organise.'

Robert Hutchins has taken office as the new prime minister. At his first press conference he swears, 'I had no knowledge of any part of the Dome's existence.' He also swears that, 'During the time that the Dome was in operation, I had no knowledge of its existence.' He also goes on to explain the he will personally do everything in his power to see that the inmates of the Dome are released, as soon as he has taken the necessary expert advice on the subject. He will also see to it personally that everyone involved in the creation and operating of the facility will be suitably punished and that includes the disgraced James Thatchmore. That is, of course, if it is proven that he was indeed involved by association and is found guilty of any or all charges.

John and Eric are shown into Scotland Yard's private conference room, in which every seat is taken by smartly dressed, high-ranking police officials, almost all of them resplendent in black dress uniforms.

Before the meeting begins, the chief of the Metropolitan Police, Sir Donald Boyd, takes Eric to one side and gives him and Molly carte blanche to continue their good work in investigating the facility known as the Dome, and they are to continue with that, just as soon as they think it appropriate.

A tall, thin elderly man with salt and pepper hair, bright intelligent green eye, dressed in a very expensive hand made pale blue suit, is sitting at the head of the table. He introduces himself as Gregory Cockwell, minister for public relations. He invites John and Eric to sit near him.

Chairs are brought in and when they are all seated at the highly polished oak table, Cockwell introduces each person in turn, the introductions complete, he turns to John and asks, 'Mr Stratton, will you please describe to us as best you can the details of your forced incarceration, and everything that you know about the installation known to as the Dome?'

He then sits back and waits for John to begin telling of his time in the Dome. With all eyes on him, a nervous John stands and begins to tell of his enforced captivity, as best he can remember, it takes him the best part of an hour to make his statement. When he has finally finished telling his tale, every person around the table stares questionably at John, as if he has been speaking in some newly discovered foreign language.

'Unbelievable,' mutters Gregory Cockwell, followed by mumbled agreement from all around the long table. Looking at John, the minister asks, 'And you are absolutely positive that the prime minister knew about this whole affair, every aspect of it?'

With a nod of his head, John answers, 'Absolutely positive, sir.' Again mumbles fill the overly hot room and rebound from the ornate ceiling.

John is asked a few totally irrelevant questions before the minister taps the table, stares at him and asks, 'And these poor people, you say that there are up to five hundred of them still incarcerated in this dreadful place?' John nods. 'Well, how soon can we get them released?'

John thinks about this question for a minute or two and then says, 'Personally,' I think this problem will need a lot of thought and even more planning, simply because you can't just open the doors and let five hundred people walk out into the wide open countryside. A team of specialist counsellors will have to be brought in to process each individual inmate, then and only then if they are deemed to be mentally stable enough to be reintegrated, can they be released. Let's not forget that some of these people have been missing for up to three years. Their cars are hidden in the basement of the complex, each of their families will have to be informed of their loved one's imminent release, some of these family members may have moved on and found new partners, formed new relationships even, in some cases remarried!

Some of the inmates may have children that they have never seen or even know about. Then there is all the false hope that families with long-term missing relatives have been through, what length of time is deemed acceptable to wait for someone? Just say that the missing person does then reappear after say three years, it would be like starting the relationship all over again from scratch and if the relationship does not, for some reason, work out, it will be another heart wrenching break-up that these poor people will have to go through. All these things will have to be taken into consideration before we make the decision to do anything.

'When I was eventually released, I didn't remember anything of my experience of the Dome, due to some kind of mind-altering drug that was administered to me on my release, whereas these people will leave the Dome with full knowledge of their enforced incarceration. They will have to deal with that fact; each and every one of the inmates will probably need counselling of one sort or another, and then there will be the claims for compensation against the government and that will run into millions of pounds.'

At the end of John's speech, everyone in the room is appalled at what has happened to the very people they have sworn to protect. Each official lowers his or her eyes and appears to be deep in thought as they wonder what is currently happening to these poor inmates, and what lies ahead for them, not least themselves because they know that they will be drawn into the affair at some point. They may even be wondering how they would have coped in a place such as the Dome.

Gregory Cockwell taps the table to regain order in the room, looking up at John, he nods his thanks. John thankfully sits down.

The old man then turns to the others assembled in the room and says, 'We, supposedly protectors of the public, have now taken control of this facility and have the man formerly in charge of the whole operation in custody, Professor Raymond Stanley is now under lock and key in the bunker. He is continuing to do his job, but under close supervision, and is more than willing to help with the release process of these unfortunate people.

'I have to tell you all that the professor has a plan in place for the eventual release of the inmates. The plan was put in place at the original planning stage.' He picks up a thick wad of papers and places them on the table in front of him, when he has everyone's attention, he places his hands palms down on top of the large stack of paper, clears his throat and begins reading, 'In front of me I have the professor's plan. As you can see, it is very detailed and some parts are complex. A team of experts and I have read and dissected the plan. We have produced a pared down version of the original idea that we can all understand.'

He picks up a few sheets of paper that are stapled together in the top left hand corner. 'It seems that, according to the professor, twenty people at any one time can be taken from the main facility and kept unguarded inside the bunker in specially prepared rooms, it will take a minimum of one hundred hours to debrief each person, so we are looking at weeks if not months to process all five hundred inmates. That is unless we can set up a separate mobile village of some sort inside the facility. That way we can then have our own team of experts on hand to help.

'This, of course, will only happen under the watchful eye of the professor. We have enough counsellors we can call on to do whatever is deemed necessary, unless anyone here, has any other suggestions?'

The question hangs heavy in the now suddenly stuffy room, as everyone else looks down at the highly polished table, nobody wanting to even look at the minister, it is as if they want nothing to do with the whole affair, to the point of trying to distance themselves from the problem all together.

Eric Morris coughs politely and says, 'There is something else that we can do, I know that if Thatchmore is found to be guilty of the charges brought against him, he will have to be punished in some way and we all know that he cannot be placed in a normal prison. So why don't we place him in the Dome itself, under guard naturally, and place him in charge of the inmate selection and release programme. We can also, if need be, place Mary Gardener, the minister for science, in there to help him, that will give them both a taste of what they themselves have created.

What we will need to do before we enter the facility is to inform the inmates they will be released soon, but the process of selection and final discharge will take a certain amount of time, so, they need to be patient.

From what we have heard today, Mary Gardener can if needed, inform the inmates of their release through the control centre using the space station. But personally I think that a matter of this magnitude should be given to the inmates one on one, in case of any questions. So we will arrange for the bank manager, who I believe is on charge, to deliver the news.

This method of communication can also be used to in the selection process, maybe we could begin with the people that have been in there the longest?'

Gregory Cockwell smiles at this idea and says, 'Yes, yes I like that idea a lot, it will keep Thatchmore out of the public eye, and at the same time give us some breathing space to decide what punishment befits his crimes. Yes, yes, that does sound rather good.' Everyone nods their agreement.

John then says, 'If I may make a further suggestion. Rather than releasing those that have been in there the longest, would it not be more compassionate to release those that have young families first. Just put yourself in the place of, say a young mother, someone who hasn't seen her children for years, she will be by now, be besides herself and desperate to see her family.'

Gregory Cockwell and everyone around the table can see his argument and nod their heads in agreement, so it is that plan that is selected and set in motion, with immediate effect.

The creators of the Dome, the disgraced prime minister, Gregory Cockwell, John and his friends who have been involved in exposing the Dome for what it is, are now standing in the underground bunker staring at a large screen. It shows the robot-like inmates of the facility, as they go about their daily routine. Mary Gardener looks over the top of her half-rimmed glasses, she is sitting at the bunker's main control panel, twisting knobs and her fingers are dancing across her keyboard at a furious rate and not once does she take her eyes from the screen.

When she completes the task, she then turns to Gregory Cockwell for permission to carry on. He nods his assent, she then begins to whisper into a round dish which is connected to a long, bright steel arm, that protrudes from the centre of the control panel. The watching audience stare at the screen in awe, as every inmate instantly stops what they were doing and like robots turn and make their way to the main square. When the square is full, a fat man who John recognises as Andrews, the Banker walks up a short flight of steps and stands looking out over the silent inmates. Mary Gardener says without taking her eyes from the screen, that what she is about to do, will demonstrate that she can contact each individual inmate, as easily as all five hundred.

The banker waves his arms for silence and begins by saying. 'Residents of the Dome, it seems that our release from this place is imminent, but I have to inform you all, that the release process will take some time to complete. From information that I have recently received, the powers that be will begin the process with residents who have young families, and the process will begin just as soon as possible.'

'On your release everyone will go through a debriefing process that will take up to one hundred hours. During that period, your families will be informed of your imminent release and brought here to assist with your reintegration.' He stops talking and closes his eyes for a few seconds, when he opens them again, he continues, 'I have just been told that around twenty residents will be released at any one time, which means the whole process will take some weeks. However, a promise of external help to assist with the debriefing has been made; and finally, the government wishes to apologise for the inconvenience that has been caused by your incarceration. We appreciate your patience during the reintegration process, thank you and good luck.'

That is all the banker has to say, he walks down the steps and heads for the bank. The reaction of the residents is subdued, some chat quietly amongst themselves for a few minutes, and then simply turn away and return to whatever they were doing before they were interrupted.

John questions the reaction of the residents; thinking that they should have been jubilant at the news of their release and that they should have been jumping up and down for joy.

Mary Gardener turns to John and says, 'It is quite simple really, with the new NYS22643 gas that we use, we can control everything the inmates do and think, even their deepest though processes, which in turn control their emotions. In truth, we can control every aspect of their lives and as you now realise, this process needs to be kept top secret. There are organisations around the world that will do anything and I mean anything, to get their hands on this system.'

A full week later and the plans have been put into place for the release of the first of the inmates. John and his friends are allowed to go to the underground bunker, so that they can watch the event unfold.

When they arrive at the bunker, Professor Stanley is sitting at another control panel staring at a large screen, his tired looking eyes dart from side to side as he stares at the screen, which is covered from top to bottom with yellow numbers, the calculations move ever upwards and disappear off the screen.

On a panel to the left a red warning light flashes, without turning around the professor points to the flashing light and says, 'Look there, yes you can look, this is all your fault, you bunch of amateurs have caused this to happen. If you had just kept quiet, this security breakdown would never have occurred.'

He turns his head and stares at John and every other face in the standing group and says angrily. 'Don't you understand what I am saying? Someone out there in cyberspace is trying to breach our security system, someone wants all the information on the Dome and I am not certain if I can stop them. Just imagine if the secrets of the Dome and its construction get out, the world could become a very dangerous place, we do have certain programs in place, constructed to divert outside interest, but until now they have never been tested. Just imagine if the Russians were to get their hands on this information, it is possible that they could turn each major city in Russia into a giant controlled Dome facility and then one city at a time until they control every capital city, in every country in the world. There is no way that we can allow that to happen, we must stop them at all costs, even if we have to destroy the whole experiment, inmates and all.'

John turns and talks quietly to his friends, as they realise for the first time that they are now way out of their depth But they are still convinced that they have done the right thing in exposing the Dome for what it is. The Professor begins to dial a number on a red phone, after a few seconds he starts talking quietly but at the same time urgently. Seconds later, he turns and says, 'That was Captain James Hewett of the SAS, Hereford.

He has deployed a Captain Tim Hunt with a team of men to guard the bunker and the Dome, but they will not be here until late tomorrow evening, I just hope that is soon enough. Because earlier, I received word from GCHQ at Cheltenham that the American's have intercepted urgent messages transmitted to foreign agents all around the world, that they are to collect as much information on the Dome, as they can get, no matter the cost. The most urgent of these messages is that, two well known Russian operatives, here in London, have received such messages, they were last seen heading out of London, in our general direction.

Descriptions of the two Russian Agents have been sent to the Captain. All we can do now is wait and hope and pray that the Captain arrives here soon enough.'

After a minute or two of silence Melissa gives a gentle cough and says, 'We can arrange immediate cover until the Captain arrives, we have some special friends nearby that will provide every bit of cover that you require, no questions asked, they are just a phone call away.'

Raymond Stanley turns and looks at the young woman for a few seconds before nodding his head in agreement. Melissa takes out her mobile and calls Colin, after a short conversation she turns to the older man and nods, saying that, 'Help is on its way.'

Colin and his SAS friends look menacing in their balaclavas and camouflage clothing, each man is armed to the teeth as they stand guard at the entrance to the underground bunker. The Dome's residents are sleeping peacefully, blissfully unaware what is going on around them. A recently requisitioned Oxfordshire police helicopter constantly searches the surrounding area with heat seeking cameras, on the hour, every hour. It's at the fourth hour that the aircrew report to the MI5 officer in charge that two heat sources have been located to the east of their position. Graham Walker from MI5 passes the information onto Colin through his communication device. Colin acknowledges that he has received the information and nods for two of his friends to follow him. The fully trained soldiers leave the bunker, in the opposite direction to that where the heat sources have been detected, and head out into the darkness. Taking the long way round to where the two men are supposedly hiding, they make their way quietly towards the heat sources.

It is almost two hours before the message saying that the watchers have been located is passed on to Graham Walker. Then Colin whispers into his head mic., 'What do you want me to do with them, detain them or make them disappear?'

Graham Walker says to detain the men if possible but to hold them somewhere safe a long way from the facility. And if possible to hang onto them until the situation at the bunker has been made safe. At least until they can be put on a plane back to Moscow or wherever it is that they have come from. But if, for any reason, the watchers put up any sort of resistance, then he will leave it up to Colin to use his discretion.

Colin and his friends silently move ever closer to the two operatives, step by silent step, they stop still some six feet behind the watching men, one is filming everything taking place in the valley below, while his companion is taking still pictures. Then Colin and one of his friends move silently forward as one to stand over the two men. Both operatives suddenly stiffen as they feel the cold steel of gun barrels touching the naked skin of their necks. They drop what they have been holding and push their hands up, in total surrender. Without a word being spoken, both are blindfolded, the two foreign agents then have their hands secured behind their backs with long white cable ties.

The prisoners are taken away and bundled unceremoniously into the back of the blue van and driven away. They are taken to the lockup and secured to chairs and placed at either end of the room, and told in no uncertain terms that they must not communicate with each other under any circumstances or their mouths will be taped up. With their cameras and the contents of their pockets laid out on the long work bench, it is confirmed that they are the two well-known Russian agents. Two of Colin's friends sit and watch the prisoners while Colin returns to the Dome and reports back to Graham Walker, he passes the meagre contents of the prisoners' pockets to the security team. The two security men inspect every item very closely but find nothing of interest.

Graham Walker from MI5 tells Colin that he has requested that the men be held in solitary confinement at Her Majesty's pleasure. They will be held at Scotland Yard until the problem with the Dome has been resolved and there is a good chance that could take a very long time. There are no further security incidents to report, so Colin and his friends are told to stand down but asked to deliver their guests the following day to Scotland Yard, where they are to hand the Russians over to the security services. They are also told that when they get close to the Yard, they are to phone a contact on the number provided who will guide them to an unused secure entrance, the building that the prisoners will be housed in is a long away from the public eye.

Simon Thatchmore the younger brother of the disgraced prime minister has managed to sweet talks his way into the prison block and stands outside the cell holding Major Jerry Keen. The major looks up at the tall thin man, with a bushy moustache and bright blue eyes and asks, 'And who might you be?'

Thatchmore looks around to make sure that he can't be overheard and quietly tells the prisoner who he is. The major stands up and walks to the bars so the they can talk quietly, they stand looking into each others eyes, finely Simon says, 'James has asked me to pay you a visit, he wants you to put plan D into action.'

The major searches the tall man's face deep in thought, eventually he says, 'You know that once the call has been made, the contract cannot be cancelled, it will be carried out to the full?'

The tall man shrugs and says, 'If that is what he wants, then that is what he'll get,' then looking around again to make sure that he isn't being watched, he reaches into his sock and passes a pay-as-you-go mobile phone through the bars. Without a word, the major takes the phone, stashes it in his pocket, and turns away. He lies on his bed and covers himself with a blanket. Thatchmore shrugs and walks away, his job done, he leaves the major to whatever it is that he has to do.

The major dials a number that he knows by heart, in his role as the disgraced prime minister's right hand man, he has used this particular individual many times before. He doesn't know who the man is but that doesn't matter, you tell him who the problem is, pay the usual amount into a numbered account, and the problem is dealt with, one way or another.

After only two rings a deep voice with an African twang to it, answers the call saying, 'Talk to me.'

The major says, 'This is the major, the problem is John Stratton, you will see his picture all over the newspapers.'

The deep voice answers, 'It will be done,' and the line goes dead.

The major smiles to himself because the elimination of Stratton will be very rewarding considering the trouble he has caused him. If he had the money himself, he would have that SAS bastard done as well. Sitting on his bunk, deep in thought, he stands and asks the guard to ask Stratton if he will come and see him, as he has further information for him. The guard takes out his radio and passes on the message. A few minutes later, the guard's radio crackles and a message comes back saying that John Stratton will be there within the hour.

When John enters the silent cell block the major is lying on his bunk with his weight on one elbow and looking directly at him, he has a broad confident smile on his face as he watches his guest walk towards him.

John stands looking at the incarcerated man and asks, 'Well, I'm here, what do you want, Major?'

The prisoner stands up confidently and walks over to the cell's bars stands right in front of John and stares into his eyes, he stands so close that John can smell his rancid breath,

'I just wanted to look at you. You think that you have won don't you? You think that because you made good your escape from the Dome and caused all this trouble, that you have beaten me. John Stratton, you may the big man now, but let me tell you this, even men like you have been known to fall and fall very heavily indeed and I can guarantee that you will come tumbling down very soon. My only regret is that I won't be there to see it when it happens.'

John looks at the major and asks, 'Have you finished, because it looks from where I'm standing that you are the one locked up behind bars, not me, you are the one that is going to prison for a very long time, not me. I will leave now, my wife and I are going out for a nice meal, and then I am going to take her to bed and make love to her all night. You just sit and think about that, Major, when you are lying on that hard bunk, on your own in the dark with your dick in your hand. So goodbye, Major, oh, and by the way, get your facts right, I was released and didn't escape from the Dome.'

With a huge smile, he turns to leave. As he reaches the door the major calls out menacingly, 'Watch your back, John Stratton, you never know when accidents can happen.'

John leaves the cell block deep in thought, asking himself what the major meant by that last remark? If he didn't know better, he might think that the major has something very unpleasant planned for him.

CHAPTER 33

John and Sarah are sitting in then garden relaxing together for the first time in an age. They sit in deck-chairs in the warm summer sunshine while watching little Molly playing in her pink paddling pool. She giggles as she squirts water into the air from the beak of a yellow plastic duck. John reaches over and strokes his wife swelling belly, Sarah links her fingers in his and tells him that she loves him with all her heart. He leans back and closes his eyes saying that the loves her just as much, if not more. Sarah sits quietly thinking for a short while before asking, 'Is it really over John, is everything finally done and dusted?'

He squeezes her hand and says, 'Well, the inmates of the Dome are slowly but surely being set free, there are more of them returning home every day, the major is safely tucked away in prison awaiting sentencing, Sam has been posted to Canada to advise the mounted police, David is back at work and is talking about running a series on the Dome in his news paper, with me as the lead, and my mother is living in her granny flat, so what can possibly go wrong?' John smiles and pulls his sun hat lower over his eyes and thinks to himself, that life just can't get any better that this.

Sarah lets out a little tut as the phone rings inside the house, she unfolds her long slightly pink legs and somehow lifts her swollen belly out of the deep deck chair. She waddles indoors and John can hear her talking but can't quite make out what she is saying. She replaces the phone and calls John, saying, 'That was David Kelvin on the phone. He says to put the TV on straight away.' John walks into the house just as Sarah aims the remote at the set and switches to the news channel. Along the bottom of the screen in large red letters are the words:

Breaking News. Disgraced prime minister found dead in wrecked car, no other vehicles involved, foul play not suspected.

The phone immediately begins ringing again, John picks it up and without speaking, stands there listening to Colin telling him that there had been no accident. Thatchmore had been hit as he left the bunker and they have found a bullet in his back, and the car crash was staged to take the heat away from the Dome. Colin warns John to be extra careful as it may be that someone is clearing up any loose ends, and at the end of the day, they are all loose ends.

John replaces the receiver and turns to his worried looking wife, who asks, 'What is it, John. It is obviously bad news?' The now tense man stands still, suddenly looking very worried.

Sarah goes to him and strokes his strained looking face and says, 'Please tell me what is wrong darling?'

He takes the woman he loves more than life itself into his arms, kisses her neck and tells her everything that he has just been told. Sarah immediately begins trembling in his arms, he feels her warm tears drop onto his bare shoulder, both of them now know the Dome has come back to haunt them.

Sir David Kelvin sits at the head of a large oak table in the conference room at the Tribute offices, everyone who has been involved in the Dome affair is there. The day's daily newspapers are scattered all over the table top, the headline on each different but all have the same meaning. Trouble is not far away for them all and they know it, but where does the threat come from and who will be the first to find out?

John and Sarah drive in silence on the journey home, silent because they are both preoccupied with their own thoughts. When they eventually pull onto the driveway, John switches the engine off and turns to his wife. He is about to speak when she places her finger onto his lips to silence him and says, 'I am not leaving you again John, this time we will stick together.'

He shakes his head and says, 'What about Molly, we need to get her somewhere safe, maybe we can get my mother to take her on a little holiday?' Sarah nods in agreement, saying that it's a good idea. They are lying in bed sleeping fitfully in the early hours of the night when the phone rings.

John picks up the receiver and says, 'Hello?' Not a word is spoken but he can hear heavy breathing on the other end of the line, so he knows that someone is definitely there, he again says, 'Hello?' But still there is no reply, not many seconds later, the phone goes eerily silent.

He looks at the receiver and knows at that moment, that trouble has found him. Three times the phone rings that night, Sarah pretends to be asleep but he can feel her whole body trembling beneath the sheets. There is suddenly an almighty crash down stairs. John ran down the stairs two at a time and finds his mother in her nightdress, standing looking at the remnants of what had once been a bay window. Fragments of glass lie all around on the carpet, a large plant pot is upside down and broken, on the now ruined cream carpet. He looks at his mother and is about to speak, when a piercing cry comes from upstairs. John races back up the stairs, again two at a time, closely followed by his mother. When they run into the master bedroom, Sarah is standing by the side of the bed holding her stomach, a look of terror on her face, she is standing in a pool of water. Joan runs to her daughter-in-law and sits her down on the bed, she looks at John and shouts for him to call for help.

John dials 999 and asks for police and ambulance, he looks at his distressed wife as she lies in the foetal position on the bed, gripping her stomach and sobbing her heart out.

She looks at her husband through tear filled eyes and reaches out to him, he sits on the bed and takes her hand in his, she looks up at him with eyes full of concern and whispers, 'It's too soon John, it's much too soon.'

On hearing approaching sirens, John runs back down the stairs as fast as he can. He flings the front door open as a police car screams to a halt at the end of the drive. Just as the first policeman climbs out of the police car, a loud shot echoes through the dark night, John Stratton flies backwards into the passage way of his house and slams into the wall, a deepening red bloodstain spreading slowly across his stomach.

Armed Police stand guard as the ambulance personnel work on John to try and save his life, it is at this time that another ambulance technician and doctor arrive on the scene, armed police shield them as the doctor goes straight to John and the technician makes his way into the house, he is urgently waved up stairs. John and Sarah are only allowed to be loaded into the ambulances when they are stable, and the police helicopter has scanned the surrounding countryside and declared the area safe.

John is in the operating theatre undergoing emergency surgery for a life threatening gunshot wound, at the same time Sarah is in the maternity unit being cared for; as the birth of her premature baby is imminent. A team of specialist nurses is standing by ready to receive the pre-term baby. Joan has phoned Molly who in turn has called Melissa and before she knows it, Melissa, Colin and one of his friends arrive at the hospital. Not long after that, Molly and her boss Eric Morris arrive, they all sit silently in the waiting room as they wait for news. Melissa and Molly hold hands as they try and comfort each other. A nurse walks into the waiting room and they all, as one rise to their feet, the nurse looks from face to face and announces, 'Mrs Stratton has given birth to a baby boy, he is small but in good hands and is being assessed as we speak. Because of her stressed state, Mrs Stratton, has been slightly sedated, but her mother-in-law is sitting with her and I will let you know of any changes.'

The nurse turns to walk away when Colin asks about John, she says that there is no news as yet, but will keep them up to date with any fresh developments.

Joan walks into the waiting room, a white hanky held to her nose, she looks around the anxious faces through tear filled eyes, and chooses to sit next to Molly. She take's the younger woman's hand in her own, and not looking at anyone else, she whispers, 'He is so small!'

Molly pulls the older woman's head into her shoulder and holds her tightly, she strokes Joan's back affectionately as she sobs her eyes out, tears of sadness streaming down her cheeks.

At the first signs of daylight, the hospital slowly but surely bursts into life as the daily routine begins. John has been in surgery for eight hours, when a man dressed in a green surgical gown walks wearily into the waiting room, he looks and sounds absolutely exhausted. As he looks around the worried faces, he says, 'Mr Stratton is out of surgery, we have done all we can for him at present. He is in an induced coma and will remain in intensive care for the foreseeable future.

Unfortunately, there is some internal organ damage and he has lost one kidney and we have had to remove part of his stomach, but hopefully he will make a full recovery. I suggest that you all go home and get some rest and we will call you if there is any change.' But as he looks around the private waiting room, he knows that not one of them will take his advice.

Molly and Melissa, have finally been given permission to visit Sarah, they walk into her private room which has an armed policewoman on guard outside the door. Sarah holds her hand out and they rush to the bedside to comfort their friend. Sarah cries as she asks what had happened to John as no-one has told her anything. Molly looks into her eyes and tells her exactly what she has happened, she also tells her exactly what the nurse has told them. Sarah nods her head in understanding. She looks into Molly's eyes and begs, 'Please, go and find out what's happening to my baby?'

Molly nods and standing up looks down at her friend, a knowing look passes between the two women. Molly has to use her warrant card to get past the police security. They allow her to see the newborn baby. She is shocked at how tiny the baby is although he seems to be perfectly formed, things are made to look worse by the amount of wires and monitors that surround his tiny body. A paediatrician enters the room carrying a clipboard, he speaks quietly to the sister in charge and looks at his charts before turning to Molly, saying, 'The tests that we have carried out indicate the baby is fine and his reactions are all normal, he will be with us for a while until he puts some on weight and can breathe on his own, but I can't see any reason why he won't have a normal healthy childhood' and with a confident nod and a smile he leaves.

Molly walks back to Sarah's room and tells her the good news and as expected Sarah asks when she can see her new baby. Molly says that she will need to let her stitches heal first. The policewoman takes out her phone and holds up a picture of Sarah's baby, silent tears run down Sarah's rosy cheeks, as she stares lovingly at her beautiful new-born son.

John is out of the operating theatre and in a private room in the ICU ward, with two armed police standing guard outside his door. He is lying, grey and unmoving on his bed surrounded by a bank of bleeping machinery, tubes seem to be entering every part of his badly damaged body. A nurse standing at the end of his bed is busy writing on a big square board, most likely it records the information given out by flashing screens and monitors. Joan looks down at her son and prays that he will recover from his horrendous injuries. Understandably, she feels under tremendous pressure at the moment. She hasn't been feeling to well for a few weeks but with everything that has been going on lately, she has put her own health to the back of her mind and hasn't said anything about her problem to her daughter-in-law, as she herself has more than enough to worry about. She promises herself that she will go and see her GP as soon as things have sorted themselves out and she has a bit more time as at the moment, she is busy looking after baby Molly.

Colin and his friend stand looking through the glass screen at John as he lies motionless and close to death. Without looking away from his friend he says, 'Someone will pay for this, let's go and talk to a certain major and see what he can tell us.' The two men leave the hospital and head for London. An hour later, they are standing outside the prison cell looking down at a smiling major.

The confidant looking man lifts himself up onto his elbow and looks from one man to the other and asks, 'Well, well. And what brings you two here, it's a shame about Thatchmore, isn't it?'

Colin asks the guard if they have made a search of the prisoner's cell recently. The guard shakes his head, so Colin says, 'Time you took a break, ain't it?'

The guard looks at the prisoner who is no longer smiling, the guard hands Colin the keys and says, 'Five minutes, okay?' Colin nods his head and slipping the key into the lock pushes the heavy cell door open.

The two men enter the small prison cell and stand in front of the now not-so-confident major, who shouts out at the top of his voice, 'You can't do this, I am a prisoner of the realm.'

Colin grabs him around the throat and lifts him bodily from the bunk and pushes him high up against the cell wall, he holds him there with one hand and stares menacingly into his eyes. Colin's friend searches the cell and finds exactly what he is looking for tucked inside a freshly made hole, in the corner of the mattress.

Colin smiles at the now shaking major and asks, 'Did you have my friend shot, you fucking coward?'

The major shakes his head in denial, but Colin punches him hard in the stomach. The blow takes all the wind out of him and he slides to the floor and sits there holding his stomach and moaning. Colin begins kicking the downed man as hard as he can, he would have quite happily kicked him to death had his friend not stopped him They can hear the whistling guard returning so they pick up the now unconscious man and drop him onto his bunk, they cover him up with a blanket and leave the cell. Colin locks the door and passes the guard the keys and says, 'He seems to have fallen over and hit his head but he's sleeping like a baby now.'

The guard shrugs his shoulders and smiles as the two leave the cells, he sits at his desk takes out his newspaper and begins to whistle the song 'Strangers in the Night'.

Sitting in their car Colin switches the major's phone on, there have been three calls made to one number. Colin presses the redial button and the phone begins ringing, a deep booming voice answers the call, 'Talk to me?'

Playing on a hunch Colin says, 'Is it done?' The deep voice says, 'Have I ever let you down?'

Colin asks, 'can we meet? I have another one for you but I don't know his name, I only have a photo.'

There is some hesitation before the deep voice says, 'You know the rules, Major.

I don't meet anyone in person.'

Not pushing his luck, Colin says, 'Okay,' and ends the call. He looks at his friend and says, 'Let's get to the bunker, maybe a certain lady can use her computer system to locate our killer.'

Colin and his friend arrive at the bunker and things look completely different, there are not nearly as many inmates left as there were the last time that they visited. But one thing that is new is that now, there are guided tours taking place inside the Dome. The SAS are still guarding the entrance, and workmen are busy erecting a steel wall which will completely seal the entrance. This shield like structure will serve two purposes; One. It will make it easier to guard, Two. It will prevent unfriendly eyes seeing inside the bunker, therefore protecting the secrets within. A large warehouse is being erected to store the outer shell of the Dome when it is finally dismantled, the inner buildings are to be left as they are and will be the beginning of a new town for young people. Colin and his friend show their security passes and are allowed entry to the Bunker.

The Minister is sitting in her usual position, in front of a bank of screens. She is still pressing keys at a tremendous rate, confident in her on ability, she doesn't even look at her keypad as her eyes follow the lines of letters that appear on the screen. Colin coughs and she stops what she is doing with her fingertips still poised over the white buttons of her keypad, she glances sideways and spits out the words, 'What do you want?'

He gives her his best crooked smile and asks, 'I take it that you have heard the news of John Stratton being shot?'

She nods her head. Colin says, 'Well, we have a lead on our assassin but we need your computer system to give us a location for him, can you help us to do that, please?'

She looks from one big man to the other and smiles a thin confident smile. 'No problem at all,' she says. She holds her hand out for the mobile phone, Colin passes her the phone, she pulls a long thin black cable out of the computer and plugs it into the phone, then presses some buttons and a wavy line appears on the screen, she makes some adjustments, and when she is happy, she nods her head to show her readiness. Colin presses the redial button on the phone, on the second ring the deep voice says, 'Talk to me.'

Colin says, 'It's me again, I really think that we ought to meet, I have £50,000 in cash for this one. I have further information on the target, but I will need to meet you in person to give you the details.'

There is a long silence on the line before the deep voice eventually says, 'I have my rules my friend and I won't change them for you or anyone else,' and with that, he hangs up.

Colin looks at the minister hopefully, she smiles up at him and passes him a slip of paper, written on it in bold black letters is the killers location.

It is early morning on a bright sunny day in June, Colin and his friend sit in their car watching the front entrance of the Brenton House Hotel in Soho, London. This is the address of the hitman, the only problem being that they don't know who he is, or what he looks like.

Colin can tell from the two phone calls that he has made to the killer, that the man is of Africa extraction. The two sit and watch as lots of people come and go from the modern five storey building, but none look anything like the man they are after. Colin has been inside and checked the hotel over and the only way in or out for paying customers is via the main entrance. The watchers take it in turns to take a break or go for something to eat, but whichever one of watching, their eyes never leave the entrance. It is just after ten in the evening when a very large, well dressed black man steps out of the hotel. He is wearing a smart grey suit as he stands on the front steps, the orange street lights reflect off the man's shiny shaved head and makes him look like an angel, complete with halo. He stands and scans the street from end to end, searching for any threat, his brown eyes study their car briefly but they have positioned themselves in such away that from where he is standing, there is no way that he can see into the car. Confident that he is safe, he begins to stroll casually down the street, his eyes searching every face that passes him on both sides the busy road.

Colin takes out his phone, looks at his friend and says, 'Here goes nothing.' He presses the redial button on the major's phone, and they watch as the black man reaches into his pocket, and takes out his phone and in a deep voice says, 'Talk to me.'

Colin hangs up, turns to his friend, smiles to him and says, 'Let's see where our black friend goes.' They follow their target down the busy street to an Indian restaurant, they watch him enter the plush looking eatery and follow him inside. The man studies them closely but when Colin drapes his arm around his friend's shoulder, all interest in them leaves the man's chocolate coloured eyes.

Having eaten their meals, they have another drink while they wait for their target to leave, when he does eventually stand up and leave the restaurant they follow him back to his hotel. He stops on the top step, slowly turns his head from side to side as his brown eyes search the street again, just as he had done before, happy with what he sees, he nods his head confidently, then turns around and enters the hotel.

CHAPTER 34

Sarah sits by John's side and holds his hand in her own. She has been talking to him for almost an hour, excitedly telling him all about their new born son and how wearing long blue rubber gloves, she has held his tiny body in the incubator. John is still being kept in an induced coma, while the doctors try their best to heal his horrific wounds. The doctors reassure Sarah that it may not seem like it but her husband is in a stable condition and showing encouraging signs of improvement. John's team of consultants are very confident that he will make a good, if not full recovery. The doctors have indicated that John will need dialysis for as long as he is an in-patient and when he is finally discharged from hospital, he will have to attend a sat-alight unit three times a week for dialysis until they can control his bloods. He will also have to have a colostomy bag, again this will only be for a short period of time, this will give his insides chance to recover. The bag will be taken out when his stomach begins working on its own again. They also inform her that John will need further minor surgery, but this will take place over the next year or so.

Sarah cries when she is finally allowed to hold her tiny son. He still has wires attached to his body, and looks so small and fragile, but the nurses have tried their best to reassure Sarah that smaller babies than her son have pulled through, and gone on to live a long, normal, healthy life. Joan has been standing next to her daughter-in-law, the older woman slips her hand into the new mother's hand and gives it a reassuring squeeze. Sarah holds onto her mother-in-law's hand as if it is her only lifeline.

Sensing that the time is right, Colin and his companion walk into the hotel, they walk confidently up to the reception desk and Colin takes out his wallet, and asks the pretty blonde receptionist if a large black man has just entered the hotel, as he has left his wallet behind in the Indian restaurant down the road. She smiles and says, 'Ah yes, you must mean Mr Jefferies in room 354, if you leave the wallet here, I will make sure that he gets it in the morning.'

Colin smiles his best smile and says that they will deliver the wallet personally, as there may be some sort of financial reward. He gives the pretty young woman a smile and they head for the lift.

Standing silently outside room 354, they listen at the door and can hear some movement from inside. Colin knocks and waits, as the door opens, a very well built black man stands there, he is well over six feet tall and almost as wide, he is dressed in a white string vest and neatly pressed grey trousers. He stares down at Colin with his chocolate brown eyes. He opens his mouth to speak, when Coin hits him in the throat with a stun gun. The huge man's brown eyes roll upwards and disappear into his eyelids as he crumples to the floor, his eyes come back into view for a few seconds, only to roll back into his head, as he slips deeper into unconsciousness. Colin and his friend drag him further into the room and close the door behind them. They pick him up and lay him face up on top of a round oak table, they tie each of his thick limbs to the legs of the sturdy table, and make

145

themselves comfortable and wait patiently for the hitman to regain consciousness.

The big man finally stirs and when he realises that he is bound to the table, lifts his head and looks around the room. His eyes try to focus on Colin and it takes him a few seconds to be able to see properly. He growls, 'Who the fuck are you?' Colin stands up and looks down at the black man.

'I am a very good friend of the man that you shot – John Stratton.'

The black man pulls against his restraints to no avail and snarls, 'Untie me, and I will fucking rip you and your friend over there to fucking pieces, you fucking cowards.'

Colin lets out a loud sarcastic laugh and says, 'You have the brass neck to call us cowards, when you shoot innocent people from a distance and think nothing of it and take the money as if nothing has happened. Well, your days of contract killing are well and truly over, as of today, my friend. Now, let me tell you what's going to happen next, my partner here will stay with you while I go and do little bit of shopping and when we are through with you, I will call a police friend of mine and you will be going to prison for a very long time. While you are locked up, I will be going through your computer and I can assure you that I will find out where you have hidden your ill-gotten gains and I will then give the whole lot to a worthy charity namely John Stratton. Because after what you did to him, he will never work again, now do you think that is fair?'

The bound man glares at Colin with deep seated hatred in his eyes and struggles again against his restraints and shouts, 'I will get you pair of bastards for this, one day I will make sure that you pay' Colin smiles at the trussed up man, turns, nods to his friend and leaves the room.

He returns an hour later, smiles at his friend who nods back and whispers something into his ear. Colin stands looking down at the prone man and smiles confidently, 'Comfortable are you Mr Jefferies?' He asks.

The large black man pulls against his restraints to the extent that large muscles bulge in his arms as they strain against the ropes, again all to no avail. Colin reaches into his inside pocket and comes out with handful of yellow capped syringes, each one filled with a thick brown looking fluid.

He spreads them out in his hand and holds them up to the prisoner, who's eyes become very large as he asks, 'What's this shit then?'

Colin smiles and picks up one of the syringes and holds it up to the light and says, 'Well, Boris, that is your name isn't it? You see my friend here is very good at searching for hidden things, but when it comes to finding hidden money on a computer, and I bet there is a lot hidden on yours, I can assure you that there is no-one better than yours truly at finding it. And I will find it. Now these little beauties in my hand are filled with pleasure, the sort that will cost you a fortune in prison, but I am going to give you these few for free.'

He removes the cap from the first needle and squirts a tiny bit of the thick brown fluid into the air. He nods to his friend, who steps forward and takes a firm grip on the man's thick black arm, holding his arm in a vice-like grip which makes the veins stand out. Knowing what is coming the prisoner struggles for all he is worth. He calls them every name that he can think off, he lifts his head and stares at the needle as it enters his vein. Colin manages to get the needle into the thick vein first time and injects the heroin. The black man lowers his head onto the table and lies still, as the drug courses through his veins, a broad smile crosses his black face. Boris rocks his head slowly from side to side, as he slips further and further into a never before visited, beautiful place.

Colin and his friend keep Boris bound to the table for around thirty-six hours, giving him another fix every six hours or so. After the sixth fix, a badly-smelling Boris is almost begging them for more, this is the time to call Molly and tell her where she can find the hitman and for a fix he will tell her everything that she needs to know, to put the major away for the rest of his life.

After a frustrating two hours of searching, Colin finally locates the hidden file on Boris's computer, the file is a detailed list of every hit that Boris has carried out. He has close to a million pounds hidden overseas, for work done on a world-wide basis, including the hit on the disgraced prime minister, Thatchmore. Colin sits and looks at the figures and decides that Boris won't need the money where he is going, so he moves every penny to another high interest account and stores the details on a memory stick. With that done, he places the stick into his inside jacket pocket. He then deletes every file except one which he sends to Molly's mobile phone. Happy with what he has achieved, he smashes the computer to bits and leaves it in a heap on the floor.

Molly and four male police officers arrive at the hotel and after showing their warrant cards to the receptionist, make their way to room 354. They open the door and are shocked at what they find. The suspected murderer is completely out of it, his wrists and ankles are red raw from his repeated attempts at escape. They all stand looking down at the man who by now smells worse than a dead dog. He has obviously urinated more than once, and also emptied his bowels, at least a couple of times. Molly moves away from the prisoner and takes out her phone and calls for an ambulance, she will let them sort him out and when they have cleaned him up and finished with him, she will take charge of him.

The baby now has a name: William Colin Stratton. A still-unconscious John is now receiving dialysis three times a week through a line in his chest, which gives his one remaining kidney time to recover from the severe bruising. The drug he is receiving for the induced coma is slowly being reduced and he is showing slight signs of improvement. It may only be the odd twitch of a finger or the flutter of an eyelid but these small things are enough to give Sarah hope. She spends any spare time that she has with her unconscious husband. She talks nonstop to him, not knowing if he can hear her or not, all the time she is with him, she holds his warm limp hand in her own.

Joan has finally found time to make an appointment, has seen her GP and is now undergoing tests for her problems, she has be will told that her condition will most likely end up with her having a full hysterectomy. In preparation for the operation she is being given drugs to increase her white blood cells, which will be vital to aid her recuperation.

Colin opens his eyes and turns to look at a naked Melissa, who is still sleeping peacefully in his arms. The woman he is deeply in love with, the woman who declared her own love for him only a few hours before, and in those few hours, has totally changed his life.

Today he will ask her to be his wife, but first he wants to thank his friends for their help and give each of them a parting gift of £50,000 Which he will take out of Boris's ill-gotten gains. After all, he won't need the money where he is going for the rest of his life. With the information found on his computer sent to Molly, he doubts that Boris will ever be released. And, just as the murderer deserves, he will eventually die in prison a sad, lonely old man.

With the band of very happy friends returning to wherever it is they have come from, Colin has made a promise to ring them if he needs them in the future. He climbs into the large transit van and heads off to see his potential father-in-law, to ask for his daughter's hand in marriage. David shakes Colin's hand vigorously and says that he couldn't be more pleased for his daughter, now all that Colin has to do is ask Melissa, but he is very confident of her answer.

Ten day's later, much to everyone's delight, John Stratton finally opens his eyes. A few days after, with Sarah holding her husband's hand, the doctor explains to John the full extent of his injuries and the future plans for his treatment. When the doctor leaves them alone they hug each other and both openly cry. John tries his best to reassure his beautiful wife that everything will, in time, be fine. When she finally stops crying he asks her if he can see his newborn son. A short while later a very happy John has tears of joy streaming down his cheeks as he is proudly holding baby William.

There is a knock on the door, and they both look up to see a smiling Colin and Melissa. Colin walks into the room carrying a huge basket of fruit with Melissa excitedly holding out her diamond engagement ring towards Sarah. John and Sarah are so happy for the well matched young couple. When Sarah asks when the wedding will be, Colin smiles and says, 'When my best man is out of that hospital bed.' Everyone smiles as Sarah examines her friend's engagement ring and tells her how happy she is for her. The upcoming wedding and the birth of his son seems to be just the incentive that John needs to speed up his recovery.

CHAPTER 35

Six months on and things are looking good all round, John is no longer on dialysis and is back at home and making a slow but steady recovery. The doctors tell him that because of the severity of his injuries, he will never work again as a serving police officer. Joan has finally undergone her surgery and has also made a full recovery. Colin and Melissa name the day for their wedding, as John is now fit enough to fulfil his duties as best man.

John is sitting at home nervously waiting for a visit from his boss Eric Morris, and hopefully Molly as well. He is pleased that they are coming as he hasn't seen either one of them for a while. When they arrive, Sarah invites them to stay for lunch and having agreed, Molly says that she will help out in the kitchen, leaving the two men to talk. Eric tells John that the inmates of the Dome have all now been released and reunited with their families. Lawyers from all over the country are hounding ex-inmates offering to sue the government for kidnap and false imprisonment. The Dome's outer shell has been almost completely dismantled, with the top secret materials placed in secure storage. Vehicles and possessions belonging to deceased inmates, have all been returned to their families. The remaining buildings will be the centre of a new village now under construction, with the apt name of Dome-Valley which is to be made available to younger members of the local community. The professor and her computers have been persuaded to make a move to a more secure location and will give added support to GCHQ in their quest to make us all a lot safer.

Eric turns to his friend and says, 'Look John, we all know that you will not return to work and it has therefore been decided that as when you first went missing, you were on your way to work, so you are to be pensioned off and will receive a full pension, which I know will be a huge relief to you both. Also the union has made sure that there will be an 'injuries while at work' payment, and that amount alone will be more than enough to pay off your mortgage and still leave you with a good few quid. If in the future you need anything, please don't be afraid to ask, because there are numerous police charities that have been specifically set up for people such as yourself, and they are more than willing to help' John is speechless and just sits there staring at the carpet. Eric can see John's relief by the silent tears rolling down his friend's cheeks. Eric squeezes his shoulder as he walks into the kitchen to fetch Sarah.

The day of the wedding has finally arrived, Colin's stagnight is spent with his SAS friends in Hereford, John refrains from going on the advice of his best friend as stagnights with the SAS are renowned for getting a little bit out of hand. Melissa and the girls descend on London's West End and end up in a club watching male strippers, thanks to Sarah. Melissa, as planned, ends up on the stage with five almost naked hunks and has a wonderful time.

At the reception, the speeches all done and dusted, Colin takes John to one side and thanks him for being his best man. He reaches into his inside pocket and takes out a small gold box and hands it to his best friend, saying, as John opens the box,

149

'This will help you and your family in the future' In the box is a credit card in John's name, he holds the card up and looks quizzically at his friend.

Colin says, 'Let's just call it a reward for services rendered, there is enough there for you to start a business, if you want, buy a new house, whatever you want, the only stipulation is that you don't ask any questions, okay?' John nods his understanding but isn't sure that he can accept such a generous gift from his friend, he will discuss it with Sarah, she will know what to do.

Colin and Melissa are waved off as they leave for their month long honeymoon on safari in Africa. Life for John soon becomes stagnant and he needs something to occupy his mind, sitting watching TV one afternoon, he sees a programme called; Baggage Wars; He watches the program me with great interest and decides that he will investigate the ins and outs of buying lost and left luggage. After all he can afford it, and it looks like quite good fun, he can always ask Colin if he is interested in going into business with him. The more that he thinks about it, the more he likes the idea as it suits his plans perfectly.

Colin and his new bride are finally back from honeymoon and have moved into a newly built house, for which Colin and his father-in-law have agreed to pay half each which will leave them mortgage free. The day after their return they are at the Stratton house showing John and Sarah video recordings of their honeymoon. When they have all watched them and viewed the still pictures, John asks Colin what his plans are for the future.

Colin shrugs and says, 'I've been offered a job at the paper but I don't really want to work for the father-in-law, I don't need to work for a long while yet, so I can just take it easy for a spell, I can always go back into surveillance work, if need's must?'

John looks around to make sure that the girls aren't within earshot and says, 'I have a plan that may be quite exciting and good fun for us, if you're interested, and I can guarantee that it will make our fortunes and secure our futures for us!'

Colin asks if it's legal. John ignore the question, stands up and indicates to his best friend to follow him, they walk into the room that John now uses as his den and sit down. John picks up the remote and switches on the TV, finds the station that he wants on i-player and presses play. They sit and watch Baggage Wars; when the episode ends Colin smiles and says, 'You seriously want us to have a go at that?'

John nods his head and says, 'I have gone into it and there are auctions all over the country, almost every week, it could be good fun, we have nothing to lose and just think of the excitement of opening those bags and boxes. We could even go into containers and lockups, if the opportunity arises.'

Colin nods and says, 'Well, we can afford it can't we. We have to spend our money on something, we may as well have some fun along the way' They talk about the endless possibilities and what they will need to get the business off the ground, like a van and somewhere to sort out the bought items.

John says that there is plenty of room in his double garage to sort out their purchases. Colin says that he still has the blue van, they can use that. They agreed to each put £20,000 into an account as starting capital. Colin says that they can just transfer money from both accounts into a new account called J&C trading.

John looks at his friend and says, 'About that card?'

Colin laughs and says, 'You haven't even been tempted to look at it and see how much is on the card, have you?'

John, looks slightly embarrassed, and shakes his head, he says, 'Okay. I will accept the card gratefully, no questions asked, on one condition, something life changing will happen soon, to both of us and when it does, again no questions asked, okay?'

Colin frowns and asks, 'Is it legal?'

John shakes his head and says, 'About as legal as that card you gave me, but I can't see any questions being asked by the authorities, anyway I have it covered. But I will say that when it happens, and it will, I promise you it will take your breath away.

The business partners travel the country buying bags and boxes, and soon find that they need to find many outlets for the various valuables they discover hidden in their purchases. So they source local antique dealers and house clearance stores. Soon they have contacts for almost everything that they find and what they can't sell, they donate to local charity shops. Melissa has taken on the job of looking after the paperwork and the accounts, they aren't making a fortune, but the boys are making a living and having a lot of fun at the auctions and simply enjoying life.

Melissa announces that she is pregnant and Colin is very pleased with himself. John and Sarah are both truly happy for their friends and can't wait for the birth, as it will make their friends' family complete, just like their own. Colin arrives to collect John to travel to Liverpool for a container auction. On the way John tries his best to wind his friend up about fatherhood, nappy changing, bathing the baby, no sleep, no sex and finally Melissa's hormones.

'You won't be able to do anything right for weeks mate, you may as well come and live with us, at least you'll get some peace and quiet when the baby's born.' Colin looks at his smiling friend and jokingly tells him to piss off.

In the container that they have just bought is some good quality furniture, which they sell locally but hidden right at he back, underneath an old blanket, they find an old fashioned safe. The safe is locked and very solidly built, so much so that it takes the two of them to lift it into the back of the van. They search every other item in the container and have no luck in finding the key. John asks his partner to fetch the auctioneer, Colin asks why and John just smiles at him, taps the side of his nose and says, 'All will become clear when we get back home.'

John asks the auctioneer about the locked safe and if he knows of anyone that can open it for them, they are given the name 'Cracker' and a phone number. Colin phones the safe cracker and arranges for him to meet them at John's house, Colin says that it will cost them £200 whether there is anything in the safe or not. When they arrive home and pull onto the drive a tiny squat man wearing the biggest glasses that either of them have ever seen climbs out of a beaten-up red Jaguar. As the little man walks towards them they see that he has a comb-over hair cut and a Mexican moustache. He is as bandy as a bulldog and must weigh, at most seven stone, wet through. He walks over to them and says, 'Where is it then?' John opens the back of the van to reveal the safe.

Cracker takes one look at the safe and smiles confidently, he says, 'Best get it inside, it might get a bit noisy, if I can't pick it.'

They carry the safe into the garage and place it on the floor, the tiny man places his bag of tools on top of the safe and says, 'Payment up front gents, if you please.' John takes out his wallet and give him his two hundred pounds.

Cracker stows the money in his back pocket, opens his bag of tricks and pulls out a roll of black cloth, he rolls the cloth out on top of the safe, to reveal a row of different shaped metal picks, he looks into the key hole with tiny torch, then selects two of the picks and pushes them into the keyhole. After about thirty second's there is a click, Cracker smiles and says, 'It's all yours, gents.' With which, he packs up his tools, and with a smile and a nod, turns and walks away. He climbs into his car and drives away. They stand and look at the safe and then at each other.

'Go on then, open it,' says John.

Colin drops to his knees, turns the brass handle and pulls the heavy door open, inside are some really old worthless papers and some cloth bags that all have pull strings. On opening the bags they find various old watches, some of them are silver and some gold, also a smaller bag that contains a mixture of women's costume jewellery.

Colin looks up at John and says, 'Not bad, at least this little lot will pay for the day!'

John says to his friend, 'Do you remember that I said our lives will change for ever one day and it may not be strictly legal?' Colin nods. 'Well that day is finally here my friend, you must promise that what I am about to reveal to you, we found in a bag, in this safe, do you agree?'

Colin nods agreement and says, 'This is all very intriguing John but get on with it as the suspense is killing me.' John takes a stepladder down from its hooks on the wall and leans it against the garage wall. He takes a hammer and climbs to the top of the steps and begins knocking some plaster away from the top of one of the grey breeze blocks, when he is satisfied he passes the hammer to his friend and reaches into the top of the breeze block and withdraws a small purple cloth bag. He climbs down the steps and stands in front of Colin and tells him to hold his hands out.

Colin gasps out loud as hundreds of sparkling diamonds rain into his hands. His eyes are as wide as they could possibly be and his mouth hangs open. He tries to speak but John places a finger to his lips and says, 'No questions, remember?'

'But there must be millions here, no-one will ever believe that we found them in the safe, will they?' Colin asks.

John smiles and says, 'Why not, this is precisely the reason that I wanted to get into this game in the first place, so that when everything finally fell into place, like it has with this old safe, it would the perfect time to retrieve the diamonds. I mean we have 'proof of purchase' of the safe, we have witnesses who will swear that we found the safe in the container, everything is perfect, now take out your phone, call your wife and tell her that we are rich, richer than she can ever have imagined.' With that he holds the small bag open and Colin pours the diamonds back in. John leaves his friend with shaking hands as he dials his wife's number.

He walks into the house and kisses his wife tenderly on her soft lips. He takes her by the hand and leads her to the dining room table and sits her down. He sits down himself and begins telling her about the container that they bought that day, and all about the nice furniture that they had found inside and easily sold. He then tells her about the safe and the strange little man, Cracker, who came to unlock it. He places the purple bag on the table in front of her and nods for her to open it. When she pours the diamond onto the table, she takes a big intake of breath, her wide open eyes go from the diamonds to his eyes and back again.

She reaches out and picks up the largest of the stones and looks at it from all angles, she finally asks, 'are they real?' John nods his head just as Colin walks in and sits down at the table. Sarah looks from one man to the other and then at the mound of sparkling stones, she suddenly jumps up and begins clapping her hands and laughing at the top of her voice. Colin says that Melissa and David are on their way over.

Melissa and her father arrive at John's house, he sits down at the table and looks a the array of diamonds that are spread out on the table, his eyes linger on the stones before he lifts his eyes to John's and asks, 'Are these stones legal, John, if so can you prove it, should you ever need to do so?'

Before John could answer Colin says, 'We found them in an old safe that we discovered hidden in the back of a container, one that we bought today at an auction in Liverpool. We have all the relevant paperwork to prove it.'

Sir David looks from one man to the other and says, 'Then I believe you are to be congratulated, now what are your plans, are you going to sell them all at once, or a few at a time?' The best friends look at each other and then at Sir David, both men shrug their shoulders and say that they hadn't thought that far ahead.

Sir David then says, 'I know some people, let me make a few phone calls in the morning and I will get back to you as soon as I know something, but for the moment, I suggest that you put these stones somewhere safe.'

Melissa speaks up, asking, 'Can I hold them first?' Her husband scoops the stones up and places them in her cupped hands, she studies the stones for a few seconds before saying, 'They don't look like much, do they?'

Colin holds the cloth bag open and she tips the sparkling stones back inside, he tightens the drawstrings and then tosses the bag to John. 'You had best look after them, mate, and please don't lose them.'

Sarah says happily, 'I think this calls for a celebratory drink.' She opens the drinks cabinet and takes out various bottles and places them on the table. Melissa takes the wine glasses from the same cabinet and asks who wants what? Someone says that they are hungry and the next thing they know, a menu is being passed around for the local Indian Takeaway. Talk soon turns to what they will do with the money that they make from the sale of the diamonds. Maybe they can all have a holiday together, somewhere hot, and for a very long time.

John receives a call from Sir David late the next morning who asks him if he and Colin can be at his home at six, as he has a man coming around to value the diamonds. John agrees that they will be there and at the agreed time, John, Colin, Sir David, Sarah and Melissa are sitting around, patiently waiting for the man to arrive. Right on time, they hear a car pull up outside. Sir David stands up and leaves the room, when he returns, he accompanied by a wizened old man who is slightly bowed over. He has yellow leathery skin, looks thin and half starved and is dressed in a once very expensive black suit. On top of his head he wears a purple and silver skull cap, in his right hand he carries a bulging leather briefcase. That looks as though it weighs a ton.

'May I introduce Mr Meyer, Mr Meyer knows more about diamonds than anyone else in London and is here to appraise your find.' The man nods his head to each person in turn and sits down at the table, placing his briefcase on the floor by his chair, he looks at John and holds his hands out, John passes him the purple bag that holds the diamonds.

Mr Meyer hefts the bag and smiles, then reaches into his briefcase and withdraws a square of black silk cloth, which he spreads out on the table. He takes out a pad and pencil, he places these next to the cloth. In an obviously well practised routine he then takes out a small black case and places that on the table. Finally ready, he picks up the purple bag and undoes the drawstring and pours the diamonds onto the black cloth. He uses his thin, boney fingers to move the stones around the cloth, when he has done this, he just sits there as if mesmerised, looking at the sparkling stones. He looks up at John and asks, 'You say that you came by these legally?' John nods his head to reassure the old man. Mr Meyer picks up the small round case and removes a silver eyeglass which he places in his right eye, finally ready the old man selects the first diamond and picks up the stone.

He studies the first stone, holds it up to the light and watches carefully as the stone reflects the light, he turns the stone over and over before he places it to one side and writes something down on his pad. The old man takes his time and goes through the same routine with each of the stones, he works silently until he has examined every single one. He reaches back into his briefcase and pulls out another bag that contains a set of digital scales. He weighs each of the stones individually and writes his findings down, humming to himself as he takes his time with his calculations. He has one last look the his list of numbers on his pad and carefully places his pencil down, he looks from one expectant face to the next. He says, 'It is a rare thing to see so many beautiful stones in one collection, you must be very proud to own them. Now what do you intend to do with them?'

Colin says, 'Please Mr Meyer, can you tell us just how much they are worth?' My Meyer looks at Colin and says, 'I can make you a cash offer, but you are more than welcome to take them elsewhere and have them appraised, but I can guarantee that I will give you the best cash price.' John looks at Colin and they nod their agreement and then John nods at Mr Meyer, the strange little man reaches into his briefcase and pulls out an old grey calculator. It seems to take forever for the small machine to come to life, he presses buttons slowly and methodically and writes down each number on his pad. It seems to take forever and the silence in the room is deafening.

Finally, he places his pencil down and turns his calculator off and looks at John, then Colin and back to John and says, 'The best that I can do is £4.750.600.00 cash.' He then holds his hands in the air and says, 'Don't decide yet, discuss it between yourselves, when you have made up your minds, David will let me know your decision. Thank you very much for letting me see the stones and congratulations.'

He packs up his things and carefully replaces them back into his briefcase. Then stands and holds out his damp, limp cold hand and shakes hands with everyone in the room, leaving David until last. He says something to Sir David that only he hears, the newspaper man shows the old man the way out. John, Colin, Sarah and Melissa all look at one another open mouthed.

Finally John says, 'Four million fucking quid, Jesus, bloody fucking, Christ.' Within seconds they are all on their feet, holding onto each other, as they begin dancing around the room.

John, Colin and Sir David are patiently sitting in the waiting room at Meyer's office, on the glass door in front of them, in gold letters, it says:

Meyer and Meyer
Dealers in Fine Diamonds

A blond-haired young woman invites them to enter the musty smelling office, when they enter, they look at one another in complete surprise because standing behind a large well used oak desk, covered in bulging folders, are obviously the Meyer twins. They are identical, even down to their purple scull caps, hands are shaken all round as introductions are made and they sit down facing each other. The twin on the left is, it seems, the one from the night before. He welcomes them all and says that he is delighted that they have made the decision to sell the stones to them. There is plenty of paperwork to be signed and countersigned by all parties involved, and when the twins are satisfied that the paperwork is fully completed, they ask to see the diamonds. When the twins are happy that everything is present and correct and all the stones have been checked and reweighed, they place them back in the purple bag and drop the bag on to a small blue tray. The blond woman pulls open a large safe door and Meyer places the tray inside. The well-oiled heavy door is then silently closed and locked.

The twins stand and the one on he left says, 'Now gentleman, if you would care to follow us please.' They lead the way down a dimly lit wooden staircase to a private garage, standing in the garage is a newish black Ford escort van, which is guarded by two very large unsmiling uniformed security men. Meyer nods to one of the men and he opens the rear doors of the van. Stacked inside the back of the van is a neatly arranged mountain of brown cardboard boxes, all of them stamped, Bank of England.

The security guard holds out a clipboard to and Meyer looks into the back of the van and counts the boxes. He turns to John and says, '£4.760.000.00 in cash, there are 176 boxes, if you care to count the them, then, if you are happy, please sign the receipt.' Colin's hand shakes as he checks the boxes and signs the receipt.

Meyer hands John the key to the van and says, 'You can keep the van, as a thank you.' They all shake hands again and the deal is done.

Sir David drives to the bank with John and Colin following him in the van. Once on the open road the friends begin shouting and stamping their feet in excitement. They follow Sir David to the bank, and as arranged, stay in the van until bank staff are found to unload the boxes. Two boxes are left inside the van, one for each of the two men, the rest of the money is deposited into the bank. When the new account has been opened and the paperwork completed, an appointment is made for the following day with the bank manager. The now very wealthy friends can finally leave and head home to John's house. Sir David has to go to his office for an appointment but says that he will join them later.

Sarah and Melissa are standing in the window waiting for the men to arrive. When they finally turn into the drive, they wave to the women and climb out of the van, John opens the rear doors. They take out a box each and walk into the house, they place the boxes on the dining room table, and stand there looking at the brown boxes, the women join them and they all stand staring at the boxes.

John looks at Sarah and says, 'Get the scissors and open it then, love.'

Sarah opens the box and takes out a bundle of brand new fifty pound notes, she breaks the seal and spreads the red notes all over the table and says, 'Oh my God, are they real?' She takes the rest of the bundles out of the box and splits them all open as well, now the table is covered in crisp £50 bank notes.

Sir David wants to do a story on the diamonds and the good fortune of his son in law. The two men involved discuss the idea at length and it is made clear that providing John's name isn't mentioned, for obvious reasons then he has no objections. The story appears three days later, and letters of congratulations roll in as well as the usual batch of begging letters which, according to Sir David, have all been professionally written, so are totally ignored.

CHAPTER 36

The two couples, now closer than ever, have taken a few months off to enjoy the finer things in life, travelling the world and spending time wherever and whenever the fancy takes them. The two men have become like brothers and do everything together, and the women have become like sisters. After returning from their extended holiday, they are enjoying an evening meal with Sir David at his home, when out of the blue the older man asks Colin and John what they intend doing with their lives. The young men look at one another and both shrug their shoulders because they hadn't given the subject a moment's thought.

Sir David says, 'Well, I have an idea for you, and I guarantee it will keep you both very busy, if you are interested, I have been thinking of moving permanently into my town house, this place is much to big for me. So how would you like to have the house as a gift and use your joint fortune to open a select country hotel? Melissa will inherit everything when I am gone anyway, it just means that she gets this house and grounds a little bit earlier than expected. Also there is plenty of room in the lodge down by the lake for you to live in. You could split the lodge into two homes, there's plenty of room for both families. Everyone is momentarily stunned, they look at one another, then all begin talking at once.

Within seconds, they are all talking about running the hotel together and the more that they talk about Sir David's offer, the more ideas for the hotel are written down. Sir David coughs and says, 'I take it that you all agree with the idea in principle then? They all nod and the look of satisfaction on the Sir David's face shows his pleasure. Soon, their family homes are sold and both families have made the move into the lodge. Plans are being drawn up for the hotel and planning permission is being sought. Local builders Lord and Sons along with some other specialist craftsmen have been chosen to do all the restoration work.

John and Colin have been to a meeting with a local man named John Shepard, a world renowned cabinet maker. After only a few minutes conversation they are more than happy that he knows exactly what level of finish is required by them, for such a prestigious project. They want work to begin right away, but he explains that he has commitments to fulfil elsewhere, after checking his diary he says that with a bit of juggling, he can maybe begin work in ten weeks or thereabouts. After a brief discussion they decide that if they want the best then they must wait until he is free. Soon the initial work is underway and the friends oversee every stage of the operation, life for both families just couldn't be any better.

Melissa seems to be getting bigger by the day and is taking great pleasure in planning her first baby's bedroom. She decides that she needs to go into town and order a silk christening gown from a lady one of the builders has recommended. Her name is Lyn Davies and it is well known locally that she hand stitches every gown she makes, and that every gown that she has created, is not only individual but perfect in every way.

The only stipulation made by Mrs Davis is that she is invited to the christening, as she is a staunch churchgoer and just loves a good christening, more so than any other religious service. Melissa tells the others what her plans are and Sarah instantly offers to drive her, but the pregnant woman insists she will be fine and that she will be back in a couple of hours at most.

When Melissa doesn't return after nearly four hours, a concerned Sarah walks over to the main house and finds the two men leaning over a table covered in builders plans. Colin eventually looks up and asks if she is okay. Sarah looks at him and says, 'I don't want to worry you Col but I've been trying to get hold of Melissa and she isn't answering her phone. I mean she has been gone more than four hours now and she said that she would be back in two.'

Colin takes out his mobile and tries his wife's number but his call goes straight to voice mail, he leaves a message for her to contact him as soon as possible as they are worried about her. Sarah finds the number and calls Lyn Davies and asks if Melissa is still there, but she tells Sarah that, Melissa didn't turn up for their appointment. Colin calls the hospital and no-one there has seen or heard from her either. Sarah calls Sir David and he says that he spoke to his daughter first thing that morning but hadn't done so since. He says that he will be right over. On the off-chance, Sarah calls DCI Molly Wright in London but she hasn't heard from Melissa in weeks but says that if there is no news about her in the next couple of hours, to let her know and she will be right over.

John and Sarah travel in one car and Sir David and Colin search in a second car, they are on the look out for the missing woman's small red sports car. For two hours they search every supermarket, hospital and garage car park, they roam the back streets and even dead-end roads. Eventually, Sarah spots the car in the corner of an overflow car park, at a local garden centre, the worrying thing is that all the cars doors are wide open. Other than glance inside and see nothing, they wait for Colin and his father-in-law to arrive before they do anything. Colin uses his specialist training as he searches the car for any clues. He finds what he is looking for when he lifts his wife's handbag, underneath the leather bag is a chilling note that only has three words written on it, and those words are: 'I want Stratton.' Colin shows John the note and both men look at one another in bafflement. John eventually asks his friend what the note can possibly mean. Colin looks at him and answers, 'It looks like someone wants you but has taken Melissa as a way of getting to you, can you think of anyone from your past that wants to get their hands on you. You must have really pissed someone off, for them to go to these lengths?'

John shrugs his shoulders and reassures Colin that there is nothing in his past to warrant this sort of thing. Colin looks all around the car park and whispers menacingly, 'They'd best not harm a single hair on her head, or by fuck they will suffer.'

Newly promoted DCI Molly Wright arrives at Sir David's house, she sits at the table in the lodge taking notes and asking questions, when she has finished, she studies her notes, looking at Colin she asks him if he wants her to contact the kidnap squad. He shakes his head and says that if it comes to that, he will make a call to Hereford and his SAS friends will take control of the operation. Simply because the hands of the police are, to a certain extent, tied , whereas his friends are more able to move around unseen and he would trust each one of them with his life and, in this instance, his wife's life.

The long awaited phone call comes at midnight, on speaker phone they all listen as the caller says in a gruff voice, 'I want Stratton, and if you want the darling Melissa back, then you will give him to me. I will call again soon, Oh, and by the way, big-bellied Melissa looks quite tasty tied naked to my big soft bed.' With that, he laughs chillingly and hangs up.

The friends all look at one another but Colin stares at his best friend and says, 'Think John, there must be someone that holds a mighty big grudge against you?' John shakes his head and then lowers his head into his hands, Colin stands up and walks to the front door and takes out his mobile phone. He talks quietly as he calls his friends at Hereford, once-more into action.

They all sit patiently and wait for the phone to ring, each of them willing the kidnappers to call. Nothing happens until late in the afternoon when Colin's mobile rings, he answers the call and excuses himself. On the way to the door he turns and says that he will be back soon. He sees his Army friends at the entrance to the estate, he shows them to the rear of the lodge where they set up camp. He explains the situation to his old commanding officer, who having listened closely, takes control, gives out orders, and the men spring into immediate action.

Within the hour, a fully functioning camp has been set up, and a command post erected next to the lodge, men wearing camouflage clothing are laying out wires, other men are carrying highly technical equipment into the lodge, where two men are connecting different coloured wires to a bank of monitors. More men are sitting at long wooden tables, turning knobs on futuristic looking computers and machines. All the while they sit with headphones on, listening. Eventually the two men who are listening, give the thumbs up. The CO, Captain Roger John Bates speaks to Colin telling him what to do. When the lodge phone does ring, Colin is to wait until he has the thumbs up from the operators before answering.

Having instructed Colin on what to do and say, he turns to the room in general and says, 'I would like to reassure you all you that we will get Melissa back, we are trained in these situations and whereas the civilian police have to follow protocol, we not only have a lot more freedom, but also a lot better equipment than civilian forces. As I speak, we have men positioned at specific points in the surrounding area. They are all equipped with tracking devices that will definitely give us the edge, all we can do now is wait for the ransom call to come through. Meanwhile our experts are analysing the note and the first phone call, to see if there are any finger prints or background noises that may give us a head start.'

He then spreads his hands wide and finally says confidently, 'And now we wait.'

The call comes at ten the next morning, the phone operators do what they have to and give the thumbs up. Colin presses the speakerphone button, before he can speak the same gruff voice says, 'I want Stratton and you will give him to me or I will cut the baby out of this lovely lady. I will then send it to Sir David Kelvin and then I will send Melissa's head to you Colin Rothe. So you will do as I say and give me Stratton.'

Before anyone can utter a single word the caller hangs up. Colin and his father-in-law both groan out loud and Sarah begins to cry into her hands, the CO looks expectantly at his men, who both shake their heads, one of them says, 'We will need more time to pinpoint him, sir.'

An hour later, the phone rings again, and the same routine takes place, the kidnapper says, 'Do you agree to my terms?'

Before anyone can say anything, John says, 'Yes, I agree to your terms.' With that the kidnapper hangs up again, everyone looks at John in astonishment.

He then looks at each face in turn and says, 'Well, it is me that they want, what choice do we have?'

The CO says, 'You could have at least given us a chance, a chance to try and locate them first.'

The phone rings again, the gruff voice says, 'Listen carefully, Stratton will walk up the northbound A34 near Didcot between 6 and 7pm tonight. A van will stop by his side and he will open the side door and get in, closing the door behind him. Be warned that we will be watching closely, any sign of following vehicles or attempt at ambush and the woman dies.' Before Colin can ask about his wife, the kidnapper hangs up.

The CO looks at his operator hopefully, the operator on the right hand side of the table says, 'All that we can tell you is that they were somewhere in the south Oxfordshire area, when they made the call.' He looks at John and asks, 'Are you certain that you want to do this John? One of my men can go in your place, they may not know what you look like.'

John shakes his head and says, 'I can't risk Melissa's life by doing that, as I said before, for some reason, it's me they want,'

The CO speaks into his radio and says, 'At least we can take some precautions.' Sarah takes her husband by the hand and leads him from the room, once outside she holds him around the neck and stares into his eyes, she then begs him not to go, saying that it is too dangerous and that she has almost lost him twice before and she doesn't want to risk losing him forever.

When they return to the room, a very tall, intelligent looking man in a black suit is standing by the dining room table waiting for John, laid out in front of him on the table is a thin silver briefcase. He asks John to take a seat by his side. When he opens the case, it is full of tiny different coloured pieces of equipment, all of different shapes and sizes and every expensive looking piece is set deep in black foam. He takes a tiny pair of tweezers and plucks a skin coloured tube out of the foam, he then tilts John's head to one side, and carefully inserts the device into John's right ear, once inserted he looks at a nearby technician and says, '1.2.3.4.' he stops counting when he is sure the device is fitted correctly. He looks at the operator, who gives a thumbs up, telling him that the sensitive device is working correctly.

The man then asks John to stand up and unfasten his jeans, he cuts a tiny hole in the seam of the waistband and pushes another tiny device inside the small incision. John refastens the jeans and looks at the technician who again says, '1.2.3.4.' and gets the thumbs up. He then goes down on his knees and drills a small hole in the heel of John's right shoe, inserts another tiny device into the hole and plugs the hole with a black putty like paste. Again, he looks to his operator and gets the thumbs up. He then sits John down and places two smaller different coloured devices on the table in front of him, ones is blue and the other, smaller one, is green.

John watches carefully as the man points to the blue tube, and says, 'This is a magnetic tracking device. Place it anywhere inside the van, and we will be able to find you.'

He picks up the other tiny device and says, 'Now, listen carefully. When it is time for you to leave, I want you to place this one in the side of your mouth and try not to swallow it, this particular device is not only a tracking device it is also a listening device, the best advice that I can give you is this. If you are interrogated, I want you to keep the device in your mouth for as long as you possibly can. If you are struck in the mouth, then I want you to spit the device into a corner of the room or if possible, somewhere out of the way where it won't be trodden on, OK'?'

John looks at the CO and asks, 'Do you really think that it will come to that?'

The CO looks at John for a full minute before saying, 'I can't answer that without knowing why they want you so badly and until we know the answer to that question, who knows what will happen?' Everyone turns to look at Sarah, as she bursts into tears and runs from the room, Molly follows her into the kitchen, she is desperately afraid for John, but does her best to comfort and reassure her friend.

The late November evening is cold, damp and dark, John shivers as he walks along the side of a very busy A34, each time a vehicle passes him, he has a feeling of dread rush through his veins. After a walk of close to a mile, each passing vehicle gives him a scare, more so now than earlier as he knows that the next approaching vehicle could well be the kidnapper's. He almost shits himself when a dark van pulls up by his side. Clutching the tracking device in his left hand he slides the door open and is instantly grabbed by four strong hands and yanked into the back, he is pushed to the floor and his hands are taped behind his back. He looks at the two menacing looking men who are both wearing black woollen balaclavas, he opens his mouth to speak and is grabbed by one of the kidnappers and his mouth is taped shut by the other one. John moves himself back into the corner of the van and pushes the tiny device deep into the lowest corner of the speeding vehicle and hopes to God that the device is working. The two men sit and stare at him with dead eyes as the noisy van trundles on for mile after mile and for what seems like hours.

It finally stops and he hears the sound of a metal shutter door opening, once fully open the van moves forward and the shutter door is quickly closed behind them. The side door of the van is yanked open and a very large man reaches into the van and grabs him by the jacket and drags him out of the van, he then simply lets go of John and he falls onto the dirty, concrete floor. A group of terrifying looking big men all dressed in black are standing all around him, each one of them staring down at him with unsmiling eyes. John looks from man to man, each one wearing the same coloured balaclava as the first two. It is obvious to John that they are some sort of biker gang as they all wear dark biker clothing and heavy black motor cycle boots. A thin man with bad breath kneels down by John's head and stares at him for a full minute before saying, 'Don't look much like a murderer and a thief, does he, lads?' The ring of men all laugh, one of them even says, 'It looks like he is about to shit himself.' Again they all laugh.

The thin man, who is the obvious ringleader tells the men to strip him to the waist and tie him to a chair, they lift him bodily from the floor, he tries his best to struggle but soon realises that it is pointless, so he relaxes and lets them get on with it. Now bound to a wooden chair the ringleader moves another chair, so that it is positioned directly in front of John and sits down, he leans in close and stares at John for a good while before taking a letter out of his pocket. He waves the letter in front of John's face and says, 'Do you know what this is, Mr John fucking Stratton? This is a message from the grave, so to speak. When they returned Ted's old van to me, there was this letter on the driver's seat, addressed to me, would you like me to read it to you? John just stares at the man, totally confused and convinced that they have the wrong man and it will all be straightened out in a few minutes and then he will be released. How wrong is he.

'The letter begins "Bert" - that is me, that is – "Bert, I can't explain my disappearance as I don't know much about it myself, all I know is that I am being held in some weird sort of place, but me being me, I have found a scam and a very lucrative one it is too. You see I have found a way to collect diamonds, lots and lot's of beautiful diamonds, a fucking fortune, enough to set us all up for the rest of our lives. The problem I had was getting them out of this place, doing the job that I have been given, maintenance man, allowed me access to all areas and I noticed over time, that when someone's released from here, it is usually with their own vehicle, but how that's done, I don't know. So my plan was very simple, I decided to hide the diamonds in my van and on my release, my and your futures would be assured.

"Well, that is what I thought, until this nosy fucking copper started poking his nose into my business and nicked the diamonds. I even kidnapped his lovely bird and hoped that would do the trick but I failed, but I did give her one before I shoved this metal bar up inside her, boy did she squeal when I did that, you would have been proud of me, bruv. Well, I find myself in a position now where there is no way out but to top myself because I am all alone and so bloody cold, colder than I have ever been before in my life, bruv. But, before I do the deed, I want to give you this copper's name it's John Stratton. I trust that you will be sure to make him suffer the way that I have suffered these last couple of days. I will die happy knowing that when you get the diamonds back, you and the lads will live long rich lives, as a reward for all my efforts. Give my best to the lads and I will see you all in hell.

"Your ever loving brother."Ted."

'Now, I can tell by the look in your eyes that you know exactly what this is all about, so the simple question is this, where are the diamonds, the ones that you stole from my brother?'

The kidnapper nods to one of his men and the tape is torn from John's mouth, taking some of the skin from his top lip with it. John licks his lips and tastes fresh blood, he opens his mouth to speak but the man sitting in front of him holds his hand up to him, and says 'Please, just don't insult me John, you see we have two choices here, you tell me where the diamonds are or we kill the pregnant bitch, simple as that. Well, what's it to be?'

John is thinking as fast as he can but nothing helpful comes to mind, in the end he goes with what he knows to be the truth. He begins by saying confidently, 'Look Bert, you must have seen on the news about the Dome and how it was run, well when I left, I went through this door and got zapped or something, after that I don't remember a single thing, so I'm very sorry but I can't help you.'

As quick as a flash and totally unexpectedly the kidnapper punches John so hard in the face that the chair that he is tied to, falls over, a dazed John takes the opportunity to spit the tracking device into the corner of the garage. John is picked up and placed so that he is facing Bert again, who says, 'Ya see John, I don't like hurting people but when they take the fucking piss, well I ain't got a lot of choice really have I? So just tell me, John, where are the fucking diamonds?'

John opens his mouth to speak, but again Bert hits him square on the jaw, just as hard as he did the first time and again the chair falls over backwards. John lands heavily this time and with a dull thud, as he bangs the back of his head on the concrete floor. When the men have picked him up again, John looks at the kidnapper with a puzzled look. Bert sighs and says, 'I am so sorry, John but I just know in my heart of hearts that you were going to lie to me again, maybe a night in this very cold lockup will loosen your tongue a little bit.'

With that, he nods to one of his men who pours a bucket of ice cold water over John's head, the sheer shock of which makes John gasp out loud. The men all laugh, as he begins to shiver uncontrollably.

John sleeps very little during the night because he is so cold, what makes things worse is that he has no choice but to urinate where he is sitting, but for a few seconds the warm flow is quite welcoming as the tepid fluid soaks into the material of his jeans. In the blackness of night, he can hear something scurrying about behind him, it could be rats scratching at something. His imagination begins to get the better of him because it sounds as if the scratching noise is now coming from around his feet, he stares blindly into the pitch black darkness and hopes that it isn't rats because he hates rats. John thinks back to when Colin tortured his prisoners and how they screamed in agony and he wonders if the same fate awaits him when his kidnappers return in the morning. His mind has been racing all through the night. As he sees it he has two choices, should he simply tell Bert what he wants to know or should he put his faith in Colin and his friends. He can see the first rays of light, as dawn creeps eerily underneath the lockup's steel shutter door.

He can hear the sound of big motor bikes arriving outside the lock up, a few minutes later he hears voices as life begins outside the lockup, nothing happens for an hour or so and then he hears the louder sound of the big van. It sounds a lot like the van that brought him here, the day before. He can hear the men talking and laughing as if they are waiting for someone to arrive. John's heart is racing as he wonders where his rescuers are, after all he has hidden the tracking devices as instructed. He begins to wonder if they had all been broken, but the technician had tested them all. John's heart flutters in his chest when he hears the sound of the key turning in the lock and the shutter door being raised. With the door up as far as it will go, the group of now unmasked men enter the lockup and instantly begin waving their hands in front of their faces, one of them shouts, 'He's fucking pissed himself, the dirty bastard,' and they all begin to laugh.

Bert says, 'Hose the dirty fucker down, lads.' He takes a step back, out of the way as the green water hose is laid out. A big burly bloke with a long ginger beard, aims the hose at John and another man turns the water full on, within seconds John is freezing cold and soaking wet again, only this time they don't stop. One man even reaches over and holds John's head still by gripping a handful of his hair, while the other man aims the water jet directly into his face. The man holding his hair has such a hard grip, that John can't move his head at all, the power of the water jet is so strong, John thinks that his eyeballs are about to explode.

The ice cold water suddenly stops hitting him and Bert again takes a seat in front of him, he sighs deeply, and asks, 'Where are the diamonds, copper?'

John realises that he has heard the very same question before, back in his room in the Dome, John shakes his head and whispers through chattering teeth, 'I can't tell you what I don't know, can I?'

Bert sighs again and reaches into his pocket and takes out his mobile phone, he lets John watch as he scrolls through a host of pictures of Harley Davidson motor bikes, until he finds what he is looking for and then holds the phone out so that John can look at the screen. Lying naked on a brass bed is Melissa, her heavily pregnant belly standing proud, she is blindfolded and tied star shaped at all four corners of the bed, exposing her most intimate place to all.

John lifts his eyes to his captor's, Bert says, 'Just say the word and Julie here will go and set your friend free, it is as easy as that.' Again John shakes his head, only now he wonders if he is doing the right thing because if he tells Bert what he wants to know, will Colin and his friends be waiting outside, and follow Julie to wherever it is that Melissa is being held. On the other hand, if Colin isn't outside and he tells them what happened to the diamonds, he will be dead, and so will Melissa and her unborn baby. All that may be irrelevant because now that he has seen all of their faces, will they have to kill him anyway?

Bert sits dead still as he looks at John, the leader of the kidnappers sits motionless for a long while before emitting a long, deep sigh, 'Well, okay then, John, you had your chance. It looks like I will have to get a bit rough with you,' he says.

'Take him, lads. In the far corner of the lockup stands a really old rusty car jack. Two of the men untie him and drag his stiff cold and wet body over to the ramp, the ramp is then raised to the correct height for their obviously well practiced purpose. John's arms are taped together in front of him and then his outstretched arms are tied to one arm of the ramp and then the ramp is then raised inch by inch until John is standing on the very tips of his toes, Bert smiles to himself as he looks into John's eyes and says, 'You will tell me in the end, copper, so why put yourself through lots of unnecessary pain?' With that, he punches John so hard in the ribs, that he is certain that the same ribs as before have been broken again.

Bert stands back and watches his men as they move a red welding machine next to John. One of the men plugs the machine into a socket. When they switch the machine on, a low humming fills the workshop. John watches as a big red tool box is pushed into position the other side of him and all the tool-filled trays are pulled open. This reveals an array of nasty looking mechanic's tools, any one of which could be used to torture him. Finally everything is ready for use.

The band of bikers all stand around looking at him and laugh at his obvious discomfort, as Bert moves a chair into position in front of him. The leader of the gang sits down, he looks up at John and says, 'This is your last chance, copper, you either tell me what I want to know or the lads here will get to work on you, and trust me you don't want that, because they are well practiced in the art of torture. You see, in our line of work, we have to deal with a lot of drug dealers who don't pay their debts, and we can't have that, can we? Because word would soon get around that we were getting a bit soft, and then people would start to take the piss.'

He sits and looks up at John for a full minute before asking, 'Well, John, what's it going to be?'

John shakes his head and Bert sighs deeply. He looks at his men, holds his hands out wide, stands up and says, 'Well I tried to help you, over to you then, lads.'

The men move en-mass, in a well practiced manoeuvre, two of the men take hold of him and secure his legs, while two more begin removing his socks and shoes. This done, they undo his jeans and pull them off. Bert chuckles and says, 'Nice boxers, John.'

John hears a soft puft sort of sound and a soothing warm splash hits him full in the face, making him snap his eyes shut. He hears a few more of the soft sounds followed by the occasional grunt and the sound of things being knocked over all around him, and then everything becomes deathly quiet, except for the humming of the welder. John blinks his eyes open to clear the sticky thick blood that covers his face, to see Colin and his friends, long black handguns held straight out in front of them, scanning the lock up for more targets. The smell of cordite hangs heavily in the air, unmoving blood stained twisted bodies lie scattered all around him.

John looks down at Bert and most of his thin face has gone, bone, gristle and the thin man's bad teeth are clearly on view. Colin rushes to his friend and begins undoing his restraints asking, 'How are you doing, mate?'

When John collapses into his friend's arms, he whispers, 'I think my ribs are broken again.'

Colin lowers his friend down onto a chair and says, 'I'll get you help soon, my friend, but first we need to find Melissa.' John nods his head understanding his friend's desperate need to find his wife as quickly as he can. John can smell the warm blood, death and thick cordite, as he looks around the lockup at the twisted bodies as the pools of blood slowly spread around each. Bodies that a few minute before had been living and breathing, but are now simply lumps of dead meat lying still and unmoving all over the blood stained floor. A the very back of the lockup against the wall, on her hands and knees is a defiant looking Julie. Standing in front of her are two of Colin's masked friends, both holding unmoving guns with long black silencers attached to the end of their barrels, both guns aimed directly at her head.

Colin walks over and squats down in front of her so that the he is at eye level. He looks into her hard brown eyes and can see the fear in them, he says, 'Look, Julie, we are SAS and you are all alone in this big bad world right now, I will let you go free, if you tell me where Melissa is being held?'

Julie spits into his face and at the top of her voice, shouts, 'You will never find the fat bitch and I hope that she and that bastard in her belly die.'

Colin stands up and Julie smiles to herself as she watches triumphantly as he wipes her spittle from his face. He sighs and whispers, 'I would normally at this point give you another chance or maybe torture you a little bit to make you talk, but I can see that will be a waste of everyone's time, and I want to get my friend here to hospital.

'Hold her leg out,' he says to his friends. With her thin leg held out straight in front of her, Colin places the end of his silencer onto the fleshy part of the thigh and without any hesitation, pulls the trigger. A deafening high pitched scream fills the small lockup. When she has finally stopped screaming, she stares up at him with hate-filled eyes, tears running freely down her cheeks, dark red blood oozing from a black hole in her thigh. He pushes the end of the silencer against the wound and presses down hard, against her leg. High pitched screams, fill the lockup.

Colin waits patiently, letting her calm down, before saying, 'Just tell me where she is and this stops now, but I warn you that I am getting mightily pissed off with you.' Julie takes a deep breath and defiantly shakes her head.

Colin lifts the gun and simply shoots her through the left elbow, shattering the bones and spraying bits of bone and thick black arterial blood all over the wall behind her, she instantly grabs her forearm with her good hand, in a bid to try and stem the blood flow, at the same instant she opens her mouth to scream but he quiets her when he places the gun against her right elbow and shouts at the top of his angry voice, 'Do you want to wipe your own fucking arse ever again?'

She groans out loud, lowers her eyes and whispers, 'Three doors up on the left, top of the stairs, first on the left.'

Colin stands up straight and asks her, 'Is there anyone with her?'

Holding her shattered elbow, black blood oozing through her fingers, she nods and says, 'Abdul. He has orders to kill her if you try and break the door down, and I promise you he will.'

'What's the entry code?' She looks down and whispers, 'four knocks, two and two.' Her chin lowers to her chest and the badly injured Julie begins to cry for the first time since she was a child knowing that the man standing in front of her can't possibly leave her as a witness. She feels the cold metal of the gun barrel on top of her head and then nothing, as she slips into the next world, her only hope is that the next world treats her better than the one she has just left behind.

Colin shouts out orders and nods to one of his men to follow him as he sprints from the lockup. Guns drawn the two men creep silently up the wooden stair case, standing outside the door Colin gives the signal knock on the door. A smiling black man in an orange turban opens the door, Colin shoots him between the eyes without a second thought, the dead man flies backwards with wide open eyes and falls against a brown wooden bookcase, his unseeing eyes still wide as they stare at nothing, but the next world. Colin turns to the bed and cuts his screaming wife free and holds her trembling body tightly to his. Her face is screwed up in agony, he pulls the blindfold from her eyes as gently as he can and says, 'It is all over now my love, all the bad men are gone.'

Melissa places her arms around his neck and whispers, 'The baby's coming, you have to do something, now.' Colin wraps his wife's naked body in a dirty sheet and hearing distant sirens heading in their direction, lifts her from the bed and carries her down the narrow staircase. Once outside on the street he passes his gun to one of his men and nods his thanks. As soon as the paramedic opens the rear doors, Colin carries his groaning wife inside and places her gently on the waiting trolly. He has to sit and watch as the two men do what they have been trained to do, within minutes they are underway, sirens clearing a path to the nearest hospital. Two more ambulances arrive, one crew takes John to the same hospital while the other crew check over the cooling bodies, just in case anyone is still alive. The police arrive at the lockup just as John is being loaded into the ambulance. Armed police officers seal off the grisly scene with long strips of blue and white police tape and await the forensic teams arrival.

John has had his ribs strapped up again at the hospital and is now sitting in the waiting room, hand in hand with Sarah, while a police officer asks him questions. But John is saying that the can't remember anything. Sir David is nervously walking back and forth and Molly is chewing her fingernails as they wait for news of Melissa's baby.

The door suddenly bursts open and Colin, wearing a green hospital gown comes rushing into the waiting room, his green hat is pushed to the back of his head and the mask which is supposed to cover his nose and mouth, is over half of his mouth and one eye, as he shouts out excitedly, 'It's happening. Any minute now, I'm going to be a father.'

With that, he goes again. They look at one another and burst out laughing, Sir David says, still laughing, 'And he's supposed to be SAS trained.'

Colin walks back into the waiting room looking stunned, his mask hangs from his left ear and he's ringing his hat in his hands. He looks from face to face, his own breaks into a wide smile as he announces, 'It's a boy, in all my time with the unit, I have never seen anything so bloody marvellous.' Everyone stands up and shakes hands and slaps him on the back, as they congratulate him.

Melissa and Sarah are sitting on the settee with beautiful baby David. Molly and the men are sitting around the table discussing everything that has happened in the last few days. In front of them is a copy of The Tribute, the lead headline reads, 'Local drug gang slain by London rivals'. With a simple phone call from John to a certain Chief Constable at Scotland Yard, all recent events in the biker gang's lock up seems to have been mysteriously covered up. Talk turns to John's treatment in the lockup at the hands of Bert and his friends. Colin opens his laptop and presses a few keys, an eerie picture of John sitting in the dark in the lockup, tied to, and visibly shivering in, his chair. They all sit and watch the whole event as it unfolds, when it is all over and the baddies all gone, everyone looks at John, and start passing comments like, 'Who's a movie star then,' and 'what's your next film role going to be?'

John sits, looks at Colin and asks, 'How did you film all that, and if you knew I was in trouble, why didn't you come in sooner and rescue me?'

His friend smiles and says, 'You seemed to be having such a nice time with your new friends, we thought we would leave you there just a little bit longer. You have to admit that it was you that volunteered to go and play with them in the first place. As for how we got the film, we drilled a hole in the wall of the lockup in the middle of the night so we had some idea of where each biker was standing when we entered the lockup in the morning. We had to keep the girl alive, because it was obvious that it would be her job to look after Melissa and she would know where she was being held.'

John nods his head in understanding and says, 'Come on mate, let's take a walk and have a quiet little chat.' The two walk outside and stand admiring the new hotel which is lit up and almost ready to open as the Stratrothe Hotel. John looks around to make certain that they are on their own, before he asks his friend, 'How come none of the others have mentioned the diamonds and how I really came by them? It's worrying me to death that nobody is asking about them.'

Colin looks around himself, and when sure they are on their own, answers quietly, 'I realised almost at once where the diamonds had come from, when you got them out of the wall but you said no questions, so for that reason alone, I never mentioned it. I was listening through headphones when Bert began reading the letter out to you and guessed that it was going to be about the diamonds, so I accidentally turned the sound off and passed it off as a malfunction saying that we would have to get a lip-reader in at some point to translate the video.

So don't worry, your secret is safe with me. The only person that you have to worry about is Sir David, I don't think he was fooled for one minute. But, I think that if he was going to say something, he would have said it by now, so stop worrying and hope that now this whole affair is definitely over and, at last, we can finally get on and enjoy the rest of our lives.'

ABOUT THE AUTHOR

Brian is a new author, he is a long-term dialysis patient of over 20 years and uses his 4 weekly sessions of treatment to write his many different genres of books, these include fiction novels, adult novels, a biography [A Badsey Boy] and many beautifully illustrated children's books.

Born in the mid 50s, Brian is a disabled man with a lifelong passion for angling, when his illness forced his retirement, he discovered his creative imagination, which shows in his love of writing.

Printed in Poland
by Amazon Fulfillment
Poland Sp. z o.o., Wrocław